River Town

About the Author:

Lynn Hobbs is a member of GFWC-Texas Federation of Women's Clubs-Marshall Women's Club, American Christian Fiction Writers, East Texas Christian Writers, North East Texas Writers Organization, past treasurer (2011-2012) of East Texas Writers Association, and a Lifetime member of World Wide Who's Who.

Retired from the Texas public school system, Lynn is a native of Houston. Married; two sons, three grandchildren, and one dog complete the family. When she isn't writing, her interests include reading, church activities, houseplants, scrap-booking and quilting. Available for speaking engagements, Lynn has enjoyed speaking at Christian Retreats, Lions Clubs, and other events.

World Wide Who's Who awarded Lynn Hobbs Professional of the Year 2012 in Authorship. A 2011 winner of National Novel Writers Month (NaNoWriMo), she completed a 50,000 word novel in 30 days. Several of her short stories have placed first and second in contests. An award winning author, Lynn enjoys hearing from her readers. Join Lynn's' uplifting Christian blog, and visit at: www.LynnHobbsAuthor.com

Other works by Lynn Hobbs:

Sin, Secrets, and Salvation

"All is not well in River Town, Texas. Its troubles will be painfully familiar to many: broken families, drugs and theft, troubled teens and hard lived lives. It sounds just like a town Jesus wants to visit. In Lynn Hobbs' latest work, he does... kind of. Susan Penleigh is God's servant making a difference in River Town. The Bible is the story of God wanting us to take up the story of the gospel as our own story. Lynn Hobbs has given us a story of what that can look like when a neighbor, a friend, a high-school employee; makes the story of the gospel her own. We need more stories like this."

**-Jeph Holloway, Professor of Theology and Ethics,
East Texas Baptist University**

"This is a great continuation of the life of Susan, a woman who has been abused, developing into 'a strong willed person.' Loved the East Texas locale for this second book as that is where I was raised and moved back to. The account of the fires brought back some scary memories as they actually happened here. Can't wait to get the third book to see where Susan goes in her life."

**-Bobby (Bob) Bell, Jr., retired aircraft engineer
Owner, former Bellsview B&B of the Bayou**

"River Town is a great book to read. The plot covered lots of activity, and held my attention well. I was anxious to keep reading to find out what would happen next; loved the suspense. It is refreshing to read a book I would not mind sharing with my 87 year old mother. The Biblical truths and teachings are shown by many characters that have an important influence on others. I always enjoy books about subjects to which I can relate. The East Texas setting was especially enjoyable. The school setting and duties of Susan also appealed to me. Perhaps it will open the eyes of people outside education to see exactly what an administrative educational aide has to do. Susan is diligent in helping those

in need. She is bold in living her Christian faith and sharing it with others. I'm looking forwards to book three!"

-Jan Bramlett, retired
Texas Public Schools

"Author Lynn Hobbs captures the continuing story of Susan Penleigh's journey to a new life with feeling and inspiration. Anxious to leave an abusive relationship behind her, Susan moves across the country to start over, only to face new challenges. Tragedy strikes the small Texas town forcing Susan to reply on her faith and new friendships to forge the life she was meant to live. Intrigue rounds out this tale of a woman's strength through intense adversity. Great read."

-Patty Wiseman, author
Lifetime member, World Wide Who's Who

River Town

Lynn Hobbs

Desert Coyote Productions
Longview, Texas

The following is a work of fiction, based on the worse drought and
wildfires (2011) in Texas history. (This author had to evacuate as wildfires
came within two miles of her home.) Any resemblance to real persons,
living or deceased, is coincidental.

Library of Congress Control Number: 2012953940
EAN-13: 978-0-9859379-2-8
ISBN-10: 0-9859379-2-0

Typeset in 11pt Book Antiqua
Printed in the U.S.A.
First edition 2012

This book is dedicated to my sister, Rhonda Flurry, and her husband, Ron; for all the years of listening to my storytelling...parts of those are included in "River Town."

Table of Contents

Acknowledgments

In continuing the journey of my main character, Susan Penleigh, (from book one; Sin, Secrets, and Salvation) I strove to have another action-packed, inspiring tale full of suspense and yet weave a clear understanding of a Christian viewpoint by her actions.
I am thrilled to complete River Town, book two in the Running Forward Series and writing on book three …the final conclusion.

Special thanks to my sons, Mike Brannon and Jeff Brannon, for all of their support and encouragement. You are both such a blessing to me.

To my mother, Lillie Clark, my husband, Jim Hobbs, and to all the rest of my family and friends; I couldn't have made it without you. Of course, I give all the glory to God, for His guidance on my hand as I wrote the book.

To each person who took time out from their busy schedule to read my manuscript and to endorse my work; I heartily thank and appreciate you. Words cannot express my gratitude.

To Patty Wiseman, my critique partner; knowing I can count on you is another blessing in itself. Thank you for another great year.

To my readers, thank you for such a favorable response to Sin, Secrets, and Salvation. Typing in my book titles at Amazon.com and leaving your review is so treasured. Your words of encouragement are greatly appreciated. I enjoy hearing from you, please visit my website: www.LynnHobbsAuthor.com

River Town

Chapter One
August 1, 2011
9:15 AM

Susan Penleigh pushed hard on the antique doorbell button. Amid the long, shrill announcement of her arrival, the shuffle of footsteps noisily approached the door. It was difficult to be patient. Sweat trickled down her back like ribbons of wetness, and her short mop of blond hair hung damp and lifeless. Today all energy was zapped, by the sticky, high humidity. Occasionally, a small gust of hot air gushed by reminding her of a blazing pizza oven.

Will this Northeast Texas drought ever end? Can you please hurry and answer the door? It is 112 degrees out here...

Air conditioned coolness blasted over her when the door jerked open.

A deep male voice lashed, "What do you want?"

She gasped, stepped back, and stared into the sneering face of a bearded, unkempt man. Long and neglected, the mass of hair surrounded a tight, drawn mouth. His rough demeanor caught her off guard. Undeterred, she coughed against her hand and held up a folded newspaper with the other.

"I read your ad about a furnished apartment. Is it still for rent?"

"Sure, come on in." A sly grin spread across his face.

Offensive odor overwhelmed her. Filth covered the room, open boxes of who-knows-what, dirty clothing, molded food on paper plates—she gagged. He reached out and grasped her arm, pulled her to his side, while awful, foul breath pierced her nostrils.

Susan's eyes widened in shock and the urge to gag subsided. A loud, blood–curdling scream erupted from her throat as she twisted away. She nearly tripped going through the doorway. Fear pounding in her chest, she reached for the brick exterior wall to catch her balance. "Get away from me!"

He looked annoyed. "You have the wrong address. This is my home." A guttural laugh spewed from his throat.

"Do not ever try to touch me again." Susan gritted her teeth and clenched her fists. "This is supposed to be 11010 Bentley Drive."

"Must be a misprint in the paper, lady, go and talk to them." He grabbed the knob and slammed the door with such violent force the hinges rattled on the wooden frame.

Susan scanned the neighborhood, but no one appeared to offer any help. Trembling, she frowned, pivoted on the sidewalk, and hurried to the car. She slid inside and turned on the ignition, adjusting all A.C. vents toward her. The blower pushed out ice cold air, and Susan savored the moment. *Thank You Lord for my Chevy Equinox and for getting me safely away from that house.* Susan looked back at the potential apartment, locked her doors, and shuddered. *The nerve of that man.*

To calm down, she studied the surroundings and noticed large cracks in the dry, red dirt. Wilted trees, unfortunate plants and shrubbery had burnt to a crisp; long dead under the extreme heat. Lawns were beige and brittle.

A movement caught her eye. Susan, still parked, raised her head in time to notice a young woman, clad in cut-off blue jeans and a halter top, darting out the side entrance of the unruly man's house. The girl jumped into an older, white car, backed out of the drive-way, and sped off down the street.

Hmm, what is she doing with him? Guess she sees something I don't. Susan briefly pondered the situation, placed her vehicle into drive, and headed out of the neighborhood.

She drove around searching for the route back to downtown, came across the town's population sign of 25,000, and laughed. "Okay, Mrs. Divorced Lady, aka Teacher's Aide; how can you start your new job in this new town if you leave the city limits?" She laughed, and her spunky attitude returned. Susan arrived within minutes, circling the town square by the courthouse. Traffic on the streets was light. In fact, except for three parked vehicles, the entire area appeared deserted.

Spotting a Realtor sign, she pulled into the slanted parking space. Powerful heat engulfed her during the sprint from the car to the building. A draining weakness overcame her, and threatened her heart rate. Inside, the smell of candles seemed out of place, but the mingling scents soothed her. Unfortunately, the air conditioner had seen better days. It labored noisily, almost in vain. Three ceiling fans spun on high speed, circulating the air, and promised relief.

A middle aged man approached wiping beaded moisture from his forehead with a paper towel. His sandy-brown hair hung down in wet ringlets. "Rick

Yeager." He extended his free hand toward Susan, and smiled.

And you, sir, better behave.

"Susan Penleigh, and I am so glad you are open," she said, shaking his hand. "It's like a refreshing, cool, oasis in here."

"Ha, I don't know who's happier about the cool part—you, me, or the electric company. We've had over 60 days in a row of at least 100 degree weather or higher. Sure can be dangerous. Please sit down." He motioned to the wrought iron chairs and a small, matching round table centered in front of a huge window, overlooking the town square. "What can I help you with?"

"Rental property, quick. My job starts in a week, and I'm running out of time. Thought I had a place lined up, but turned out to be someone's home."

"Whoa, what happened, where did you go?"

"11010 Bentley Drive," Susan replied, glancing out the window.

"I know the owner, guy with a beard?"

"Yes." She gave the Realtor her full attention.

"He's Wes Harper, local carpenter. Does great work, too."

"A high level of testosterone is all I noticed and a filthy house. Needs to keep his hands to himself." Susan frowned and gripped the side of her shoulder strap purse.

"He can be bold, but he's harmless. Wouldn't hurt him to consider a wife."

"And why am I not surprised by your statement?" Susan looked up into Rick's blue eyes and raised an eyebrow, "So, he's not married?"

"No ma'am. Could I get you something to drink?"

"Thanks, but I really need to start looking at other rentals. Do you have anything available?"

"Several, furnished and unfurnished. What do you have in mind and what kind of price range?"

"I'd prefer furnished. I'll be working at River Town High School and need something nearby, if it's affordable."

"Ma'am, excuse me for meddling, but how tall are you…what, about five foot three?"

"Close. Why?"

"Discipline is horrible here. Those older kids will chew you up and spit you out. You won't stand a chance. They don't want to be taught anything, and you'll end up being the scapegoat. The school board will insist you are an incompetent teacher. Seen it happen too many times."

"Mr. Yeager, I've always wanted to make a difference in the lives of students. I left Seattle, Washington and relocated to this small town in Texas to help teach. I am even more determined after talking to you. Thanks for the warning, though."

"Fair enough. Follow me and we'll drive a few miles through the forest to the river. Housing there should be within your price range." He grabbed a black, Stetson hat from the wall rack and held the door open for Susan. Outside, he stopped to lock the office. She was quick to shove dark shades over her eyes, as the blinding sun bore down upon them.

True to his word, Susan found herself in a thickly, wooded region. His massive black, Toyota Tundra truck zipped along, and she drove behind in hot pursuit. He eventually braked and reduced speed. She quickly viewed the hilly East Texas terrain from her side car window.

Over thirty cabins and bungalows hugged the banks of the winding river. Paved roads were a relief. *At least I will not be isolated or have to deal with a muddy road this winter.* She pictured herself fitting into the neighborhood with total ease. Empty tennis courts loomed ahead at a local park surrounded by a tall cyclone fence. Susan slowed the car as she noticed shimmering sand caught up in swirls of hot wind under a volleyball net. *I can almost visualize a game. Almost hear shrieks of laughter explode as young adults run toward the net, and kick sand under their feet attempting to clobber an out of bounds ball. Looks inviting…maybe in the fall of the year.*

Trees were scattered around the park providing shade, and at the entrance a huge sign displayed the map of a bicycle trail. Susan chuckled as she read the words 'For your enjoyment. Enter at your own risk.' *Ahh, liability, still sounds like fun. Have not been on a bike in years.*

Rick turned into a long, circle drive about a mile past the recreation area. Susan parked her car behind him and walked briskly to his idling truck.

"Excuse my reckless driving. My mind was miles away." He cocked his head to the side and motioned toward the house. "Care to check it out? I think you will approve."

"Yes, let's go, and I hope we haven't gotten off to a wrong start. I am thankful for your help." Susan gave him a brief smile. Rick returned the gesture, climbed down from the Toyota, and grabbed a folder from the seat. Now a perfect example of a professional Realtor, he escorted Susan to the bungalow. She surveyed the area as they approached the front door. Round, white, glass bulbs of a six foot tall hobo light sat majestically in the middle of rambling brown ivy. Landscaped timbers on all four sides, formed two levels containing dry stalks of something undistinguishable, obviously planted long before the drought took hold. Rick unlocked the door, and Susan stepped inside the house while a strong, fresh, paint smell engulfed her.

"Clean." She muttered, while ambling into the open area. Modest furnishings appeared to be in satisfactory condition. She examined the couch and matching love seat and made her way to the kitchen. Taking note of the sparkling stove and refrigerator with labels still stuck to their fronts, she saw the information packages on the counter. "Brand new warranties?"

Rick nodded and pointed toward the rest of the house. "Two bedrooms, two baths, on the left." He paused as she cast a glance inside the rooms. "Kitchen and dining on the right, you have seen that, and laundry room near the pantry— is just past the kitchen. At the end of the living room, you can go through the sliding glass doors and walk out to the covered patio." They meandered to the rear of the house as he talked. "It has a grill, and near the river, is a fire pit, and seating for twenty. Of course, I wouldn't recommend having friends over *now.* Folks get cranky and short tempered in these overheated days."

"I agree, and we all try to avoid stress, Mr. Yeager." Susan leaned out the back door and peeped outside, "I am impressed. It is exactly the right size for me…how about the price?"

"Trash pick-up included…six hundred a month plus lights, gas, and water."

"Not bad, and the deposit?"

"Four hundred on the house, none on utilities—they are in the owners' name. So the utility bills will be mailed to you, and no pets are allowed."

Susan did a double take at the Realtor. "A rare bonus on the deposits, but a shame not allowing a pet."

Rick shrugged his shoulders. "Damage is not worth it."

"Well, I still want this place. You have got a deal."

He opened his folder and handed her several stapled pages. Susan reviewed the document and signed each designated line. "Looks like a pretty standard contract," she remarked, and wrote a check.

"Yes, it is." Rick detached a copy from each original page, gave the copies to her along with a set of keys, and took her check. "I'm glad you like the house." He shook her hand again.

"I'll contact the moving company in Seattle to bring my belongings. Should only take one trip, and I will be settled here in a few days. Until then, the motel I saw in town will be perfect for me." Susan retrieved car keys from her purse while she and Rick sauntered out the entrance.

Susan kept going.

Rick chuckled. "Mrs. Susan, aren't you going to lock your door?" He stood near the hobo light while she turned and came back.

"Oh, I am too excited." Susan sensed her face heat up and imagined she must be blushing.

"Here, I will do it." His key clicked in the lock.

"Thank you, and I cannot wait to get moved in."

"Here is my card. If you ever need help with anything, let me know."

"I do appreciate your kindness." Susan stuck his card into her purse as they ambled down the driveway, in no hurry despite the heat.

"Hey, you have a new neighbor. A moving van is unloading around the corner."

"Where? I don't see it." Susan squinted against the sun and raised a hand over her eyes.

He nodded toward the grove of tall, pine trees further down the road.

"Hmm…good eyesight, I can barely see the end of the van."

An abrupt noise of squealing tires ended the conversation. Startled, Susan quickly looked in all directions. Rick gasped and raised his head toward the road. Wide-eyed, they watched two police squad cars race by without sirens. Lights flashing, the vehicles speed increased, and the roaring sound of engines changing gears penetrated the air.

Susan, clutching a purse and car keys, managed to cover her hands over both ears until the rumble grew less intense with distance.

Rick stared at the cars departure and appeared lost in thought. He grimaced at Susan and climbed into his truck.

She entered her car and lowered the window.

"Busy neighborhood," she yelled, as they drove off in the opposite direction.

Wonder if I have dead bolts...

Chapter Two
August 1, 2011
2:00 PM

Rick pondered possible illegal activities in Susan's neighborhood which escalated to numerous scenarios. Overcome by these ideas, he accelerated unconsciously, and the massive Toyota truck responded swiftly.

What about Susan? Will she be safe? Sweat rolled from his forehead, leaving a long, wet streak across his cheek. He wiped it, absentmindedly, with the back of his hand. *Two patrol cars passed her house and went toward my own property.*

A low growl inside his belly reminded him of a missed lunch. He regarded the time of 2:05 displayed on the dashboard, and scowled.

I smell trouble, and it's Cotton Taylor. He's up to something, and what a rogue of a neighbor... Ahh, enough of this!

Popping a Bob Wills CD disk in the player, Rick's deep voice rang out vigorously as he sang along. "Deep within my heart lies a melody, a song of old San An-to-ne...Ee-ha!" He added a shout, and drove faster, tapping his left foot on the floor board in rhythm, while the lively western swing music lightened his mood.

Alarmed by an abrupt, loud roar, Rick's enjoyment came to an immediate halt. He frowned at the interruption, briefly unable to identify it.

Sounds like sirens. He glanced at the rear mirror. Dancing red and blue lights penetrated his whole being. Rick's shoulders slumped, and without hesitation, he steered the truck off the road. Quickly, he rummaged haphazardly through the glove box. Its contents spilled across the floorboard, while his heartbeat grew extremely loud, pounding rapidly inside his head. Papers retrieved, he swiveled around in the seat, and snatched his billfold from a back pocket.

Observing the patrol car parked behind him, he contemplated the situation, and grimaced. As the officer approached, Rick bolted forward and jabbed the disk players eject button with his finger. Instantly, the music stopped. He rolled the window down and peered into a face he recognized.

"I need your driver's license, registration, and proof of insurance. Where are you going in such a hurry, Rick?"

"Home." Rick handed the required information to the officer.

"At seventy miles an hour?"

"Seventy miles an hour? I didn't realize I was going that fast, George, uh, I mean Officer George…"

The officer laughed. "Rick, we've known each other for years. Today's your first time to get pulled over by me, and let's make it the last. Tell you what, focus more on driving, and I'll give a warning. Don't want you getting killed or killing innocent people by not paying attention." He handed the license and papers back.

"Thanks, George. I mean it, sorry this *ever* happened."

George silently wrote the warning, gave it to Rick, nodded, and walked away.

"Whew! Have to leave you at home old buddy." Rick grabbed the Bob Wills CD off the seat and placed it back inside the disk holder. "You and the Texas Playboys can't travel in my truck."

He positioned his turn signal, made eye contact with George, and waved while easing onto the nearly deserted road. The officer returned the gesture while speaking into the car radio. Moments later, George resumed driving, following behind Rick. Traffic increased until Rick could no longer see the deputy in his rear view mirror. He sighed deeply and immediately felt the heavy weight of tension lift from his body. *I have to be more alert…*

◆ ◆ ◆ ◆

River Town's recent addition of a Dairy Queen remained successful, despite the counties poor economic woes. Rick supported it often. The tall, red and white sign bearing the DQ logo caught everyone's attention. Business boomed, all traffic on Highway 59 flowed directly into the town and right by the new establishment.

Rick swung by the restaurant and slowly maneuvered to the drive through lane. One car ahead of him sped away, and he was suddenly next to consider food options. Taped on the menu display, a homemade sign informed customers of the malfunctioned microphone, and to please drive forward to order. He did.

13

"You're late, Mr. Yeager. What can I get for you?" A teenage girl leaned out the side window, pen and paper in hand.

"Oh, I'll have a double-meat, Belt-Buster, combo meal with fries, and a diet Coke. Are you doing okay, Cindy Lou?"

"Yes, sir, thank you." Nodding, she scribbled the order. Turning to enter codes in the computer, she calculated the cost, told him the amount, and he paid with cash.

"Keep the change."

"Thanks." A quick shove and the cash register drawer closed. She spun on her heels and handed his request to the cook.

"How has your day been?" She chatted, selected a jumbo size paper container, pressed it against a lever on the drink machine for ice, and another for diet coke.

"Interesting. Someone leased a house earlier and is determined to work at the high school. Looks like we have a new resident in River Town."

"Wow. Doesn't happen every day…new at school, I mean. So, who are we talking about?"

A snap-on lid was positioned in place, and she grasped a straw. Circling back, Cindy Lou faced him, beaming a bright smile, and lowered the drink out the window to him.

"Her name is Susan Penleigh from around Seattle, Washington."

"Hmm, big city."

"Mrs. Penleigh struck me as a nice lady. Someday, who knows, I might be able to introduce her to Texas bar-b-que. Of course, the county wide burn ban is now in effect, and no one can cook outside. She is very nice, though."

"Well, that settles it, Mr. Yeager. We need nice people." She pressed the sanitizer pump, spread and rubbed in the liquid, briskly cleaning her hands. "Won't be much longer on the burger and fries."

"Great." He surveyed the area. "I'm your only customer?"

"Yes, but believe me, we were mobbed earlier."

A low rumble of conversation developed nearby and Cindy Lou twisted to one side, frowning over the counter at the cook. It steadily grew in volume, until one couldn't help but overhear the loud talk coming from the kitchen.

"I know you're working by yourself in there." Cindy Lou put both hands on her hips and raised her voice. "What did you do, Jason, put that police scanner back on?"

"I sure did," Jason answered.

"It gets on my nerves. Turn it off," Cindy Lou commanded.

Jason remained calm. "No. We need to be aware of what happens in our county."

"Hey Jason, can you hear me?" Rick called out.

"10-4." Jason replied using a familiar police code.

Rick leaned his head out the truck window and spoke loud, "I saw two deputies race toward the river less than an hour ago, Jason, any idea why?"

"Shots fired from a high powered rifle were reported. The game warden told a state trooper a deer poacher is nearby." Jason emerged from the kitchen and lounged against the door frame.

"How do you know that?" Cindy Lou stepped back from the counter, folding her arms across her chest.

"From leaving the scanner on." Jason dashed to the kitchen as a timer suddenly buzzed.

"Sounds like I need one." Cindy Lou continued, "My dad suggested a scanner to raffle off for our cheerleader fundraiser."

"What a prize…now, *I'd* buy some of those tickets." Rick adjusted his seat belt. "His idea needs to be launched. Tell Caleb I said hi."

"Sure. He's home, you know. Dad got laid off yesterday in the final phase of downsizing the plant."

Rick whistled and slowly shook his head. "Hard to imagine…well, he and I go back a long way. We grew up together. When you return home, mention I'll see him soon."

"Orders ready." Jason's voice rang out inside the empty restaurant, and he plopped Rick's order on the counter.

Cindy Lou made rapid strides to retrieve it. Carrying the package to the window, she carefully handed Rick the food.

"Cindy Lou?"

"Yes sir?"

"Trust God."

"Thank you for reminding me, and Mr. Yeager… I'll give Dad your message."

❖ ❖ ❖ ❖

Rick clutched the steering wheel and drove responsibly. *Don't want George coming after me.* He pictured a stern expression on the officer's face, and realized he didn't want to disappoint his friend

16

George. *He'll be proud I'm not endangering anyone by driving careless. And I have to help Caleb...laid off work and raising four kids...*

His stomach groaned, and minutes from home, hunger got the best of him. The scent of fries and a hamburger assaulted his nostrils until his mouth watered, and he ripped the top of the bag open awkwardly using one hand. Clutching several long, warm fries in his fingers, he popped them in his mouth and moaned as the flavor seized his taste buds. *Umm!*

He pulled into his driveway, parked, locked the Toyota truck, and ate fries all the way inside the house. Kicking off his boots, he set the food on the table, and enjoyed what was left of the meal. Thoughts of how Caleb can feed a family of four kept running through his mind as he roamed into the living room, flopped his lanky frame in the recliner, and decided to watch television. Rick blinked, unaccustomed to heavy eyelids before the ten o'clock news, but today's dreadful heat took its toll, and left him weak with total exhaustion. Overcome by blissful sleep, and unaware his gentle snore grew in volume, hours passed by swiftly.

A loud intake of air suddenly shot up from his throat while an offensive snarl emitted from the back of his nose. He jerked awake, but dazed, and stifled a laugh, remembering the loud, slumbered sound. His eyes wandered to the wall clock, and he stared at it for a while. Amazed, the fact registered, it was indeed 8:15 at night. He had been asleep since 3:00 in the afternoon.

Wrestling with an idea, he determined what course of action to take. *And there is no plan B. I have to do it.* Exhilarated with new found purpose, Rick entered the bedroom and changed into a worn t-shirt and paint splattered blue jeans. He gathered chest waders, a bow and quiver of arrows, rushed out to the garage and loaded them in the Jeep.

Where are those waxed, chicken boxes I get from the packing house? Searching, he finally pulled two boxes from a shelf. A can fell, and bounced repeatedly on the concrete floor, banging louder each time it landed. Rick grabbed the boxes. He glanced outside and could barely see moonlight. *It's dark enough.* Locking the house, he tossed the special containers into the Jeep, turned on the ignition, and headed to the river.

Leisurely passing by Susan's vacant house, the entire neighborhood disappeared as woods surrounded both sides of the road. *I wonder if Susan goes to church. I should have talked to her more when I had the chance.* Rick exhaled, pulled into a gravel driveway, unlocked a six foot long, galvanized gate, and entered. The rough drive across the metal bars of a cattle guard jerked him around more than it jerked the Jeep. He stopped to lock the gate behind him, slowly glanced around his property, and listened.

So far so good, nothing but chirping crickets.

He continued the drive.

Half an hour later, the gravel road ended, and a bumpy, dirt trail took him directly inside the woods. Sharp sticks of dead brush scraped against the vehicle reminding him to slow down, and be patient. *The drought did dry the mud holes. At least I won't get stuck.*

Dodging scattered pine trees involved a constant, hard turn of the steering wheel. Changing gears, he shifted to neutral, and let the motor idle. His wrists were being challenged, and he flexed one hand at a time, opening and closing fingers as muscles relaxed. The drive resumed for another mile when he gratefully saw the expanse of water looming before him, accented by the moonlight.

Pausing to enjoy the view, Rick jumped as the cell phone vibrated. Surprised by the call, his fingers darted into the pocket, curled tightly around the phone, and quickly withdrew it. Pressed against his ear, he answered before looking at the caller I.D. information.

"Hello?"

"Rick? Hi, this is Susan. I didn't call at a bad time, did I?"

Astonished it was her; Rick gulped and almost choked as he swallowed. "No. No you didn't."

"What are you doing?"

"Ahh, just hanging out. What about you?"

"I was watching the news on television, and statistics were given claiming this was the worst drought in history for Texas. Is that true?"

"Yes. It has affected all of us, in one way or another. Working at the school, though, you should have no problem."

"Well, I was concerned, after all, I am moving there and don't know anyone."

"Susan?"

"Yes?"

"You know me, okay?"

"Okay."

"I was wondering…I don't know what you'll think about it, but …I'd like for you to go to church with me, sometime."

"Rick… I will. I want to."

"It's been awhile since I've gone, and I've been thinking about it."

"I'll look forward to it. Thanks for asking me."

"Thank you, and Susan, try to hurry and move in."

"I'll see you soon."

"Alright, call me when you get back."

"I'll do that. Goodnight, Rick."

"Goodnight, Susan."

Realizing his chest was heaving up and down, Rick smiled and considered his phone call. *I am as excited as a teenager!*

Grabbing his bow and arrows, he set off to the edge of the river with determination.

Briars tangled across his pants legs while he walked through the thick brush. No wind blew in the intense heat, and Rick's sweat-drenched clothes clung sloppily to him. He located the landmark, an enormous cypress tree, and quickly found his john boat which he'd shoved under brush on the river bank. Easing inside, he pushed off from the land, and the boat darted across the water. In total silence, he paddled gently, swirling the aluminum paddle in the water, making left and right half circles.

Familiar night sounds surrounded him. He slapped at mosquitoes buzzing around any exposed skin. A lone coyote's howl echoed from a nearby slough. Frogs croaked in a rhythm that suddenly grew loud, only to abruptly cease minutes later, and start over again. Turtles, perched on floating logs, appeared startled by the approach of the john boat. Rick watched while one turtle after another, quickly dove off and splashed deep into the water. Slow to bob their heads up, he noticed they kept their distance from him as ripples in the water circled out.

Rick heard a *clunk* sound and had a fleeting concern, hoping whatever fell over in the boat wasn't important; but it reoccurred, again. Something knocked hard at the side of his boat. Grabbing a huge floodlight he kept in the vessel, he rose up, shined the light out, and flinched.

Four feet of a wide, knobby tail flipped around, slid underwater, returned, and rammed straight into the boat. *I must be close to a gator nest. Lord help me! I pray for Your help, and I stand on Your Word...* Rick quickly tried to recall the correct scripture... *God is our refuge and strength, a very present help in trouble. Psalm 46:1, in Jesus name I pray, Amen.* Rick's faith was strong, and he experienced a rush of peace as he prayed. He knew everything would be fine. He clutched the aluminum paddle, stuck it in the water, and expertly fled the area. Shining the flood light for the second time proved the alligator was gone. The water was no longer churning, and Rick looked up at the sky.

Thank You Lord for being with me in my time of need, to God be the Glory.

He continued on, maneuvered to the land across the river, and tied his boat secure by a clove hitch with a square knot on top, looped through a gnarled cypress knee. Shoving red, night vision goggles over his eyes, he scanned the area.

Nothing moved.

He crept along deeper into the dark woods and emerged near a small clearing where he had planted, and faithfully watered, a patch of rye grass to attract hungry deer. The corn feeders were empty, and he made a mental note to replenish the containers. Hunting was a natural way of life in East Texas and one Rick enjoyed. Ready to forge ahead, he was about to turn when it happened.

A four point buck gracefully inched into Rick's view. It stepped lightly. Rick stiffened instinctively and remained still. Adrenalin rushed through his veins as the buck bent his head and nibbled vegetation. Rick positioned an arrow, drew back on the bow, and let the arrow fly.

Yes! Perfect shot! Momentarily stunned, the large buck bolted, and galloped wide open for thirty yards before collapsing. Ricks heart raced.

Twigs snapped nearby. He stood, and listened, unnerved. *That's not natural…*

Suddenly, an explosion, KA-POW, sounded directly behind him, and he instantly heard the whirling swoosh of air as a bullet flashed by a few feet from his shoulder.

"Hey!" He shouted. "Who is out there?" Anger surged, while he glared and glanced in all directions.

Two hundred pounds of an expert hunter, Cotton Taylor, grunted and emerged out of thick brush. He sidestepped a rotten oak branch and held his high powered rifle pointed toward the sky. "Rick, I didn't know you were here."

"What were you *doing*?" Rick hastily extended his arm out reaching for the man, but Cotton jumped back, and dodged.

"Look at you, Mister bow and arrow! What were YOU doing?" Cotton raged.

Rick's anger left. "Fair enough. At least I didn't nearly kill someone."

"Hey, I apologize, that was too close." Cotton edged forward and shook Rick's hand.

"Well, help me dress and quarter this deer. I'll get the chicken boxes from the Jeep."

Cotton nodded and hastened to where the deer lay. Rick rushed back with the boxes. They made fast work of skinning and preparing the animal. Both fell silent, and finally, placed the meat inside the two boxes.

"Thanks, Cotton, this is going to the Martin family. Caleb has four kids and got laid off yesterday."

"You're going to *give* it to them?" Cotton frowned.

"Yes."

"I sell one chicken box of quartered deer meat for $20.00. A man's got to make a living in these hard times."

Rick eyed Cotton's face. "I guess you are the poacher the law is after."

"I guess so." The eye contact held as Cotton raised an eyebrow.

"Well, I can't say you are right or wrong. We're both hunting illegally at night."

Cotton spoke fast and loud. "You are just as guilty as I am."

Rick raised his hand to quiet him. "Hush, voices carry far out here. Okay, okay! You get one box, and I get the other. Now, take your deer meat and go."

Cotton nodded, slung the rifle over a shoulder, lifted the heavy box, and groaned. He huffed by the patch of rye grass, and veered off to the thick woods, quickly becoming indistinguishable in the brush.

Rick glanced in Cotton's direction, mumbled to himself, and gripped the remaining box. His own legs wobbled from the weight, but he managed to carry it to the boat. Worn out, he forced himself to exert some energy, and paddled routinely back to his property. Tying the boat, he reviewed Cotton's intrusion, shook his head, and hurried to load the box in the Jeep. Rick climbed in behind the steering wheel, slumped in the driver's seat, and drove away.

I'm as guilty as Cotton. Just because I'm giving the meat to Caleb, still doesn't make it right. This is the wrong way to help Caleb. Lord, forgive me for hunting illegally.

Driving to the Martin home gave him time for a clearer perspective. Relieved, shades of guilt vanished as he vowed to never hunt illegally again. Rick turned onto a county road and arrived in less than an hour. He was able to park in front of Caleb's house, and was thankful he wouldn't have to walk far. As soon as he stepped out of the Jeep, dogs barked and appeared out of nowhere surrounding him.

Someone turned on the porch light, and a voice yelled, "Who is it?"

"It's me, Rick."

Caleb Martin hurried out the front door, and Rick approached, carrying the box.

"Here, got something for you." Rick handed Caleb the long, chicken box amid all the dogs still barking, and running around.

"Shoo! Get away dogs," Caleb hollered. He eased the box down and opened the lid. Caleb gazed at the meat and quickly looked at his friend. "Thanks, Rick."

Rick nodded and got back in the Jeep. He cranked the motor, backed up, and left. The interior lights of the vehicle were dim, but he noticed how grimy his clothes were. A wave of weariness washed over him as his tense body relaxed, and sank against the seat. He yawned, and his eyes, stinging with sweat, kept watering.

Good to see Caleb...

Chapter Three
August 8, 2011
8:00 AM

Teacher orientation was unfamiliar to Susan. All staff met in the auditorium for a warm welcome. Each received a tote bag of various office supplies, a lunch provided by the local administration, plus the privilege of being an attentive audience for several motivational speakers. New employees were announced and applauded.

School would not start for another week while classrooms, bulletin boards, and hall posters would be prepared to encourage students to excel.

Grateful to be included, Susan even enjoyed her lunch. She relished the last bite of crisp, fried catfish, and with a twist of her wrist, flung the paper plate into the trashcan. Indeed, she had her fill of fish, along with spicy, curly fries, jalapeño hushpuppies, creamy cole slaw, and pinto beans cooked with bacon, onions, and garlic. *Yum! Love this southern cooking!*

Another speaker was announced over the intercom. Everyone hurried toward the auditorium, but Susan bustled out the building. Mr. Monroe, the high school principal, left a voice message on her home phone, earlier; requesting she leave today's assembly at one o'clock, and report to his office.

So ready for my new job and relieved moving days are over—I am finally settled into my bungalow. Susan walked briskly toward an older conglomeration of buildings, ran up a row of worn, concrete steps, and tugged one

26

of the double doors open. A vast hallway lay before her and sported hundreds of old lockers on each side. Memories flooded her mind as she briefly recalled her own high school in another town, where she always tried to get a bottom locker. Inevitably, a tall student would end up with a bottom locker and due to Susan's shortness, they would trade. A quick glance at room numbers on doors she passed, assured her she didn't have far to arrive at the principal's office. Susan scrutinized the area. The drop acoustical ceiling had several tiles slightly ajar from the metal, support frames. *Hmm, sort of shabby. Forgot this is the oldest wing of a one hundred year old school…*

Her low heels echoed with each step in the deserted hallway.

At first the brown spot above her, on the overhead ceiling she approached, appeared to be the size of a tiny splattered pancake about two inches wide. *Too dark for a water ring from a roof leak.*

Susan was about nine feet from the door with a protruding sign that displayed Rex Monroe's name and title when the spot moved. Mesmerized, Susan stopped and stared while the object descended. It shrieked at her and flapped wide, open wings.

A bat! Headed straight at her, Susan's defense mode kicked in and her arms instantly covered her face. Another shriek screamed out above her head. Trying to hurry toward the principal's door, her right ankle weakened, and she stumbled side-ways to the floor.

"Help…anyone…help!"

She heard the gusts of air as wings fluttered around her and ducked her head. Terrified, Susan realized she couldn't tell if the shrieks came from her or intensified from the bats. Crawling to the door, her body inched along, while she dragged the brand new designer handbag in earnest. A slight nudge against her shoulder by a bat flying too close, proved to be more of an experience than she cared to have. In sudden anger, adrenalin rushed through her veins. Susan bravely stood up, wobbled, and defiantly opened the office door.

She fell inside. Afraid the bats might follow; she instinctively drew her leg back, and kicked the door shut with a fierce motion. Exhausted, she remained still, lying on the linoleum floor until her breath returned to a normal pace.

No one is here. I have to get to a telephone…

Susan pulled herself up using a file cabinet for support, tucked her loosened blouse back into her skirt, and smoothed the disarrayed hair-do in place. She sank into the chair behind an L-shaped desk, dialed the superintendent's office, and heard a prerecorded message. Frustrated, Susan ended the call the same moment an adjoining door burst open. A man entered and glanced at Susan as they held eye contact. He stopped in the doorway and frowned.

"You must be Rex Monroe." Relief flooded over Susan. She stood up and held herself erect.

Obviously annoyed, his head jerked at an angle and thick, red hair flew haphazardly across a wrinkled forehead. "You must be the source of all the unwanted commotion."

"Excuse me, but bats are the source, and I managed to dodge them. I am Susan Penleigh."

"Penleigh—we do not have a bat problem. Occasionally, a few of our taller students will jump in the hallway, with their arms extended out, touching a few of the ceiling tiles that come ajar. Maintenance is required to daily position the tiles back in proper order."

Hmm, your students continue their bad habits, while maintenance follows after them and repairs the damage? How appalling. Susan's emotions raced, and she wanted to argue against his reasoning, but held her tongue still and listened. She grasped the arm of the chair and mutely sat down. It appeared he took her lack of speech as agreement. He spoke in a less sharp tone.

"Yes," he sighed. "It is possible, one or two bats could enter the hallway through the small cracks. The older ceiling area above the tiles is their habitat. You can watch them return in the early morning through the opening of the old, brick chimney. They keep mosquitoes away. Let me introduce myself, Rex Monroe, principal of River Town High School."

"Mr. Monroe, bats can carry rabies and should not be allowed to remain near the children."

"Mrs. Penleigh, our school will be shut down if the public learns of any bats. I will reiterate; we do not have a bat problem. Understood?" He narrowed his eyes and glared at her.

"Loud and clear, sir." Susan held her head up, remained calm, and refused to display an agitated response.

"Good. At this point, I will conduct an interview concerning your future employment. You may be seated, Mrs. Penleigh."

And I may not want you for my employer, Mr. Monroe, but what a challenge!

"How fast can you type?" He sat rigid in a nearby chair.

"Typing fast is not my strongest asset. I am accurate, though. I completed the "No Child Left Behind" three day course and passed my tests with a 96 grade average. I have my paraprofessional certificate and have been finger printed, as required, by Texas law to work in a public school. Also took training for substitute teaching and teacher's aide."

"Any bookkeeping experience?"

"Yes, I was treasurer at my church for four years."

"Mrs. Penleigh, I realize you applied and received employment here for a teacher's aide position. Unfortunately, some people take my no-nonsense policy on privacy as a personal attack, and I've lost another secretary this past Friday. The position remains available, and I want to recommend you to the school board for the job. Your pay will show a substantial increase."

"How substantial?"

"That salary is budgeted for an additional ten thousand dollars."

"Job description will include what, Mr. Monroe?" Susan brushed a speck of lint off her skirt.

"More training will be necessary. I'll enroll you in workshops for attendance, discipline, and 'PIEMS.' Have you heard of 'PEIMS,' Mrs. Penleigh?"

"No, I have not."

"It is a state legislated program that pulls from all school districts and builds one elaborate database of

30

information. There will be forms to complete for state security clearance, and you will need passwords to do the daily, and six week, state reports on each category. Of course, you're responsible for all bookkeeping, including fund raisers, and writing and processing purchase orders."

"I can multi-task, Mr. Monroe."

"And I am not through with your instructions, Mrs. Penleigh. List and maintain inventory in each room at the high school, schedule parent conferences, order all office and teacher supplies, ahh…" He paused. "Oh yes, students are allowed private visits with their probation officer during school hours. You will be notified on who the judge has ordered to attend State School while incarcerated, and who has been released and is returning here. I'll need to give you a current Teacher Handbook and a Student Handbook. Study both of them, you'll need to know the rules. I will tell you we do have one registered sex offender enrolled in our eighth grade. Some of our students are on probation for assault, burglary, or substance abuse."

With a frown, his long fingers swept through the mass of red hair, and he turned to stare out the window, obviously in deep thought. In a lazy motion, he strolled toward the desk and resumed his imposing behavior.

"You admit and withdraw students using T-Rex, the state's approved software, not a fax machine. Answer the phone and distribute all mail. Learn how to fix a jammed copy machine, install staples in it, and change toner and ink cartridges. Oh, and monitor each teachers use of the copy machine by code. You'll set a maximum monthly limit and give me that report. I'll have a representative from the office supply company make an appointment to train you. You collect grades from teachers through our new computer software. You will be a Grade Book Trainer and assist the teachers daily in this task. That's all I can think of, but I'm certain there is more." His frown deepened. The lines took on a semi-permanent mark cutting into his skin.

"As long as my job description does not include bats, I think you have a secretary." Susan smiled.

"Ha! Sounds like a plan. I will call Eunice and Lloyd and get it rolling." Rex reached for the phone.

"Eunice and Lloyd? Who are they?" Susan leaned forward.

"Eunice is my father's sister, and Lloyd is my second cousin on my mother's side; both are on the school board. You just got hired as a secretary, Mrs. Penleigh."

Wow. No time to be apprehensive. Susan tried to appear pleased with the new situation and politely smiled from ear to ear.

He began relating her information, loudly, to someone on the phone, and Susan took this moment for a private prayer. "Lord, I pray for Your will, guidance, and protection in my new job and surroundings, and I surrender as Your servant. I pray You will accomplish Your work through me. In Jesus holy name, Amen."

Susan was immediately aware of the silence that hung in the room. Raising her head, she noticed Rex

Monroe watching her, and barely audible, he finished his conversation and hung up the phone.

"Did I overhear you whispering a prayer, Mrs. Penleigh?"

"Yes." Susan opened her purse, took out a prayer book, and handed it to him. "Here, you can have this copy. I like to pass them out." She smiled again.

"No, thank you."

"Do you pray, Mr. Monroe?"

"No, Mrs. Penleigh. Some of us have different religions. You may return to the assembly now."

"And you may want to read this sometime." Susan set the candy-apple red prayer book on top of the desk, and left it with him anyway. *Sure is noticeable against the drab grey office furniture. Maybe he will read it later.* She walked to the front door, cautiously opened it, and peeped into the hall, only to jump back inside the office.

"Four bats are still clinging to the corner between the ceiling and top of the walls, and I'm not going out there."

"I'll get something." He went into the adjoining room and returned with a long-handled, straw broom. "Get back," he instructed, stepped out of the office, and slammed the door.

Susan heard Rex hit the walls with the broom, it would swish and thud. Finally, by the sound of his shoes striking the floor, going away from the office, he must have chased the bats down the hall. A loud banging noise ensued, beating into the linoleum floor as Susan listened. Abruptly, a frightful stillness materialized, and remained, until Rex Monroe suddenly yelled at her.

"Bring me a lid from a box of copy machine paper."

Shaking, she searched a closet and found what he wanted. Taking the lid, she opened the door and shoved it down the hall. It slid all the way to him. Rex grabbed it, walked a few feet further, and bent over a lump on the floor. Susan looked wide eyed at the broom—it was broke in half. Frazzled, she continued to watch. He used the end of the broke, jagged handle, and pushed the dead bats into the cardboard lid he held on its side.

"I am taking this mess to the incinerator. Be right back." He carried the lid with both hands, used long strides to walk to the end of the hallway, and exited out the rear door.

Susan's attention was drawn to the ceiling, and she scanned the area. "No bat problem, indeed." A chill raced up her spine while she waited anxiously for her new boss.

Within minutes, he returned and called maintenance to clean the hallway. "Go on back to the assembly, Mrs. Penleigh, we have everything under control."

Susan grimaced and left. Her strength returned with each step down the now empty hallway and she made her exit from one of the heavy, double doors. Fresh air and sunshine greeted her outside, and she momentarily stood on the sidewalk and basked in it. Shaking her head at the recent turn of events, Susan went straight to the newer buildings, located the one for the remaining assembly, and found a seat inside.

The small audience of employees looked straight at the speaker, and in all appearances gave the woman their full attention. Susan could not keep her mind on one word being spoken. She noticed the obvious, intense expressions on most of the faces and looked around again. *I must be missing an interesting speech.* Seconds later, Rex Monroe arrived and sat a few rows across from her.

"Psst!"

Susan heard the intrusion and turned to see the jolly face of the lady sitting to the left of her.

"I'm Izabella. Welcome." She spoke barely above a whisper in a refined, southern accent.

"I'm Susan, and thank you."

Izabella proceeded to pull out a notebook and pen from her tote bag, scribbled something in a hurry and handed both to Susan.

Are you a teacher? I have been the Special Education Coordinator here for years.

Susan read the message and wrote her response, *Secretary to Mr. Monroe.*

Izabella scribbled across the page again. *We have to talk, soon.*

Susan smiled at her, and tried to concentrate on what was being told to the audience from the podium. Quickly getting her own notebook, Susan jotted down a quote the speaker shared with the audience.

"This is a new beginning——give the children the best you can——treat them like family."

It brought back memories of her own family. In a reflective mood, Susan's mind wandered to the life left behind in Seattle.

Susan and Dave had three children together from their past marriage. Daughters, Karen and Molly were both married and lived in Seattle. Son Scott, also married, recently joined the service and was stationed in Virginia. Susan didn't blame her grown children for spending so much time with their dad and his new wife, Marta, since he got out of prison for insurance fraud. *Out on a technicality. They are Christian kids, wanted to give him a chance, and be supportive of him.*

Dave and Marta would be cordial to Susan in front of the kids, if they were at an event like festivals, or parades, or anything public. If the kids weren't there, they wouldn't speak or acknowledge her presence. Pretentious people.

I refuse to be bogged down in more drama concerning Dave and Marta and their actions. I tried several years of it until after the kids married.

And then there is Mark Shackelford and his granddaughter Lucy. We planned a new life together. Another heartbreak…

Too painful to remain in Seattle.

At least Mother is happy. So proud she married the nice deputy, Wyatt Clark, and moved to Houston, Texas.

Susan was suddenly aware of the audience applauding and many rose from their seats to leave. Rex Monroe beckoned at her with his finger. Susan promptly nodded, and made her way towards him, still pondering about her married children. She pictured her naïve kids with what they were manipulated into and tried to shake the past off before anger took hold.

Maybe that is God's Way to put Christians near Dave and Marta. Maybe, through the kids, they'll see how Christians treat others. Maybe God wants Dave and Marta to realize their wealth with arrogance is not the Christian way. Maybe...

Waving to Izabella, she caught up with Rex Monroe and walked beside him.

"We have a lot of work this week in preparation for a smooth school year, Mrs. Penleigh. I want to help organize you and discuss scenarios you may encounter next week when school starts."

"Thank you, I don't know what to expect."

Chapter Four

August 15, 2011
6:45 AM

Rick opened the door and stepped inside. He raised his head and recognized some of the seated customers packed in the Red Clover Café. Brilliant sunshine glistened through the front windows and settled on the early morning breakfast crowd. Noisy chatter surrounded him as voices rose to heights of excitement. A sudden hoot from a nearby table rang out, followed by light-hearted laughter. Finding an empty stool at the counter, Rick made his way, nodding at the locals he knew.

"George Lodi, how are you doing?" Rick slid on the stool and grinned at the next occupant.

"Can't complain." The deputy tipped his hat.

"Seems hotter than usual at daybreak." Rick grabbed a napkin and wiped his brow.

"Last night's 85 degrees didn't help any." George dipped a homemade biscuit into a small bowl of sausage gravy and took several bites.

The waitress hurried to Rick, smiled, and set a cup of coffee in front of him. "Black, no cream, right?"

"Yes ma'am. Thank you." The aroma of yeast biscuits hot out of the oven penetrated the room, and tugged at his nostrils, until he could no longer resist. "I'll have the same thing George has, but throw some scrambled eggs together."

"You want ketchup or hot sauce with those eggs?"

"Both, and make that Louisiana hot sauce, please."

38

"Will do." She wrote on an order ticket and scurried off towards the cooks' window.

"Bastrop County wildfires in central Texas are raging. I saw the news again today. Evacuees may need our motels. Live reports on television show the fires are spreading fast. My heart goes out to those people." George drank a long swallow from his glass of milk.

"This drought is dangerous and tragic. Wildfires burning up peoples' homes and their livelihood is disappearing. Lake Palestine has dried up, nothing left but large cracks in the bottom. Not even any mud left. All the marinas have closed. Closer to home, Lake O' the Pines and Caddo Lake are way down. The speaker yesterday at the Noon Lions Club was from the Texas Forestry Service. I was appalled to hear how even the trees are dying and ranchers have to sell their cattle because nothing is growing to feed them. Price of hay has shot up; no one can afford it."

George glanced at his friend. "That explains the new posters plastered all over town. Jacksonville, Texas is having an auction out at their sale barn this coming Saturday. Might consider bidding on a black angus. Sure would be great in my freezer."

"Delicious steaks, a two hour drive there wouldn't be bad. I can borrow a cattle trailer if you are serious." Rick turned to look as the waitress approached, placed the food in front of him, and scampered away. He doctored his eggs, took a bite, and sat with his back facing the entrance.

A lull in conversation made the slam of the front door sound extra loud, and both Rick and George spun around on their stools, each staring at the new customer.

An attractive young woman, dark hair shining in the sunshine, emitted an air of unmistakable confidence in her Red Cross uniform.

George gasped out loud and nearly fell as he stood.

She continued toward him, and he seemed mesmerized, until he finally spoke.

"Megan Depp," he managed to say.

"Yes, how did you know?" She gave him a dazzling white smile that complimented her creamy completion.

"I caught the interview on the morning news. You are with our local Red Cross, and your team will take supplies to Bastrop County. Deputy George Lodi, how can I help you?"

"Nice to meet you. I was told to hand deliver this envelope to you before we left. A friend of mine said I could find you here and stressed the urgency of the matter." She placed it in his open palm and pivoted. "Got to run." She returned to the door in a flash as George called out to her.

"Who is your friend? How long will you be gone?"

"Oh, you know the mayor, and I am staying for the duration. There is a lot of work to do."

"They need all the help they can get. I'll thank the mayor for this, later. Take care and be safe, Ms. Depp."

"You too, Deputy Lodi." She sailed out the door, and his gaze continued after it slammed shut. Moments later, he glanced down, ripped the envelope open, and read the message.

George, watch out...Tessa Yeager is back in town.

He frowned at his friend, Rick Yeager, and stuffed the note into his pocket.

"What? What is it?" Rick raised an eyebrow concerned.

"Oh, small town gossip. I don't pay attention to stuff like that." George slapped some money down on the counter and left in a hurry.

Chapter Five

August 15, 2011
7:30 AM

Susan, overwhelmed by many procedures from the past week, none that were flexible, established a workable routine. Stacks of enrollment pages from new students sat alphabetically with rubber bands holding them secure, in an attempt of order for this first day of school.

The phone rang constantly; two fights had taken place on the school grounds. Two teen girls tangled on the school bus. When the yellow bus finally did arrive at the school and opened its door to unload students; one girl threw the other one out the bus door. She landed in the grass, legs and arms flinging in all directions, while the remaining students rooted for their favorite girl to clobber the other one. Another fight with two teenage males broke out inside the cafeteria; because of both incidents breakfast was served late to prevent a food fight, and Mr. Monroe's car had yet to appear on campus.

It was now 7:45 AM.

Earl Tillman arrived first, River Town High's Vice Principal, and he literally dragged some teenage girl into the office by her arm, while a second girl ambled in and sat down.

Susan recognized the first one. She was the cute girl that fled the house of the obnoxious Wes Harper two weeks ago.

Shouting vile remarks, she pranced before her latest victim, the other teen girl, who was slouched on a bench in Susan's office.

"Harper, sit," Tillman instructed the long legged, foul mouthed girl. She opened her lips, drew her breath in loudly, and panted noisily. Chest rising and falling in an agitated manner, she flung her arms out, draping them over the sides of the chair. Her jaw tightened, she sat defiantly rigid, clearly upset. A frown set in, disturbing Harper's young features, and it deepened as her eyes darted to the victim.

"Call 911, Mrs. Penleigh. We have an altercation." Tillman stood with his head cocked to one side.

"Don't you do it, lady!" Harper, a menacing smirk on her face, leaped from the chair, and hurled herself towards Susan.

Tillman grabbed the back of the girl's shirt and pulled her away.

Susan dialed the number with a fury and she requested help from the dispatcher. "This is Susan Penleigh. I'm the secretary at River Town High School. We have two girls fighting this morning. Don't know who started it, or what it involved, but both are sitting in my office."

"Ma'am, use different rooms and separate them immediately. I'll have a deputy there shortly."

"Thank you," Susan managed to say before glancing at Earl Tillman. His muscles were bulging taut, exposed from the short sleeve shirt he wore. *Reminds me of a drill sergeant and his first day at boot camp.*

"I was told to separate them in different rooms and help is on the way." She looked Tillman square in the face.

He opened the office door and yelled at several students passing by. "Guys, tell Coach Ramsey to hurry to the office." They scrambled off while Tillman stood in the doorway.

Harper remained as frisky as an untamed animal mauling at a possible meal. She would not calm down. Coach entered the office in time to remove her from the other girl, before more harm could ensue. Coach Ramsey left escorting Harper out the door by her left elbow.

Susan considered the wound on the other girl. One eye was badly swollen, and dried blood caked on her face around her nose.

No nurse available, only one for the entire district, and today, she was at the elementary.

"I'm going to get ice from the break room. Do we have baggies around here?"

Tillman leaned over and clicked one switch from a long row on the intercom.

"Mrs. Merry, could you please send someone to the office with a quart size baggie and a twisty tie?"

A loud female voice quickly flooded the office in reply. "Yes sir, no problem, sir."

He flipped the switch back into neutral position and smiled at Susan.

"On the way."

Susan stood up, walked from her desk, and looked out the window at the parking lot as two sheriff's deputies arrived in a patrol car.

44

"That was fast," she announced and turned around. "Help is here." She nodded at Tillman.

The door opened and a harried looking employee, obviously from the cafeteria with an oversized apron on, handed a fistful of loose baggies and ties to Tillman. Ducking her head down, she left as fast and quiet as she had arrived.

Susan reached over and took them from him. "I'll get the ice," she informed him and slipped out the side door to the employee break room.

A sudden knock grew intense. Tillman threw the office door open and greeted the arriving officers. "Gentlemen, welcome. Please come inside." He read the name badges; Deputy Hughes, and Deputy Lodi. He ushered them into the office as Susan reentered the room with a baggie full of ice cubes. Placing a paper towel down on the injured girls face, she gently laid the homemade ice bag on top.

"Hold this so it doesn't fall."

The girl took control of her ice bag and watched Susan.

Tillman buzzed the intercom and instructed Coach to return the girl. Coach Ramsey promptly dropped the girl off at the office and left.

"I'll need your names, ladies," Deputy Lodi addressed the teen girls.

"Ula Mae Miller, and our tigress is Shelly Harper," Tillman responded first.

"And," Deputy Lodi continued, as he caught Susan's glance, "will you be so kind as to provide me with their parents' names, home address and phone numbers? I also am required to have their social security numbers for identification purposes."

"Of course." Susan went to one of several filing cabinets and pulled a drawer open, rummaged through the files until she removed folders for both girls involved.

She handed them to Tillman. He scanned through one of the folders and gave the information to Deputy Lodi while Deputy Hughes talked on his cell phone, obviously to the dispatcher.

Parents were notified by Susan; two were tracked down at their jobs, and a message was left on Wes Harper's answering machine. Eventually, two parents arrived, except the disgusting Wes Harper, whom Susan dreaded to see again. Much to the parent's dismay, they were too late. Both teens were on route to the juvenile detention center. Deputies legally secured the school by removing them.

It all happened quickly and without any turmoil.

Mr. Rex Monroe made his morning appearance at that time. Much to Susan's relief, he ushered the parents into his office. Before he closed the door, he stopped and addressed Susan.

"Mrs. Penleigh, your instructions are to physically collect 1st period, written attendance lists from all classrooms. No data will be entered into the computer until the end of the week when we roll over to the new school year."

"Why?" She asked exasperated.

"This would bring the Jr. High kids forward to the High School roll and delete the graduating seniors from the previous year. For a more accurate list, attendance is obtained manually to ensure all new or transferred students were accounted for, as well as recognizing any drop outs that didn't return. These will have to be tracked down, by you, and reported on your state reports. We have eight periods in a day." He entered his office, and Susan stood up to leave hers.

Hmmpf! Run, run, run! Do I ever catch up? And how can I possibly enter attendance for each period with each teacher for the whole week on Friday?

She marched around all day a few minutes after the bell rang signaling the beginning of yet another period. Lunch came and went, while she chomped down on a salad she'd grabbed and brought back to her office. Her door remained permanently open as the noise of chattering students swept by while they hurried to classes.

"Mrs. Penleigh?" A timid girl entered the room.

Susan looked up from her meal. "Yes? May I help you?"

"I do not feel good; I need to call my mother."

Susan scooted her name plate out of the way and placed a telephone on top of the counter for the girl to use.

"Is there anything I can help you with?"

"Oh no, Mrs. Penleigh, I have been feeling nauseated in the mornings for a few days. Mom wants to take me to the doctor today if it happened again, and it just happened a while ago."

"What is your name, dear?"

"Monica, Monica Cooper." The girl brushed a loose strand of long brown hair behind her left ear.

"Monica, is this a long distance call?"

47

"No ma'am, it is local."

"Good, I don't have to stop and record it, or use a code for it to go through. Please call your mother while I finish my lunch."

Monica dialed her mother and spoke in a low voice. "Mom, I do not think I can do this … I cannot help it, I feel bad. No, ma'am, I haven't thrown up, but it could be I got nervous from the fights this morning. The kids were picking on Shelly Harper again, you know about her parents, and she went ballistic, swung her fists around and hollered. You know how they can provoke her. It made me queasy, and I just feel shaky inside … Okay, Mom, I'll get my things ready, thanks, I'll be waiting for you in the office."

She hung the phone up, and Susan tried to make the girl comfortable.

"I'm sorry that fight upset you, Monica. Please sit down. I take it your mother is on her way to get you?"

"Yes, and we will go to the doctor, so I will have a doctor's excuse when I return today."

"Great, I hate to see you start out the new school year with unexcused absences and possible truancy issues."

Monica smiled. "Oh, I usually don't have a problem with that. I don't want to get mixed up in something that is none of my doing."

"You are referring to this morning's fight?" Susan spoke gently.

"Yes, see Shelly has to live with her uncle because her mom and dad are both in prison. She hates it there, and everyone picks on her. It just makes her so mad, and the instigators never get in trouble, either. It is not

48

fair; none of it is fair to Shelly. She really is nice, Mrs. Penleigh."

"I am sure she is, Monica, but I'm not allowed to discuss any student or express my opinion about anything that deals with school. I do understand your concern, though. Please have a seat and try not to exert yourself. This morning is already over and all we can do is learn from it." She smiled at the young girl. *Hope my encouragement helped ease her nervous stomach.*

"Here, read this while you wait. It's got uplifting short stories." Susan handed her a small magazine she brought from home and placed inside her desk drawer. Monica became engrossed in the stories, and Susan tried to finish her lunch. Peace surrounded the room, and Susan treasured it. Even the phone momentarily stopped its insistent ringing.

Susan jerked when a woman burst into the office and rushed to the girl's side.

"Oh, Monica," The woman lamented, and bit her lip.

The girl looked up, obviously grateful to see her. "Mother, this is the new secretary, Mrs. Penleigh."

"Bernice Cooper." She blurted. "Thanks for taking care of my daughter. She has a time coping with stress. Her stomach knots up when anything gets out of hand. I called our doctor, and he is going to work us into his schedule this afternoon. She will probably be prescribed medication."

"It should make Monica's school days a lot smoother," Susan assured Mrs. Cooper, and handed her the notebook to sign her daughter out of school.

49

Bernice glanced at her watch, filled in the time of departure in the appropriate slot on the form, and quickly wrote the reason why Monica was leaving. She walked to the door and suddenly stopped. "Where did you get that magazine?" She looked at her daughter, and Monica clutched it tightly in her right hand.

"Mrs. Penleigh let me read it while I waited for you."

"Take it with you, please enjoy it." Susan nodded.

Bernice looked at the magazine again and raised both eyebrows as a smile quickly formed on her beaming face. "It's been forever since I've seen one of those. Such great stories! When my mother was in a nursing home, I sent her a subscription for that same one."

"Well, feel free to read it."

"Thanks, I will, and call me Bernice. I'd like to invite you to our church sometime. Chapel of Christ is located on the corner of Gentry and Broadway in the heart of downtown. Service begins at 10:30, Sunday school at 9:30. We would love for you to come."

"Appreciate the invitation." Glancing at Monica, she smiled. "Young lady, you get to feeling better, and Bernice," she glanced at the woman, "please call me Susan."

"Sounds like a done deal." Bernice shook Susan's hand again while Monica grabbed her backpack, and the two waved at Susan as they left.

Most of the salad still sat in the to-go box from the school's cafeteria with her own balsamic vinegar dressing that tempted taste buds of many casual dieters. Susan shut the door and returned to the salad, alternating between crackers and bottled water, and soon wiped out the meal.

Someone knocked and entered through the open door at the same time.

"You must be the new secretary, hope you can stay awhile. We sure need a lot more help around here, but one thing's for sure, we always have plenty to keep us busy, ha. I am Lester Davis, Lester to you, and I do maintenance here, and also bring you the mail. "

"Susan, Susan Penleigh, and can I help you bring those inside?" She looked at the three tubs of mail he sat on the floor.

"Oh no, ma'am, they are way too heavy. Let me scoot by you and take them into the break room. The mail slots on the side wall are listed with each employee's name, and you will find there is never enough time to sort through this and stick it all into the proper slot." He carried two tubs past her, and sat them near the mail area in the adjoining room. "I mow grass at the school on Saturday's, and I always bring Saturday's mail inside this break room first. You can count on it being here on Monday morning."

"Thank you, Lester." Susan followed him, grabbed a stack of mail from one of the tubs, and began inserting each to the correct person's slot.

Simultaneously, the phone rang on her desk. Hurrying back, she snatched at it. "Good afternoon, River Town High School." She reached for a pen, listened to the caller, and began writing on her daily notebook. "Mr. Monroe is not available at this time, Mr. Whitman. I'll give him your message, thank you for wanting to include us in your cookie dough fundraiser program." She hung up the phone and ran into Lester as he went around her desk carrying in the last tub of mail.

"Might as well get ready for interruptions, Mrs. Susan. It's harder to get things done around here than you would think." He chuckled while she returned to pass out the mail.

"Lester, someone has already put something in a few of these slots." Susan grabbed a folded page that was lying in her own mail slot and slowly opened it.

"Oh, that has to be from Mr. Monroe. Always check your mail a few times a day. Mr. Monroe inserts notes to us whenever something crosses his mind. You don't want to miss something important he might suddenly want you to do."

"Thank you, Lester," Susan called out as he left. She read the instructions that were indeed from Mr. Monroe. "Make a copy of the new checkbook balance with the added deposit and a copy of the activity page for the cheerleaders with the added deposit recorded, and put both copies into the yellow inter-office mail envelope. Address it to Mrs. Celia. Also, put another copy of the check into a new folder, place that folder on top of the checkbook inside the file cabinet, and lock it."

Susan sorted mail as fast as she could go and heard the muffled conversations of the parents finally leaving Mr. Monroe's office from the other side of the break room.

"Mrs. Penleigh?"

Rex Monroe must be in my office now. She retrieved her note from him and walked through the open doorway into her office. "Yes?"

Rex stood in the middle of the room like a train about to charge down a mountain.

"Need I remind you of our privacy policy? I will not tolerate anything being repeated that happened this morning."

"That is not necessary, Mr. Monroe. I read the policy and signed my agreement to it." Susan briefly exchanged eye contact with him when a different woman entered Susan's office.

"Mr. Monroe? I sure do need your help, sir."

She appears to be deeply troubled. Susan momentarily forgot Rex Monroe's attitude and gave the woman her full attention.

Rex turned toward the intruder. "How may I be of service to you?"

"I'm Iris… Iris Livingston, and ah… it is about my sister. You remember Patsy Garrett, don't you? You went to school with her right here in River Town, years ago. Well, she is not quite right, you know, and I am trying to help her get on social security. The most stupid thing came up about her gender. It was never recorded on her birth certificate if she is a boy or a girl. So I thought if I had a copy of her school records here, it would say if she is a boy or a girl."

"Yes, I do remember her. Have a seat while I get my secretary to get those records."

He glanced at Susan. "I showed you last week where the old records are kept. Mrs. Penleigh, please bring me Patsy Garrett's folder while I visit with Mrs.

53

Iris Livingston." Susan noticed the brand new gracious smile that suddenly appeared on his former hostile face.

"Yes sir." Susan grabbed a set of keys from the desk drawer and left immediately.

Upon her return, she found both laughing, clearly enjoying each other's company. "Sir?" Susan interrupted and handed Rex Monroe an old yellowed folder.

"You could have merely put it on the desk, Mrs. Penleigh. " He cleared his throat and opened the folder. Flipping through several pages, silence draped over the room as Susan stared at him, and Iris Livingston sat waiting for his decision.

"Well, it has never been selected here, boy or girl. No one ever checked either box on the form, in all these years. Funny, why no one checked boy or girl." He looked up from the folder and addressed Iris Livingston. "She is a girl, isn't she?"

"Yes, she is, her name is Patsy, after all." Iris smiled.

Rex grabbed a pen from Susan's desk, held the yellowed form toward both women, and marked a check in the small box with girl next to it.

Susan gasped audibly. *He has just changed an official document.*

Rex glared at Susan. "Here, make a copy of this form and give the copy to Mrs. Iris Livingston."

"I have to maintain security on those records. No one is allowed to alter any document. How do you know she is really a girl?"

"Mrs. Penleigh, do not question my decision."

Iris Livingston laughed. "It is okay, Mrs. Penleigh. Mr. Monroe is just helping. I knew I could count on him. Thank you, Mr. Monroe." Her face beamed with obvious admiration.

"Forgive me for being so blunt, but have either of you ever looked under *her* dress? Do you really know she is a she?" Susan continued.

"That will be enough, Mrs. Penleigh. Are you refusing to carry out your duties?" Rex Monroe's face flushed a sudden bright shade of red.

Susan scowled at him, took the form to the copy machine, laid the old form onto the scanner, and selected one copy. Within seconds, it shot out into the tray, and she quietly gave it to Mrs. Livingston.

"That will be all, Mrs. Penleigh; you may return the folder to the old records section of filing cabinets."

Susan quickly went down the hallway, dropped the folder off at another room, and continued the fast pace. *Mmm, mmm, mmm…what a mean, arrogant man…*She walked briskly to each classroom, gathered the day's remaining paper slips, and hurried back to her own office. Silence greeted her, and she peered out the window looking at the parking lot. *What a relief…Mr. Monroe's car is gone…*

Susan stapled each teacher's attendance slips together, recorded the daily total to her notebook, and called the information in to the superintendent's office. She leaned back in her seat. *There, at least I finished that today.* A glance at the wall clock seemed to verify her weariness. School had been out for over an hour.

After all three tubs of mail were processed, Susan grabbed her purse, locked her office door, and left for the day.

◆◆◆◆

She drove her car to a nearby grocery store, and ran inside, stopping at the deli.

"I would like one order of the grilled chicken, please. Do you offer the combination salad of chopped broccoli and celery with walnuts and raisins?"

"Yes, ma'am." The employee donned tight plastic gloves and snapped them with a loud pop at each wrist.

"I'll take both."

The clerk nodded and dished out the items in to-go containers.

"Mrs. Penleigh."

Susan turned to see who was calling her name. Unsure what to expect, she looked directly into the face of Shelly Harper.

"Shelly? It is Shelly Harper, right?"

"Yes ma'am. Surprised to see me? The judge rushed our cases into court because he wanted me and Ula Mae back in school right away. We are on probation. Do you live near here, Mrs. Penleigh?"

"Yes, I do."

"Well, my living conditions are awful."

"I know where you live. I met your uncle."

"He is so creepy."

"How old are you, Shelly?"

"I turn eighteen in September, this is my senior year. An older guy I know said I could move in with him, but he gets in more trouble than I do. He is back in prison for armed robbery."

"Shelly, I have been invited to the Chapel of Christ church this Sunday, at 10:30. Why don't you join me there?"

"I know where that is. Okay, I will go."

"Do you have a Bible?"

"No ma'am."

Susan reached inside her oversized purse and gave her a small, compact Bible, along with a red prayer book. "You do now."

Shelly tilted her head at Susan. "Thank you."

The clerk handed Susan her packaged meal, turned, and addressed the younger patron. "What would you like to order?"

"That sounded good. I'll try the same thing she got."

The clerk smiled and set about filling the order.

"You'll like it and Shelly…" Susan turned to leave.

"Yes, ma'am?"

"Don't cast your pearls before swine."

"I like that. Is it a Bible verse?"

"Yes it is. Matthew 7:6"

"I will read it. Thanks, see you tomorrow."

"You too, Shelly."

Chapter Six
August 17, 2011
4:30 PM

"Susan?"

"Yes."

"Hey, this is Rick. Am I calling at a bad time?"

"No, I'm in the recliner, and my feet are elevated. Did you know it is mandatory to relax after school each day?"

"Ha, and whose rule is that?"

"Mine. Of course, I recommend this for everyone. You don't have to work at a school."

"Lady, I could not work at any school. I'm afraid my mouth would get me in trouble, and ol' George Lodi would carry me off from there."

"Now that *is* funny, but I think you are more of a gentleman than you portray. Besides, George has been at school, earlier. You missed your chance."

"He's come and gone? Hmm, certainly tells me how things are going at your new job."

"Not so bad."

"I was hoping it would be agreeable. Listen, I want to run something by you. We talked before about going to church sometime, and tonight is eating meeting…"

"Eating meeting? Pardon me for interrupting, but that is my kind of church. I used to bring a covered dish to them for years!"

"It will be a great way for you to meet everyone. We have ours on the third Wednesday each month. What do you think, want to go?"

"I'd like that Rick, thanks."

"Okay. Dress casual, jeans will work. It starts at 6:30. I'll pick you up at 6:00, and we'll swing by, and get a bucket of fried chicken."

"Sounds like a great evening."

"All right then. See you soon." Rick ended the call. *Oh, I can't wait…*

Shower and shave did not take long. He opened the medicine cabinet, scanned several bottles, and considered what aroma would be casual. *There it is.* Rick grabbed and applied Cool Water after shave. The smell engulfed him and it was pleasing. *Perfect.*

A search through his adjoining closet found the pressed blue jeans fresh from the cleaners. Starched and bleached white, the short sleeved shirt was next. Rick dressed, snatched socks from a drawer, and hurried to tug on his Justin Ostrich boots.

Inspecting his hands demanded a quick run to the sink. A vigorous nail-brush scrub, hair combed swiftly, and Rick was ready to go. *What time is it?* He grabbed his Citizen Eco Drive Chronograph, noticed he had ten minutes left, and slipped on the watch. Rick glanced around the room and spotted the black Stetson hat he always wore. Cocking his head to the side, he adjusted the hat in final preparation, smiled into the wall mirror, and crammed his billfold into a back pocket. Keys in hand, he left the house, locked it, and headed for the huge, shiny, black Toyota Tundra truck.

Minutes passed, and Rick pulled into Susan's driveway, at straight up 6:00 pm. He quietly parked the truck. Greeted by the dreary, beige lawn, he walked by the landscaped area of dead stalks and brown ivy. *Too hot to work on this.* A slow, sorrowful shake of his head, expressed the shock as he once again encountered severe drought damage. *I will never get used to this. Maybe I can help Susan clean out the flower bed, if the heat ever lets up.*

A loud knock on the door, and it opened almost immediately, which brought him face to face with the one he often thought about. Each with a half-smile, he gazed at her, and she beamed at him. They continued eye contact until Susan broke the moment.

"Let me get my purse and keys."

"Sure." Rick nodded at Susan. She darted off and raced back. The oversized black, patent leather purse hung from her arm and swung into everything it came in contact with. Rick dodged it, and escorted her down the sidewalk, after she locked the house. He nearly stumbled as he stared down at her with admiration.

"You look great." Rick smiled.

"Thanks, so do you."

"I have to say being with you reminds me of a happy, spring day; birds chirping and all."

Susan blushed, and at a loss for words, gave a lopsided smile. *I only picked out the blue jean capris, white peasant blouse, and white sandals to feel cooler in this heat.*

Rick held the passenger door open on the truck and helped her inside. "We could almost be twins." He laughed.

"Blue, white, and black… ha. Great minds think alike."

He hurried to his side of the truck and jumped in. "Except for that massive purse." He teased.

"Hey, I am prepared." Susan tried to set the purse on the floor board and it wouldn't fit.

"Here, plenty of room in the back seat." He reached over and groaned audibly as he swung it over to the empty seats behind them. "Girl, how can you carry that heavy thing around?"

"I know it's heavy, but I need everything in there."

Rick smiled, backed out the driveway, and took off toward the church.

"Do many come to the eating meetings?"

"We usually have about thirty-five or forty. Some are terrific cooks, I might add." He noted a slight nervousness on her part and rambled on. "Most are working people like us, probably be a lot of fried chicken bought for tonight."

Susan poked him in his ribs and laughed. "Shame on you! Now I'll start to smile every time I see fried chicken tonight."

"And I'll whisper, 'stifle, stifle' and give you a kick under the table." He winked at her. "That reminds me, we'd better get our fried chicken. What do you like, white meat or dark? Crispy or original?"

"If it were just me, I'd prefer grilled, but who doesn't enjoy fried every now and then? Crispy would be good, and a bucket of mixed dark and white meat will work."

"Done deal." Rick changed lanes to exit, zipped down a few side roads, and cut across an empty parking lot. The KFC chicken sign loomed ahead.

"You make a great GPS, I was lost. Nice driving, Rick."

"Thank you, ma'am." He eased into the take out lane, ordered, proceeded to the next window, and paid. He turned to Susan and spoke in a matter-of-fact tone. "Now this is something I am also familiar with, every drive through in town."

"That could be remedied with my expertise in cuisine. I'm good for one home cooked meal a week, if you are up to it."

"I'd like to try." Rick reached for their order and cautiously drove back onto the main road.

"Great, I'll have fun picking something out." Susan smiled.

Traffic increased. Rick carefully maneuvered around a stalled car at an intersection and signaled a right turn. Susan watched as he focused on driving until they entered the church parking lot. It was nearly full.

"We made it." Rick sang out. "Here, let me help you." He exited and opened her door. Susan stepped onto the pavement while Rick retrieved her purse and handed it to her.

"Thanks." She looked around at the few people walking ahead of them.

Rick grabbed the bucket of chicken, and the keyless remote beeped loudly as he clicked to lock the truck. Side by side, they strolled towards the entrance.

Several children, obviously of elementary school age, rushed past them and barged inside. An older woman stood at a nearby table as the group scampered towards her. Shouts of "We're hungry!" filled the dining room, and the kids jumped up and down, clearly excited.

"Whoa, hold on a minute. Wash your hands first, and then stand in line at the buffet tables," she instructed the young group, who scattered to the rear area marked with men and women restroom signs. A quick glance at the couple still standing at the open door, brought a warm smile to her face, and she made rapid strides to them. "Welcome, come on in. Rick, who do you have with you?"

Rick and Susan both regarded her.

"Mrs. Cleburne, you do amaze me. I could stand here and watch you corral kids all day. This is my friend, Susan Penleigh. She works at the high school."

"Nice to meet you. Rick and I go back a long ways. In fact, I taught him in Sunday School when he first moved here."

"Oh, the stories you could tell," Susan prompted.

"No, she's can't; I was already a grown man." Rick steered Susan away and placed the KFC bucket near the other food dishes. "We're hungry, too, Mrs. Cleburne." He called out to her and laughed while they got in line. Other introductions were made. Rick and Susan filled their paper plates, enjoyed their meal, and fellowship. Susan met and talked to many people, and her face glowed with contentment.

The youth volunteered for cleanup duty, and Rick and Susan said their goodbyes.

Rick drove them back to Susan's house and parked in her driveway. "Our evening is flying by." He glanced at her, and she made no effort to move.

"Let's just sit and talk awhile. Tell me about yourself, besides Mrs. Cleburne being your teacher." Susan chuckled.

Rick narrowed his eyes at her. "Oh, there is not much to tell. I was raised in Lufkin, Texas. Graduated, spent four years in the Air Force, got my Realtors license, and moved here."

"What about your family? Did you ever marry?"

Susan suddenly seemed serious to Rick. He studied her a moment, she sat still and appeared to have patience. *She is so comfortable to be with.* He sprawled back in the seat and smiled at her. "Well, I am the oldest of four siblings. A younger brother and two sisters round out the family. They are scattered all across the states. I haven't heard from any of them in months. Our parents passed away years ago." He leaned forward over the steering wheel and slid the palms of his hands across the top. Rick swallowed hard and darted his eyes towards Susan. "Yes, I did marry. My wife wasn't ready for marriage, liked to flirt around; and sure didn't want to be tied down as a mother to our little girl. My wife's behavior worsened until she ran the streets and clubs like a wild teenager, which she made look exciting to our child. We finally divorced. After our daughter turned eighteen, they both left town together. Haven't heard from either of them."

Susan flinched, reached out, and rubbed the back of Rick's neck in circular motions with the tips of her fingers. "It's a wonder you aren't one big knot."

His hands visibly relaxed on the steering wheel and hung motionless as he turned his head to face her. "What about you, Susan?"

"My husband was a ladies' man. Cocky, good-looking, smooth talking; you know the type. We

64

married young, and I'll never forget the first time he put me down. I was so naïve. I can still remember being so shocked at what he said and did." Susan paused, looked out the window, and continued. "We were buying groceries, and I was dressed in jeans and a pull over sweater. I was about nineteen years old, and he was five years older. I didn't realize it at the time, but I was standing in the middle of the aisle, reading the label on a can, making sure it contained the ingredients I wanted. He walked up from behind me, jerked a hold of my arm, pushed me to the edge of the aisle, and yelled, 'Move! Get out of her way!' I turned to see a young woman in a business suit that had stopped pushing her shopping cart. She made eye contact with my husband, slowly looked me up and down, and thanked him. He stood there with a sheepish grin on his face. She walked on by with her high heels clicking against the shiny tile floor. I should have left him then, but I didn't. The only good that came from our marriage was our children, one boy and two girls."

"I think I've heard all I can stand about him. Glad you have kids." Rick squeezed her hand, and Susan yawned. "Girl, I'm keeping you out too late. I forgot you get up early for work." He smiled, reached, and gently pushed a fallen curl back from her forehead.

"Rick, let's finish this talk later, okay?" Susan yawned again.

"Yes ma'am, we will."

Rick helped Susan out of the truck and escorted her to the front door. She unlocked it, turned, and stood in the doorway. "Goodnight Rick, I sure enjoyed our evening."

"So did I Susan. Goodnight." He tipped his hat and left.

Rick drove home whistling all the way. He finally angled off the main road and steered onto his street. Something thrown on the side of the curb caught his attention. He slowed his speed and stiffened when he recognized what it was. *My clothes!* Rick clicked on the high beams on the truck, and identified articles of clothing that were strewn at least a half mile from his house. *On each side of the street!* Rick pulled into his driveway and parked near the entrance of his house. He jumped out.

The front door was wide open with a gaping hole in it. "Door knob and lock removed?" Rick sputtered.

Clothes spilled out in the doorway and onto the yard. Many still in the clear plastic bags from the cleaners. Empty coat hangers lay on the ground amongst the pressed shirts and pants.

Rick swayed in anger, grabbed his cell phone, and called 9-1-1. "My home has been vandalized, and the perpetrator or perpetrators may still be inside. I just got home, and the door is wide open." Rick gave his name and address and was told to return to the truck, and wait inside.

Two deputies he wasn't acquainted with arrived within minutes. The two officers went into the house, secured the area, and came back out.

"Mr. Yeager, do you know why anyone would want to trash your home?"

Rick's voice croaked. "Trash my home?"

"Yes sir, every mirror is broken, everything is smashed or ripped. Complete disaster."

Rick ran through the open doorway and stood in the topsy-turvy mess that once was his living room. He groaned as his eyes scanned the destruction. *Why? And why so brutal? I don't dare tell Susan, she'd be too frightened it might happen to her.* He stepped into another room, kicked an overturned ottoman out of his path, and felt his stomach knot up from stress. *This has to be a random act of violence.*

Chapter Seven

August 19, 2011
7:15 AM

Susan awoke early with ample time for leisure morning coffee. *Haven't heard from Rick since the eating meeting, and I have to stop being so quick to not like Mr. Monroe. We clearly don't know each other's ways yet.* She sipped again, enjoying the taste of a strong hot brew, and savored the aroma as it arose from the cup, taunting her senses. Another cup and a daily prayer to the Lord, and Susan scrambled from the kitchen to dress for work.

Minutes later, purse and car keys in hand, she dashed out to the Chevy Equinox.

Neighbors were leaving also and waved to her as they drove by. Susan returned their friendly gesture, backed out of her driveway, and heard every motorist's dreaded sound.

Ker-plunk, ker-plunk, ker-plunk…

"Oh no, not a flat tire," Susan groaned and stopped the car immediately.

Jumping out, she hurried to the rear of the vehicle, confirmed the flat tire and opened the trunk. Susan bent over and a struggle to remove the spare ensued. Both hands held tight to the large bulky tire, which she rolled close to her chest, tugging upward in an awkward, lifting attempt. It slipped and fell, heading down hill in the direction of the road. Susan's adrenalin surged, and she ran as fast as she could go; when a male voice yelled, "I got it!"

She saw a long legged man rush toward her and grab the bouncing object in mid-air.

"…Oh, I cannot believe this. Thank you!" Susan stopped running and spoke between gasps until slowly her breathing returned to normal.

"Whew! That was close. Glad to help. Logan Wakefield, at your service, ma'am." His slow, southern drawl captivated her, as did the slight graying hair at his temples. Susan managed not to stammer a response. *Hmm, how did that song go? 'You had me at hello?'*

"Susan…Susan Penleigh." She blinked and recognized an encounter of genuine kindness. "How nice to meet you and what great timing." She motioned with her hand toward the tire.

"So is this something you do often?" He grinned at her.

"What?" Susan queried, and turned her head to the side.

"Bounce tires around?"

"No way." She laughed. "I couldn't handle many flat tires. One surprise was plenty."

"A mere delay. Let me help get you on the road."

"Thanks, a lug wrench is in the car and other tools, as well. I do appreciate this, Logan."

"You're welcome."

Susan walked to the trunk while Logan rolled the tire along.

He grabbed a crow bar, squatted down, and popped the hubcap off. Susan set it upside down next to him and handed him the lug wrench.

"You haven't lived here long, have you?" Logan took a lug nut off and placed it in the palm of Susan's hand.

She pitched the lug nut inside the hubcap. "No, and Logan; this isn't how I wanted to meet my neighbors. Hope I'm not keeping you from anything."

"No ma'am, I keep my own hours, and it's a pleasure to meet you. So, how do you like River Town?"

"Oh, I love it, but how can you keep your own hours?"

"I'm a self-employed computer technician, and thankfully, I stay busy." He removed the other lug nuts and passed them to Susan. She grinned, took careful aim, and tossed each one into the hubcap.

"Well, that is great information." Susan turned to look directly at Logan. "I am somewhat technically challenged myself."

"See, you needed to meet me and didn't even know it." He laughed, pulled the tire off, and replaced it with the spare. Susan gave him the lug nuts. Logan tightened them back into place and pounded the hubcap into position.

"There, all done." He got up off the driveway, gathered tools, and returned them to the car. "If you don't mind my asking, where do you have to be this morning? Hope this doesn't make you late."

"I work at River Town High School. I actually got up early today, and in spite of what happened, thanks to you, I have plenty of time to get there. Maybe I can repay the favor. Apple pie or something."

"I would like that. Cooking or baking does not work for me. Now I can Bar-B-Q, but if you smell something awful in the air, it's probably coming from my house, and I have scorched another pot of beans." He raised an eyebrow and quickly cocked his head towards her.

"I'll see what I can come up with." Susan grinned. "Thanks again, Logan."

"Anytime, and my house is right across the street." He turned and sprinted away as Susan climbed back into the vehicle. She turned on the ignition, drove off to work, and hummed a tune. *Interesting morning.*

◆ ◆ ◆ ◆

Another hectic day lined itself up with demands that kept Susan hopping. Her smile and a burst of energy, ensured a productivity level even Mr. Rex Monroe might notice.

Susan jumped as the room filled with a loud blast of noise from the intercom unit. *I'll never get used to that buzzer.*

"Susan?" A female voice spoke as static crackled in the line.

"Yes."

"It's me, Izabella. I'm not bothering you, am I?"

"No ma'am, you most certainly are not. How are you?"

"Fine, Susan. I thought it might be a good time to have our talk together."

"I would love that. How about lunch in the school cafeteria?"

"Lunch A or lunch B?"

"I can do either, Izabella. Which do you have to take?"

"Lunch B will work. That's on my schedule, and my oh my, Susan; do not mess up a schedule around here, ha!"

"Wait; don't tell me about your schedule. You cannot stand someone and want to be moved to another class…oh no, Izabella, you *are* the teacher, you *cannot* be moved, ha."

Izabella played along. "Oh, how did I get to be the teacher?" She moaned out loud until both women burst out laughing.

"See you for lunch, girl." Izabella clicked off, and Susan dove into her work.

Several interrupting phone calls later, she retrieved last month's unopened bank statement, and processed it. Susan made copies of the ledger pages, and copies of all statement pages, front and back. These copies were stuffed into large, inner office envelopes, addressed to people at other offices, and she pitched them in the outgoing tub of mail.

A bell rang close to her ear, which caused an involuntary shudder on her part. Her head throbbed from all the daily bells that designated each of eight class periods. Not to mention hearing it twice again each period; once five minutes after, and the tardy bell at ten minutes after the class began.

She couldn't forget the loud buzzes from the intercom, or the constant ringing of the telephone. *Yes, the noise level is excessive. Might not hurt to wear ear plugs…*

A glance at the wall clock showed it was close to noon. Susan recalled her lunch invitation. *Izabella is such a fun person!*

She locked the office door and took off to enjoy her lunch. Scanning the hallway ceiling for bats, she breathed a sigh of relief.

"What was that for?" Rex Monroe spoke behind her.

Startled, Susan whirled about. "Oh. I didn't see you. I cringe remembering the bats. It was a scary experience. Is the problem being addressed?"

"Yes. Measures are being taken to prevent their return. Of course, we remain quiet about the issue, Mrs. Penleigh." He walked to a nearby door and entered a classroom.

Susan hurried to the cafeteria as the bell rang and soon chatted with students while standing in line. It moved swiftly, and a teenage boy handed her a tray from the top of a huge, slightly wet stack.

"Thanks for your kindness." Susan smiled at him. He smiled back. Food selections were made; she grabbed her utensils, a drink, paid the employee at the cash register, and looked around for Izabella.

Laughter penetrated the entire area where Susan spotted her. Approaching the table, Susan pulled a chair out to sit with Izabella's friends.

"No, wait Susan; I reserved a place for us in the corner." Izabella rose and turned to face those still laughing. "I'll see you guys later." She guided Susan away from the lively group and toward the quiet, more private, reserved table. No one sat nearby at all, and Izabella motioned for Susan to be seated.

"We need to talk. I need to make you aware of some alarming details. First of all, I am not here to gossip. I am here to alert you to many dangerous, safety issues."

"Izabella, I appreciate your concern, but a local realtor has informed me of the lack of discipline here at the high school. Believe me, upon my arrival to River Town, I have been warned."

"It is so much more than ... to be warned, Susan."

"Okay, I will listen. You have obviously given a lot of thought about the subject."

Izabella sighed deeply. "Where do I begin?" She smiled at Susan. "Eat your lunch, dear, and let me ramble."

Susan nodded, attempting to understand, and convey encouragement to her new friend at the same time.

"Sometimes incidents are not listed as accurately as possible. If all discipline was coded true to the violation, our state funding would be greatly reduced. This is why our school has a discipline problem. No one will accurately code the incident like it should be coded, according to the state rules. When the reports go in, everything is covered up. If they did report accurately, then our school would be considered "At Risk." State funding would immediately dwindle. Ours is not the only school that practices this method."

Susan's voice cracked and betrayed her attempt of calmness. "Method? Sounds more like open lying to me,"

"It is a money thing; it is *all* about the money. The school keeps the money coming in. We have three fourths of our discipline students leave here thinking they can get away with anything. They end up in armed robbery, making and selling drugs, violent

74

family abuse, burglary, home invasions, rape, or credit card fraud. Read the local newspaper. Someone from River Town High makes the newspaper at least once a week in the police report. It is a proven fact. No gossip."

"So, those in charge of the school are not doing the community any favors by keeping the school open with incorrect discipline reports?"

"Correct. All they are doing is simply talking a good show. Grades are down, pregnancies are up, and the dropout rate is not accurate, either. Everything shown on reports to reflect progress is being made, when just the opposite is true. "

"It's not fair to hear only your side. I respect your right to an opinion, but schools can be wrongly labeled. Many could be working diligently to prevent what you claim is happening. I say this because often things are not what they appear to be. Any examples?"

Izabella stopped and took a bite from her taco. "I don't know if I can give you all of them right now, but I will inform you of the more dangerous ones."

Susan looked at her and noticed the strained look on Izabella's face. *This really is hard for her to reflect on, much less discuss any of the incidents.* Sprinkling parmesan cheese across Italian food, Susan thoughtfully twirled some spaghetti around the meat balls on her plate and slowly ate her meal, as she listened to every word.

"We had one student, who in all appearances, seemed like a sweet kid. You can only imagine how shocked the entire community was when he was arrested for forcibly raping a little fourth grade girl. He was only in the sixth grade at the time." Izabella sighed loudly.

"He went off to the state correctional school and returned the following year. Long story short, he was in and out of trouble for his remaining school years, and raped again; finally got involved in a home invasion.

"That has to be an isolated incident."

"No, it is a mere drop in the bucket. A perfect example of not giving correct discipline, and a perfect example of how horribly that student's attitude grew bold and hurt the community."

Izabella looked at Susan. "I don't want you to become a fatality here while someone gets away with who knows what."

"I wasn't aware I needed to be so cautious."

"Can't leave Charlie out. He got away with a lot, too."

"Charlie?"

"Yes. A woman moved to our town with three teenage daughters. Charlie decided he was going to date the youngest one. Somehow, he obtained her home phone number. He called constantly every night, until the mother, who was a single parent, told him to stop. She told him her daughter was entirely too young to date, and for him to leave her alone. Charlie followed the girl through the school halls and into her classrooms, and let everyone know that he *was* going to date her. Finally, the oldest sister argued with him inside a classroom that he was *not ever* going to date her.

"Charlie actually fought her physically and hit her with his fists, until an ambulance was called to carry her to a hospital. Her spleen was torn. The following day, the mother came to the school demanding justice. No one told her the only way she would get justice was to legally file charges on him herself. Charlie was suspended three days for fighting. The mother decided the only way to keep Charlie away from her daughter, and keep her family safe, was to move. That is exactly what she did, and our school district lost three honor students, but kept Charlie with his failing grades. He later beat up a girlfriend, finally married, and beat up his first wife. That was his first prison sentence. He was also in a different home invasion.

"There have been a total of seven home invasions in our town in the past two years…each by young thugs, and thankfully, all were caught. I can't help but see a pattern was established in high school of getting away with anything. In a home invasion, the home owners are home when the intruders enter. Usually, the intruders are high on drugs, and do not reason like we do."

Susan pushed her plate aside. "I understand what you are saying. It is a different world than when I went to school."

"Yes. Be careful, a lot of people are related. They take care of their own."

"Thanks, Izabella. I appreciate your concern, but please realize that I *do* intend to make a difference. I *do* have the students' best interests at heart, and I want to get acquainted with all of them. They have a voice, and I want to hear it."

"I think you will do well here at River Town High; if anyone can, I honestly think you have a chance." Izabella grabbed her tray and left. Susan sat contemplating the history of the school.

"Mind if I join you?"

Startled, Susan glanced up from her plate and smiled at Earl Tillman. "I would like that." She extended her arm out and gestured toward the table.

"Good to see you having lunch here and not confined to that office. Trying to eat while you work is not a healthy routine for anyone."

"So true, and I enjoyed intermingling with the students while I was in the lunch line. They are at such an impressionable age."

"Mrs. Penleigh, that is the whole key to our students, intermingling. You, being new, may not be aware of the poverty level here. We are talking third generation welfare and an area where jobs are scarce. Unfortunately, in all appearances, it is popular to be a thug in today's American high schools. Let me assure you, most only want attention. They don't get it at their homes, those who do have a home. Often, they are not encouraged to succeed, and are abused, with drug addicts for parents."

"Like Shelly Harper?"

"Yes, exactly like Shelly Harper. They just don't realize the only way out of this vicious cycle is education. Without it, they have no promising future. Yet, they fight it. They don't try to learn, they don't care about attendance, it doesn't matter they missed lessons and are sure to fail exams. They want to fit in and belong, and for that reason they cling to the wrong peers."

"Mr. Tillman, surely not all students can be put neatly into such a category. For example, it is true most male students wear the baggy pants that fall below four inches of their belly button. I see them walking down the halls with their hand constantly clutched onto their belt buckle, holding their pants up. For every ten I see dressed that way, I notice two that are not. Those two young men can clearly think for themselves and do not follow the others."

"We have a long way to go here at River Town High, Mrs. Penleigh, but we are working to improve the situation."

'That's what it's all about. Improvement will make a positive difference in their lives. I guess I should not say this, Mr. Tillman, but there are times when I get so furious at seeing these young men walk around holding their pants up. I wonder how would they feel if women marched around clutching their bra constantly?"

Earl Tillman threw his head back and gave her a deep, belly laugh. "Oh, Mrs. Penleigh, that made such a funny picture in my mind." He chuckled, and people sitting at other tables turned towards him, and smiled.

Susan blushed when she noticed others smiling in her direction. "Well, I am glad no one else could hear me."

She reached for the slightly toasted garlic bread that accompanied her spaghetti and meat balls. The slight crunch of the first bite amazed her with a perfect taste of just the right amount of soft butter and creamy garlic. "Mmm! This is delicious! What great cooks, I'll probably gain weight here."

Tillman chuckled, and Susan finished her meal while he picked at his. The bell rang shrilly as he took one last bite..

"Let's do this again." He grabbed his tray and shoved his chair back.

"I'll look forward to it." Susan stood and looked around as he left. A crowd of teens walked past her in a hurry, their voices rising in bubbly excitement about something inaudible.

"Hey, where do these trays go?" She called out to them.

"Over there, through that doorway." A young man with baggy pants pointed to the other side of the room.

"Thank you." Susan quickly put her drink and napkin on her tray with the partially empty plate and utensils. *I like this, I will so return to the cafeteria.* She smiled at everyone, made her way to the area with the conveyer belt, and set her tray on it.

"You certainly have good food here." She told a cafeteria worker who was removing trays from the opposite end of the slowly moving belt.

"Thank you for the compliment. I'll be sure and tell the others."

Susan nodded again and left to make the rounds to gather attendance slips from each classroom.

"Hi, Mrs. Penleigh," A student called out.

"Hi, dear," Susan answered. Her smile lingered. *What a nice way to finish off a Friday, and Rex Monroe still isn't ready for me to sit at my computer and enter this week's attendance data…*

80

Chapter Eight
August 20, 2011
7:00 AM

Rick awoke, head pounding, in a suite at the River Town Inn. *My new residence.*

Necessary toiletries spilled from a plastic Walgreens bag and covered the top of a nearby dresser. Slowly, he left the bed and shuffled his feet to view the late night purchases he'd made Wednesday; after his home had been vandalized. In a daze, he stared at the assortment and rummaged through all of it, until he found something for a headache..

Who trashed my house…or should I say who created a crime scene…and why?

Rick opened the tiny refrigerator, grabbed an open bottle of water, and gulped down the headache medication. *Maybe my house made the news by now.*

He snatched up the remote and turned on the television. *Rats…it's Saturday morning cartoons.* A fast click and off it went. *So much for watching the news.* He placed the remote in the side pocket of the recliner. *That was my routine at home, always knew where it was.* He shook his head.

Suddenly, a shrill whistle rang out. Rick flinched and fumbled with his cell phone before he answered it. "Hello."

"Rick Yeager?"

"Speaking."

"Detective Broussard. We tracked your laptop and 48 inch, flat screen television to a pawn shop close to

81

the county line. Serial numbers match, but no sign of your guns."

"I was hoping they would have showed up right away."

"Hard to tell…depends on the desperation of the thief. Sometimes they sell for a quick buck on the street or wait for a better price. Either way, we will continue. Our investigation is far from over."

"Any fingerprints?"

"No leads at this time. We are finished with your house, though. I suggest you get pictures, and have your insurance agent verify the damage, before you contact a cleaning service."

"Good point, I will, and thank you."

"Anytime, and I'll be getting back with you later."

Rick ended the call, and at breakneck speed; dressed, brushed his teeth, and was out the door. Sorting out priorities, it occurred to him to change the locks on the house and install dead bolts. He yanked the cell phone from his pocket and, from pure memory, dialed his buddy.

"Amos, how's the insurance business?"

"Hey, Rick. I've been busy, but nothing new, lately."

"Well, there is now. Can you meet me at my house on short notice?"

"As many customers as you've sent my way, I guess so. I'll be there in ten minutes."

"Thanks, Amos. I'll be waiting on you."

Rick cranked the Toyota Tundra and eased out of the crowded parking lot. *Wonder why the River Town Inn is so busy? Nothing going on around here, must be evacuees from Bastrop County. Could the wildfires still be spreading?* He dismissed the thought and concentrated on his own situation. *Why didn't I get a security alarm service monitor on my home? I'll check the price; it is possible I can afford it. Don't plan on being a sitting duck, again…*

Arriving home, Rick parked the truck, and stared at the house. *Neglected for three days, it looks different. It's not the same. It will never be the same.*

Amos drove his Volkswagen Jetta in and parked behind the Toyota. Rick hopped out of the truck and strolled down the driveway to meet him.

"Appreciate you coming, Amos." Rick shook Amos's hand.

"What's going on, Rick?"

"I called a report in on the 800 number to the main insurance headquarters Wednesday night, but I couldn't let you in until today. The authorities are done with it, so come check it out. Vandals got my home while I was at church."

"Sorry to hear that, Rick. Let me take some pictures." Amos went back to his car and returned with a notebook and a camera. "At least you were gone when it happened. We've experienced a rash of home invasions all over the county. Busting in while the owners are home, hard to imagine, isn't it? Some people are totally nuts."

Rick pushed the door open, and they entered the living room together. Large chunks of jagged mirror pieces, once adorning the entire wall, lay stuck into the couch, coffee table, and floor. Rick noticed a gallon jar of cherry peppers shattered across the carpet. A vinegar smell hung in the air, and round, green

83

peppers the size of extra-large jawbreakers lay helter-skelter on everything in the room. Amos pointed to a golf club at the end of the couch and nodded at the holes in the wall that once held the mirror.

"Looks like someone was angry. What did they steal?"

"Enough. My laptop, television, and all of my guns are gone."

Amos scribbled on his notebook and wandered into a bedroom. Deep cracks ruined the mirror on the heavy oak dresser.

Rick was slow to enter and gazed at the dresser. "Looks like a huge spider web, doesn't it?"

"Yep, and I'd say whoever did it took aim with that golf club for a center shot." Amos kicked shoes out of his way and proceeded to the closet. Not one item was left on any shelf. No articles of clothing could be seen. Rick tripped over a metal wall hanging tangled on the floor with a busted wall clock, and Amos grabbed his friends arm as Rick steadied himself.

"Come on. I've seen enough. What's the kitchen like?" Amos glanced at Rick

"Too nasty; busted windows, broken dishes, and food from the refrigerator tossed about."

"Hmm, I'll make a quick run through the rest of the house, stay here." Amos took off, clicking scene after scene with his camera.

Rick glanced in dismay at all the mess. Lost in thought, he jumped when Amos returned.

"You're right Rick. The kitchen is the nastiest room. Let's get out of here."

Weary, Rick led Amos outside.

"Go ahead and call the cleaning service, and I'll turn the rest of this in. Did you get a case number from the police?"

"I did, but it's at the motel. I'm staying at the River Town Inn."

"That's okay, I know Broussard, and he'll give it to me. Get some rest, Rick."

"Thanks Amos, I will."

They both left at the same time, and Rick realized he'd missed breakfast. He drifted into deliberation and zipped into a Subway Restaurant. His to-go order was quickly processed, and he returned to the Inn.

Rick stepped inside the rented suite and flopped onto an over-sized recliner. Drink on one side and napkin on the other, he ate a 'Big Philly Cheese Steak' sandwich, slow, savoring each bite. The television remote was in the side pocket of the recliner; Rick retrieved it and turned the set back on.

"Breaking News" trailed across the bottom of the screen as the disturbing video showed wildfires in Bastrop County, Texas destroying homes.

Rick leaped from the recliner, stood closer to the television, and stared in horror. Sincere and instantly, he prayed out loud. *Father, I pray for comfort and help in abundance to all those who encounter any hardship. Lord, forgive me. I thought my situation was bad, but they have nothing…*

Chapter Nine
August 21, 2011
7:30 AM

Sunday arrived. Susan awoke and wrestled with the idea to exercise. She focused on the alarm clock, slipped out of bed, and with a mighty stretch she heard her ankles pop. *Maybe later I can try sit ups, I have all day after church to get healthy. Church! I have to hurry…*

An hour flew by, and Susan was transformed in a pale, summer green pant suit with white pumps and matching bag. Thankful her hair cut only required quick brushing; she accomplished a neat hair-do without major effort. No frizzed hair, no cow licks, merely brush and go. Glancing in the mirror, lipstick was applied, and a light spray of perfume completed her grooming. Susan dashed through the house, and grabbed her purse and car keys from the kitchen table.

The bible she used daily, with highlighted scriptures in pink and yellow markers, sat by her bed. Susan snatched it off the night stand, hurried outside, and left in her car.

Chapel of Christ proved easy to locate. All parallel parking was taken near the church and both adjoining parking lots were full. People meandered in small groups toward the entrance while others strolled past many empty vehicles along both sides of the street. Susan zipped into an adjacent lot marked "For Customers Only." *Clearly the bank is closed today. No objection should be made.* She parked on the corner and made her way across the street.

I don't know any of these people. She rushed by strangers and entered the crowded church as the choir began to sing. Slipping into one of the back pews, she glanced around for a glimpse of Shelly, or Monica, or Bernice. *Nope. Never find them in here. Too many people.* Susan settled back and enjoyed the service. Later, she became lost in the large crowd and got turned around trying to find her parked vehicle. The crowd thinned considerably when she finally spotted it. Parked right next to the Chevy Equinox was Shelly's car.

"Mrs. Penleigh, over here." Shelly waved from the entrance of the church, bounded down the steps, and ran towards her.

"Glad you made it. We will have to do this again." Susan met her on the lawn, and they hastened to the parking lot. "Are you hungry? Do you want a hamburger or something?"

"I'm fine, filled up on granola bars and milk, earlier." Shelly pulled a package of gum from her purse, offered it to Susan with raised eyebrows.

"No, thank you. What are your plans today?"

Shelly popped a piece of gum into her mouth and shook her head.

"Might as well not have any. Uncle Wes said I have to clean house and wash clothes. He just throws things down and walks off. I am not his maid, Mrs. Penleigh."

"Need some help?"

"Are you serious?" Shelly stopped walking and opened her eyes wide.

"Sure, why not?"

"Why? I will tell you why, Mrs. Penleigh, it is my uncle. He is awful. You will not want to be near him."

"I have met him, and I agree with you, but I am going there to help you and not to sit and visit with him."

"Ha, okay, let's do it then. I would love some help."

Susan got into her car and followed Shelly. They arrived at 11010 Bentley within minutes.

Can't believe I'm back here! Susan pulled into the drive way and parked like she belonged there. Shelly was already out of her car waiting at the side door of the house. She frowned at Susan. "Are you up to this?"

"Lead the way, Shelly. It won't take long with the two of us cleaning at the same time."

Shelly opened the door, and a sour smell stuck in Susan's nostrils, making her gag.

"Open the windows. Leave the door open. I don't care how hot it is, get some fans going." Susan choked, and Shelly hurried to oblige.

"Which way to the kitchen?" Susan yelled.

"Who wants to know?" Wes marched into the room, and Susan saw the shocked look on his face. "You again." His voice hardened, and he shouted, enraged. "Well, just what do you think *you* are doing in *my* house?"

"I am a friend of Shelly's." Susan remained calm and looked straight into his eyes.

"Shelly does not have any friends." His face flushed a light crimson color.

"She does now, and you leave me alone or I'll call 9-1-1." She held up her cell phone and glared at him.

He extended one hand towards Susan with all fingers stretched open, in all appearances to stop her. "Okay, okay, I'm out of here." He turned, and left, slamming the door on his way out. It wasn't long, and Susan heard a truck race its engine. One peep out the window, and Susan beamed.

Shelly entered the room. "What is going on?"

"Your uncle just drove off in a red truck."

"Yee-hawh!" She yelled.

"Let's knock this out, girl." Susan looked around. "Where are some trash bags?"

No time to waste, they each hurried through the living room, kitchen, and dining area; threw empty drink bottles, old to-go food cartons, papers, junk mail, etc. into large trash bags.

"Line the bags outside against the house. Get them out of here. Let it be his problem to carry them off. I'll gather dirty dishes and stack them to wash. Shelly, try and get a load of clothes going in the washing machine. Do you have Pine-Sol to mop with?"

"Yes, it is under the kitchen counter."

They scurried throughout the house, each with their own task, and after two hours all clutter was gone, dishes were washed, clothes still washing and towels were folded. Susan finally mopped the floors.

She glanced at Shelly and noticed sweat dripped off both of their faces.

"We got that foul smell out of here. I'll help close the windows, and you turn the air conditioner back on. I love that fresh clean smell of lemon pine-sol."

"I feel like we were in a television commercial." Shelly laughed.

"Girl, nobody works that hard in a commercial. I think we are done. Wes can clean his own room, and you can clean your bedroom after I leave. The

89

bathroom will be a breeze with everything else done. It won't take long. You have got a routine going now."

"Thanks, Mrs. Penleigh for all your help. This house has not been clean for as long as I can remember."

"You are so welcome, Shelly, and who knows? Your uncle Wes may return and think it smells like sunshine in here. Maybe he will try and help keep it clean. I have to run, let me know how things go, okay?"

"I will, and thanks again. No one would have helped me like you did. I'll never forget the drastic change that took place today."

"Maybe it is time for a change. Luke 6:31 is referred to as the golden rule. 'And as you would that men should do to you, do you also to them likewise.' In other words treat others as you would like to be treated." Susan raised an eyebrow, and Shelly nodded.

Susan walked outside and climbed into her car. *Didn't realize how tired I am. Sitting down in this car seat gives me a sensation of falling into a recliner, except for having to use my right leg and foot to drive.* She counted eleven, large trash bags; stuffed full.

This was so worth it, in more ways than one.

◆◆◆◆

Logan waved at Susan when she turned into her driveway. *What a perfect opportunity to flash him a dazzling smile.* She made the effort, displaying the white porcelain caps on her front teeth, and chuckled. *My dentist would be proud.*

Not trusting her instincts, a cautious peep in the rear view mirror of the car, and she immediately shifted her weigh in the seat. *I'm getting too old for this. Oh, he is crossing the street. He really is coming. Calm down, girl…*

90

Susan exited from the Chevy and slung the white bag over her right shoulder in a casual manner.

"How is your day going?" He called out and approached the rear of the car.

"It has been interesting, why?"

"I figured out how to enjoy a back yard wiener roast in this sweltering heat wave we are having."

"Seriously? Is it possible?"

"Of course. I spent the afternoon at Lowe's and found a commercial size shop fan on wheels with a heavy duty extension cord."

"Logan, I do not know about you, but I have not eaten since a few oatmeal cookies this morning with coffee. Help me crank up the fire pit. I have grated cheese, pickle relish, a package of ballpark franks, a can of chili, bread —but no hotdog buns."

"That will work. I'm game if you are."

"Count me in. I'll change out of these clothes. It will not take long. Oh, this will be fun, Logan."

"I'll be wheeling the shop fan over and get the cord. Do you have any firewood, or charcoal?"

"No, I don't. This is unreal, Logan. Both of us are drenched in sweat and here we are planning to cook outside and have hotdogs." She shook her head. "Funny thing is, I cannot wait."

"Me either. I will swing by the store and grab a bag of charcoal. By the way, Susan, I am glad you are hungry. I have not eaten much today, either." He laughed and walked away.

Susan unlocked the front door and entered the house. She stopped to remove the white pumps from her feet. *Oh, they hurt. No wonder Shelly said she felt like she cleaned in a commercial, I cleaned house wearing low heel pumps!* Susan chuckled aloud picturing a 1950's television commercial where the women wore dresses and heels while they cleaned.

Now I have to find something to wear…modest but cool.

Susan dug through her summer clothes and decided they would still be entirely too hot to wear outside. Wearing anything of knit material would be like sitting in a sauna wrapped in three, heavy, oversized beach towels. She found a pair of blue jeans cut off a few inches above the knee, a short sleeved, batik-lace, cotton blouse and slipped into the cooler outfit and sandals. *Okay, off to prepare for the meal…*

Onions were chopped in record time, and she placed the other ingredients on the counter, adding napkins, plates, and eating utensils. Susan checked the patio, wiped off two trays, filled a cooler with drinks, and set that outside by the lounge chairs. Pulling their backs upright, she quickly adjusted the chairs into a sitting position for their meal.

"Looks inviting." Logan walked into her back yard and carried a new, bright orange outdoor extension cord.

"Hey, that was quick. Make yourself at home. I don't have a clue if there *are* outside plugs."

Logan glanced at the walls and spotted one. "Yes ma'am, well, one anyway, and it's in a good location." He plugged the end into the socket and looked the area over. "I like how you have us sitting here, next to the house. We'll have the fan on us. I'll go get it and roll it over. You can find some matches while I'm gone, and later we'll work on a fire in that pit. I won't be gone long."

"Sounds like a plan." Susan nodded as he left.

She hurried inside and found a box of matches in the pantry, dropped them off on the patio, and opened the door to the small outside, storage closet. *I thought I saw a water hose in here.* She tugged and pulled the tangled mass of hose out of the closet and attempted to straighten it out. Sweat popped out on her entire body. She heard the grinding noise of Logan's commercial size fan being rolled closer to her back yard and gave an audible sigh of relief.

"Hold on, I'll help you, but let's try the fan first." He pushed the massive fan onto the patio and positioned it about two feet from their chairs. "Alright lady, hold on, I'm fixing to plug it up." He grabbed the end of the extension cord and inserted the fans prongs into it.

Immediate noise rocked the whole neighborhood as the machine kicked in at high speed.

"Whoa. Tie me down, this is amazing." Susan lifted her arms into the air. Her hair was blowing straight out at about thirty five miles an hour, and she did not care that her blouse was flapping in and out away from her body. She knew she was still decent, but probably looked like a tornado got a hold of her.

"Oh, Logan, I have never cooled off so fast in this heat."

"Maybe I should turn it to medium speed." He yelled over the gyrating, loud rhythm.

"No, stand over here with me first. You have to experience this, Logan."

93

He gave her a double take as he glanced in her direction. "...Okay." He walked towards her, and his body swayed when the full impact of the breeze hit him.

"Best thing I ever bought," he mumbled and eased his arms up into the air.

"It's sort of like going down a roller coaster. The rush of air is exhilarating. "

They basked in the moment for a while, each silent, as their bodies stood unaccustomed to the massive wind.

A dog suddenly sprang from around the corner and barked viciously at the fan. The bright red collar he sported announced an owner did claim him, but the daring stance he rigidly placed his legs into displayed total independence and an ensuing war. The hair stood up on his back, and he continued to bark nonstop, as if in a trance.

"That's my next door neighbor's dog. He is protecting me. I do not think he is ready to leave," Susan hollered while she lowered her arms.

"Well, he is fixing to be history," Logan shouted and walked toward the fan. Reaching over to the control knob, he turned the fan to the slow position.

Susan's flying hair fell down instantly into a disarrayed mass clustered about her face, and the ear-deafening sound of the fan was abruptly silent.

The dog raised his head toward Susan, gave a tiny yelp, turned tail, and ran. Logan looked satisfied as the dog left.

"Well, he was a good guard dog, and we've all made a grand discovery; what a fan. Susan, you might want to go brush your hair, and I can only assume that I need to do the same thing."

"Would not hurt." She glanced at his hair and nodded.

They departed, and Susan was surprised the day was quickly slipping away. Shadows fell across the lawn, and dusk approached with all its remarkable grandeur in the sky. A splendid array of colors, yellow, red, and shades of purple, displayed brilliantly. Tree tops stood majestically in black silhouettes against the last bits of colored sky.

Mellow, she entered the house going straight to the bathroom to freshen up.

"Yikes." She laughed at her reflection in the mirror and brushed her hair back into its usual style. *I'll picture us in front of the fan from now on, arms raised and all.* Susan laughed aloud again, and discovered she could not wait for Logan to return.

A knock on the front door made her run to answer it.

"Well, hello. You must be my new neighbor, Susan?" Logan bowed.

"Yes sir, I am." He caught her off guard, and she tried to come up with a clever reply. Eyeing the bag of charcoal he carried, she quickly teased, "Hmm, and you must be Logan. I have heard of you. Don't tell me I'm about to be impressed with your cooking skills."

"Yes, you are in for a rare treat. May I join you in the back yard?" He held the charcoal toward her, a look of clear amusement on his face.

"Of course." She narrowed her eyes and smiled.

He quickly leaned forward and lightly brushed a kiss upon her cheek.

A warm glow crept over her, and she blushed while glancing into his face. A sudden impulse on her part brought a finger to his lips. He tried to bite her finger and growled.

Surprised, she jerked her finger away. They both laughed, and Susan spoke first.

"Goodness, Mr. Logan, you must be hungry!"

"Actually, I think the wolf says something like, 'and the better to eat you, my dear,' and even raises both eyebrows to get his point across."

"Oh no, I'm not inviting a wolf in. Now, you have to turn back into Logan the tire changer."

"Well, okay, as long as you *don't* change. Susan, I like you just the way you are."

"Well, thank you, Logan. Come on; let's work on that fire pit." She ushered him through the house and into the back yard.

"First, I'll need some kindling."

Susan walked across the huge concrete circle with the fire pit situated directly in the center. She and Logan both glanced at the nearby woods, and they hurried to collect fallen, dead branches. Logan broke them into several pieces, squatted down and put them in the pit, pouring charcoal on top.

"Before I start the fire, we need that water hose. Where did we leave it?"

"Near the house. I have to find a water faucet. I haven't cooked out before, so I am not familiar with this back yard." Susan scanned the lawn and noticed one a few yards from the pit. "Well, aren't you a handy faucet?" She retrieved the hose and pulled the twisted mess toward the pit area. Logan grabbed it from her, quickly untangled it, and attached it to the faucet. He turned it on, and water gushed out full force. "Okay, it works. We are safe, now." He turned the water off, and left the hose within their reach.

"Bring on those matches, girl."

Susan handed him the box, and he lit the fire with only one match. "It is so dry. I have always spent at least five minutes trying to get the kindling to catch on fire under the charcoal. Not this time." Logan looked out at the surrounding woods. "We better dose this fire as soon as the meat is cooked. I heard they have a burn ban in a few counties north and east of us. I have never seen it this dry."

"Dry and burn bans are both new to me. I carried rain gear in my car every day when I lived around the Seattle area." She turned as she talked. "The hotdogs are on a tray inside. I'll go and bring them out. Make yourself comfortable."

Logan sat and waited while she hurried into the house. Within minutes, she returned with the tray and quickly inserted two hotdogs onto each metal holder.

Logan ran to help and held the meat on the fire, turning them over every so often.

"Is two enough, or do you want more?" Susan glanced at him.

"Two is plenty. I like mine nearly burnt on the outside. How about you?"

"Same here."

Logan handed her the meat when they reached the right texture. She used a table knife to slide them off the hot metal prongs and back onto the tray.

They both stood up and gazed at the fire.

"Sure got dark quick." Susan looked at the sky and noticed a few twinkling stars.

"We have to tell some ghost stories. No camp fire is complete without a scary story."

"Logan, we are not camping out."

"I don't care; we have a fire glowing in a pit."

"It's not about some creepy thing that makes you jump, is it?" Susan shuddered. "Our food is getting cold and it is still hot out here."

"Okay, tell you what, we will go eat, but then I am going to tell a ghost story that is guaranteed to scare the socks off of you."

Susan chuckled. "…I guess I am in for it now."

"Oh you are! Let me flood the fire." He grabbed the hose and saturated the entire pit with gushing water until all embers quit glowing, and the charcoal sat protruding from a pool of murky liquid.

"Done." He turned the water off, and they walked inside the house and washed their hands.

Susan put two slices of bread on each plate, and he placed the hotdogs on top.

"I like the way you have everything laid out. What a variety. See, a man would simply cook the hotdog and maybe squirt mustard across it, or if he was out of mustard he would grab whatever was in the refrigerator; ketchup, maybe even barbecue sauce."

"Barbecue sauce? Hmm, you may have something there." She placed a cover over a small bowl of chili, and heated it in the microwave. In less than a minute, using hot pads to grab the bowl, Logan took over the chili and stirred the hot, bubbly mixture, while he whistled. Each added other toppings until they ended up with a massive mound of pickle relish, grated cheese, chili, and sprinkles of chopped onion.

"Wow, I don't know if I can eat all of this or not." Susan looked at her finished masterpiece and could not see an inch of either hotdog.

"Knife and fork is the only way. Umm, looks delicious."

"We will have to eat in here. I don't trust myself outside with this—I might spill it." Logan gazed at their plates and nodded.

They gingerly sat down on bar stools at the counter, and Susan turned to face Logan. "Would you like some lightly spiced, iced tea? I left the cooler of can drinks out on the patio."

"Ice tea would be great. Thank you."

Susan got up, brought two large ice tea glasses out of the freezer, and filled them with ice cubes as the glasses quickly frosted. She opened the refrigerator, reached inside for a gallon of fresh brewed tea, and retrieved two twigs of fresh mint in a vegetable chilling drawer. Rinsing those off quickly, she poured the tea and added mint to each glass.

Logan drank immediately when she handed him the chilled beverage, and Susan climbed back onto her stool.

"Oh, I do like the tea…most refreshing." Logan took another long swallow.

"Glad you enjoy it. Have all you want." Susan said grace, and Logan quickly bowed his head. She cut into the hotdog concoction and took a bite. "Nothing beats outdoor cooking. "Thanks, Logan; this was such a great idea."

They slowly finished their meal. Afterwards, Logan closed containers, and helped load the dishwasher, while she cleaned the counter and ran the garbage disposal. Suddenly, the kitchen was clean again.

"Susan, how about sitting out back with the fan on low?"

"Sounds relaxing."

"If it gets too unbearable with hot air rushing by, we can always come back inside to the air conditioner."

"Okay, let's give it a try."

Light escaped out the back window of the dimly lit living room, across the entire patio. Logan turned the fan on and positioned it towards the chaise lounge chairs. Nestled in a more darkened area, the chairs were about two feet apart from each other. Susan and Logan approached them and sat. They leaned back and stretched their legs out on the lounge chairs, gazing up at the stars.

"Ready for that ghost story?" Logan raised his head and glanced her way.

"I don't believe in ghosts, but sure, I'm listening." Susan noticed a mischievous grin on his face.

"Well, legend has it there was a mean old stepmother named Betty. Every night when she went to bed, she locked herself inside her bedroom. Betty's husband and step kids would hear her chanting in a low voice." He rose up again and looked directly into Susan's eyes.

He spoke in a voice barely above a whisper. "There were four kids, and they all told the same story later on in their life."

Susan tried to keep a straight face and not ruin his story by smiling.

"Go on," she encouraged him.

Logan returned to his usual way of speaking. "Years later, completely white headed, she was skinny, weak, and dying. Doctors said nothing else could be done for her. She was at home, and three of the now grown kids were watching over her. Betty could not talk. She was lying on the couch, and the three women took turns dabbing chopped ice, held together in a small hand towel, onto her cracked dry lips. After a while, the first woman got up, and the second woman sat on the edge of the couch to continue.

"The woman leaned over, and got closer to apply the cool towel to Betty's lips. At that moment, Betty raised her right arm, placed it around the woman's neck, and with super human strength, Betty began forcing the woman's head down to her open mouth. The woman screamed and tried to break the hold Betty had on her and cried out for help. Betty kept her mouth wide open and attempted to smother the woman's screaming mouth with her silent open one.

"Finally, one of the other sisters ran into the room. It took both of them to jerk Betty's arm away that was draped around the woman's neck. Betty never got to cover the other ones mouth with hers."

Logan paused, and demonstrated with his own arm, the hold Betty had around the other woman's neck.

"Everyone decided Betty was a witch and was trying to suck the breath out of the other woman. She needed the breath of life to live, without it she would die, and she laid right there on that couch and died."

Logan sat up on his lounge chair and swung his legs over the side.

"Then, a year later, the woman who had the encounter with Betty's super human strength, well, her son wanted to spend the night at the same house to be with his grandfather. The young boy was eight years old, and had spent a happy day helping his grandfather with errands. He also wanted to sleep in Betty's bedroom, with its large bed. The grandfather saw no reason why he couldn't sleep there. As soon as they quit watching television, the old man told his grandson goodnight, and entered Betty's room with him. The grandfather grabbed the covers and draped one side of them back to prepare the bed for the boy. He crawled into the bed, and said his prayers, while the grandfather tucked the grandson back under the covers. Moonlight gently cascaded into the room from the double windows over the bed.

"'If you need me for anything, my bedroom is next to this one. Just holler, okay. I will hear you.' The grandfather assured the boy and left.

"The little boy laid there glancing across the palely lit room and couldn't believe he was finally inside this room. Betty had never allowed him or anyone else inside it. After Betty died, the child's grandfather

102

gathered all of her belongings, and gave them to Betty's own son from a previous marriage.

"Later that night, the boy dozed off to sleep comfortable under the covers, when he suddenly awoke, and heard a shuffling sound in the living room.

"It sounded like Betty.

"He remembered she didn't pick up her feet. Betty always scooted along wearing her house slippers. The sound grew louder, and the boy realized the shuffling sound came into the bedroom. He stiffened and braced for whatever it was. The sound suddenly stopped at the foot of the bed. He peered from the covers and turned cold, there was a chill in the air, and to his surprise the covers were moving. He raised his head and saw nothing, yet the covers continued to slowly pull away from him, toward the foot of the bed.

"Frightened, he opened his mouth to scream for his grandfather, but not a sound emerged. He tried again, and a squeak came out. He inhaled roughly to force a verbal sound, any sound to be vocalized, and nothing happened but quiet exhaled air. He tightened his grip on the covers as they were now forcibly being pulled away. So strong, and yet methodically slow, the pace continued until no cover was near his chin. In fact, the covers were indeed half-way down his pajama top.

"Finally, he managed a blood curdling scream, and trembling with fear, he gave another mighty yell, hollering for his grandfather.

"As the story goes, the old man's feet hit the floor, and he ran into the boy's open bedroom door. He flipped the light switch on and gasped out loud.

103

"He looked in total amazement at the covers draped at the foot of the bed, all pulled in the same direction, laying in long rows with the material falling onto the floor.

"The grandfather's voice shook, and he spoke in both English and broken German. 'I have to get you out of here. *Gott 'n hamel,* help us all.' He gathered the child up into his arms, and carried him out of the room. A quick slam of Betty's bedroom door, and he took the boy into his bedroom. The old man had twin beds, each against a wall, across the small room from each other. Nothing else was said, and nothing else happened. The grandfather did lock the door on Betty's room, and no one ever entered it again. Years later, after the grandfather died, his children decided to sell the house as none of them wanted to have any part of it."

Logan slowly leaned near Susan. "Boo!"

"Aagh!" Susan screamed, and burst into laughter. "Logan, I might have known that was coming. You got me good."

"I was hoping you would still be thinking about Betty." He chuckled. "I couldn't resist. Guess I'll leave now, can't have us late for work tomorrow."

"What a story." Susan stood and reached to pull Logan up from his chair. "Thanks Logan, I enjoyed it." They walked inside, to the front door.

"If you don't care, I'll leave the fan here and get it sometime tomorrow."

"No problem."

"I think I might pick it up on my lunch hour."

"Whatever works for you. I'll be at school."

"Okay, see you later." He placed a hand under her chin and lifted her head ever so slightly, giving her a kiss as he looked into her eyes.

"Ma'am, I *will* see you again."

"Yes sir, you will." She smiled. Logan turned, and walked across the street to his own house. Susan went inside and shut the door. *Oh, how nice…what a fun evening with Logan.*

She locked up the house, made her coffee, showered, and hopped into bed. Reaching over to the night stand to set the alarm clock, she jumped when the phone rang.

"Hello?"

"I am not calling you too late at night, am I?"

Susan recognized Izabella's voice. "No, of course not." She sat up in bed.

"I wanted to talk to you about something, and it may take a while, if that is okay with you."

"Talk away." Susan scooted towards the alarm clock and quickly set it.

"There is some positive help for our failing students. Mr. Monroe does not know about it, though. You know how he is, everything has to be his idea, and he has to get all the credit."

"Wait, are you talking about Mr. Rex Monroe? Is this the same Mr. Rex Monroe who is not friendly, or cheerful, or encouraging?" Susan laughed.

"One and the same. My, you catch on quick, Susan." Izabella chuckled.

"Carry on, you have got my full attention."

"Well, I do not know if you have become acquainted with Mr. Fred, as the kids call him. He is an English

105

teacher who has taken a lot of kids under his wing and has decided to give them private tutoring for free. He does this in the back room at the local library. The board of directors there let him have use of the room every afternoon, Monday through Saturday, from four to six o'clock. So far, he has twenty eight students. Besides myself, Mrs. Anita Gillis and Mrs. Barbara McFarland enjoy helping. We have all been most successful in bringing the children's grades up in English and math, as well. The students not only understand and complete the lessons, but retain the knowledge. Fred said some of the kids will stop and explain a problem to the others. He said they get along well with each other, and they all behave. That is something in itself, right there."

"Izabella, I think it is a shame they have to hide such a tremendous program. I mean, after all, the adults are volunteers, and what they do during their free time is their own business."

"We were hoping you would see it that way. It has been suggested that you may be interested in sharing some office skills with the after school group. Our school policy does not allow for students, even those seniors about to graduate, to be office aides. Mr. Monroe became furious the last time it was mentioned at a board meeting to simply place it on the agenda for open discussion. He flatly denied any good would come of it, insisted the students would spy on him, and repeat everything they overheard."

"He wants total control, Izabella. That's what it's all about concerning Mr. Rex Monroe." Susan inhaled and exhaled loudly.

"That and the money. Do not forget the money."

"Oh, I know. I have met some students already who only need a chance, just one decent break, and yes, Izabella, I would be proud to help."

"Great. Susan, some of them do not know how to operate a fax machine, much less a copy machine. I am sure they will never get an office job from what they are taught here. This school district is not offering them the skills they need to get an office job."

"Count me in. Is there anything else I can help with?"

"Yes. There are two clubs that I am a member of. You might be interested in both of them. Would you like to join the FBLA?"

"Is that the Future Business Leaders of America?"

"You are familiar with it?"

"Of course I am. It is a great organization. What is the other one?"

"I sponsor the other one, it is Christian Athletes, and I could use your help."

"Izabella, sign me up for them. I would love being a part of both. Let me know when and where they meet next, and I will be there. Tell the others they can count on me."

"Thanks, dear. I knew we could. Christian Athletes meet next Monday before school at the flag pole. The FBLA is tomorrow, after school. Let's get off the phone, and I'll remind you of the meetings. Get some rest before you encounter Mr. Friendly in the morning."

"I will, and Izabella, thanks again."

Chapter Ten
August 22, 2011
6:45 AM

Rick gulped lukewarm coffee and considered his home. *Sparkle Cleaning Service will earn every penny of today's job with me. Ought to help the local economy.* Aroma drifted from the buffet table as Rick selected warm banana-nut muffins and orange juice. *Nothing like a free continental breakfast.*

"Good morning." An elderly couple interrupted his thoughts, and he nodded at their polite greeting. Stuffing a large portion of warm muffin into his mouth, he snatched at a napkin and headed for the exit door.

Humid outside air engulfed him, creating stickiness between his clothes and skin. Rick stood on the sidewalk at River Town Inn and reflected, again, about the packed parking lot. *Has to be some evacuees from the wildfires.* He rounded the corner of the motel to get his own parked vehicle. *Might as well run by Lowe's Building Center and get a new set of locks for home.*

"I can't believe this." Rick stopped his approach. "I *cannot* believe this." He repeated as Deputy Lodi strolled towards him.

"Looks like your truck got broken into. One of the occupants here reported seeing the busted windows. Must have happened during the night, and by the way, it was the only burglary." Rick sidestepped the patrol car, lights still flashing, and walked, with caution, over crushed glass from the Toyota Tundra's front windshield.

"Bold, weren't they? Must have made a lot of noise to bust in like that." Rick looked at his friend.

"Yep, and especially with this many people around. Rick, don't touch anything, but see if you notice anything missing."

"Seems like a new routine for me. I did the same thing at my house last week."

"Oh?"

"Left a mess there, too." Rick peered into the front seat and saw the large compartment door hanging open under the dash. He glanced at the floor board. "Ha, they even left the crow bar they used to pry open the locked glove box. He leaned closer to the truck door and shook his head. "Well, my GPS is gone. Guess I should have slept with it." Rick grumbled. "No need to lock anything up, is it?"

"Sorry Rick. What brand did you have?"

"Garmin."

"Serial numbers saved anywhere?"

"No."

"I'll put it in my report. Want me to call Enterprise for you?"

"No, I can get them to bring me a rental car. Thanks, anyway, George."

"They may not be open this early, and I know the manager. He lives down the road from me." George Lodi stopped writing and glanced at Rick.

"Okay, do it. Appreciate you." Rick grimaced as George pulled his private cell phone from his pocket.

"Deputy George Lodi here. Hey, a friend of mine needs a car, can you come out to River Town Inn? I'm in the parking lot with him; you'll see my black and white with the lights flashing. Yeah, can't miss it. Thanks, buddy." George clicked the phone off and looked at Rick. "He's on his way."

"Great. Thanks man." Rick let out a loud sigh.

"Let me get back to the report. We'll notify you when we are done with your truck."

◆ ◆ ◆ ◆

Rick caught his ride and filled out paperwork at Enterprise to rent a brand new, blue Dodge truck. Back on the road, he hurried into Lowe's and purchased new locks with deadbolts. The drive to his neighborhood was uneventful, and he relaxed. Total amazement overcame him when he did arrive at his house. It was a beehive of activity. People were coming and going from the busted front door. The cleaning service van was parked near the front entrance. Workers hauled trash out and into a massive waste disposal truck parked at the curb.

"Focus on the positive," Rick said to himself and parked in the driveway. He grabbed the Lowe's bag and walked to the garage.

"May I help you?" A man called to him as he tugged a large, broken lamp across the lawn.

"I'm the owner. I'm here to change out the locks." He waved and opened the garage door, searching for his tool box.

"Ah ha!" Rick muttered. "The one thing the crooks didn't find...don't tell me I can't camouflage something." Rick pulled the deflated children's bounce

110

slide off the metal toolbox and unlocked it. "Yes sir, last year's garage sale purchase came to the rescue." He remembered how the previous owners gave him a deal on it, and said to reinforce the one hole with new duct tape. He retrieved the tools he needed and went to complete his task.

By mid-morning he was already drenched in sweat. *Two doors done and only one more left. Time to cool off on the back patio.* Rick strolled through the house to the kitchen, dodged a few workers, and grabbed an ice cold bottle of water.

He pulled a cushioned chair out from the round patio table and cranked the handle to open the umbrella. Rick flopped into the cozy chair and drank a long swallow of ice water. He wiped beaded moisture from his face with his shirttail, and sweat simply reappeared. Tired, he rubbed his eyes and took another drink.

Something moved.

Rick narrowed his eyes and looked across the river. He got a brief glimpse of a man and saw the person dart behind a tree. Rick sat perfectly still and watched. Several feet farther into the woods, another figure emerged and joined the first man. For a split second, these two men glared at Rick, until suddenly they turned, and went deeper back into the woods. *What in the world is that all about? Illegal fishing, maybe? Catfish traps?*

He guzzled the rest of the ice cold water and walked to the side door. The procedure to replace locks grew routine, and Rick finished in a few minutes. He returned to the garage with an assortment of tools and the Lowe's bag, which he locked inside the tool box. Satisfied everything was back in order; Rick locked the garage and walked back to the rental truck. He turned on the ignition, and the air conditioner vents blasted cold air full force on his face.

He left and drove past a few houses before he spotted Susan's. *I need to check on her one day. Make sure she's okay. Warn her to be careful.*

He looked around the neighborhood for anything that would seem out of place, but didn't see anything unusual. Out of habit, he glanced into his rear view mirror. Sunshine reflected off a chrome bumper from the black car behind him and almost blinded Rick. He flinched and continued the drive back to River Town Inn. He swung into the parking lot and saw the same black car flash by him. *What was he doing still behind me?*

Quick to get another look at the car, Rick raised his head and barely caught the back license plate. *Only red letters and numbers on it, hmm, where could that be from? Guess I'm getting too suspicious…I've had enough of this…*

Chapter Eleven
August 22, 2011
7:00 AM

Susan arrived at work early and sorted through tubs of mail Lester Davis had brought to the employee break room on Saturday. Silence was welcomed, and her pace quickened to distribute every letter and magazine into each mail slot. The walls were covered with posters to inform employees about health insurance, weekly cafeteria menus, workman's compensation, teacher retirement, abuse centers, and various hot lines available to contact.

What caught her eye was the spot where a poster was missing.

Hmm? As precious as the space was, many posters overlapped each other…what was removed, and why is the spot empty?

She turned in slow motion and tried to reconstruct in her mind, what had been on the vacant spot of the painted wall.

The whistle blowers hot line; their toll free, phone number. That's it. The one where you report wrong doing by any employee, and you will not get in trouble. How convenient for Rex Monroe it disappeared. He is the only one I know who would benefit by it being gone.

"Hello, hello. Anyone here?"

Susan heard someone in the adjoining office and looked around the corner through the open doorway. She saw a well-dressed man, clean shaven, who obviously must be a parent or a salesman.

"Yes, may I help you?" Susan noticed his brilliant smile and wondered again who he was.

"You are Susan Penleigh, are you not?"

"Yes, I am. You must have a student here who attends our high school."

"No, actually *I* do not, but I owe you a tremendous apology for my rude behavior."

"Pardon? I am sure we have not met, and I most certainly would recall anyone's rude behavior. I can hardly picture you being rude to anyone, sir." Susan tried to practice the graciousness she previously witnessed as southern hospitality.

"Let me introduce myself. I am Wes Harper." He gazed into her eyes and then lowered his head.

Susan gasped and frowned at the man. She bent her head closer to him and rudely spoke in a sharp tone. "What kind of joke are you playing, sir?"

"I can assure you ma'am, I am not playing a joke on you. Forgive me for intruding on your day, but you made such an impression on me, and my niece Shelly, that I wanted to personally thank you for everything you have done. Again, I am so sorry for the way I have treated you in the past. I was drunk when I first met you, Mrs. Penleigh, and totally wrong to try and touch you. I beg your forgiveness. I have never met a woman like you, and Shelly deserves you as a friend. Offensive as I have been to you, and to Shelly, please let us start over. My past pulls me down, and often, my habit is to wallow in self-pity and get completely drunk. You have made me ashamed of myself, and of my actions. You, Mrs. Penleigh, have sobered me up. I want to thank you for that, and for coming into Shelly's and my life."

"I...I don't know what to say, Mr. Harper."

"Well, I do. I came home the other day, and saw eleven bags of trash on the side of my house. Talk about facing reality, it was shocking. I thought how those bags represented my own life. I hauled them all to the dump, came home, and made myself as clean as the house. You opened my eyes, Mrs. Penleigh, and I had to come and talk to you this morning. Please forgive the treatment you encountered from me in the past."

Susan looked intently at the handsome man on the other side of the counter. *I can't believe this is the same man. Maybe it is a fluke, and someone is indeed pulling my leg. I will have to agree with this man and get him out of my office.*

Susan glanced again at the man, wrinkled her face, and exhibited a concerned expression, complete with raised eyebrows, and she held her mouth in a straight line.

"Mr. Harper, you are forgiven. Please put the uneasiness behind you. Forward is the only positive way to go."

"Thank you, Mrs. Penleigh. I will go now and leave you to your work." He smiled and walked out her office door.

Susan hurried to the window. *He cannot be Wes Harper. There is only one way to know.*

She watched the man stroll onto the outside parking lot, and nearly choked when he climbed into the same red truck she saw leave Shelly's house.

Oh nooo. It was him.

Susan adjusted the blinds on the window as her mind tried to process the unbelievable information.

"Ma'am?"

Susan turned her head to the woman who entered the office.

"Hello, how can I help you?"

"I am the substitute for Mrs. Harris."

"Mrs. Dawson?"

"Yes, are you the Mrs. Penleigh who called me?"

"Yes, I am, and you will be in Room 382 in the next wing, second door on the left. Susan smiled and handed her a folder. "This is for you. I included the information you will be needing. Attendance slips, lesson plans, discipline forms, lunch schedule, please return it this afternoon." Susan gave her a typed page. "I will need you to sign Mrs. Harris's Absent From Duty form as her substitute, also."

Mrs. Dawson signed the form with a pen attached to the counter by a chain.

"One more form to sign, proof of you working here today, strictly for payroll. Also, something new we are doing." Susan handed her another page. "This is an evaluation page that will be held in great confidence. Mr. Monroe wants to know how well his teachers left their class prepared with lesson plans, and how the students behaved in the teacher's absence. If you have any trouble let me know, your intercom buzzer is located on the wall behind your desk. Do not hesitate to call, and I hope you have a great day, Mrs. Dawson."

"Thank you, hopefully I will with all this help." She raised her folder, nodded toward it, and left.

The phone rang piercing the treasured quiet time. The daily hub of officials and students rushing in a whirl of alternating levels of activity and noise had begun.

"River Town High School."

"Mrs. Penleigh?"

"Yes, how may I help you?"

"This is Bessie Wilson, I drive bus #4 and some students threw paper out the window, and I have been pulled over by a deputy. He is telling me that I am responsible for littering, and I do not think I should get a ticket." Her voice broke, and she quit talking. Susan heard Bessie inhale deeply, and barely audible, a sob escaped.

"Hang on; let me see if Mr. Tillman is here."

Susan buzzed Earl Tillman's office on the intercom.

"Tillman here."

"Mr. Tillman, I have our bus driver, Bessie Wilson, on line two. She needs to talk to you immediately."

"Thank you, Mrs. Penleigh. Transfer the call, please."

Susan punched the numeric code for the transfer to his phone and said a quick prayer under her breath. *Lord be with Bessie Wilson, help her in her hour of need.*

"Mrs. Penleigh?"A student walked into her office, and Susan immediately noticed the blood covering his hands.

Genuine concern took over. Susan rose from her chair and walked to him.

"What happened to you?"

"I have been bleeding, ma'am," he stammered.

"I can see that. What is your name, young man?"

117

"I am Kendrick Vargas. They call me Kenny."

"Well, Kenny; let me look at your hands. Hold them out for me to see and spread your fingers open."

He did as instructed, and Susan's heart broke when she looked at his bloody hands, and imagined the obvious pain he must be suffering.

"I see where you have blisters that have burst open. They are bleeding, and inflamed. Even your calluses are bleeding. Kenny, what have you been doing?"

"I chop firewood for my daddy, ma'am. He only has one arm, and he cuts pulp wood. I help him every day when I get in from school. I chop it so he can sell it the next day while I am here. Sometimes, I cannot do my homework because there is so much to chop, and sometimes it gets dark, before I'm finished." He shrugged and formed a lopsided smile.

"Kenny, do you have any gloves to wear when you chop firewood?"

"No, ma'am."

"Kenny, you are bleeding. Your fingers are nearly raw. They could get infected, and you would not be able to chop for a long time."

"Yes, ma'am. That is why I came in here. I heard you have Band-Aids."

Susan took in his thin, tall frame and guessed he was about sixteen or seventeen. She pondered about his future and resolved, then and there, to make a difference.

"Kenny, follow me to the sink in the break room. I want you to hold your hands out, and I will run water over them, and then, carefully dry them. I have some antibiotic crème to apply, and I will wrap your wounds in gauze."

He did as he was told, and she cleaned and dressed the wounds satisfactorily.

"Now, I want you to sit in one of the chairs against the wall and wait for me. If the phone rings, do not answer it. Tell anyone who comes in that I had to go to the restroom, and I told you to sit here and wait for me, okay?"

"Okay, Mrs. Penleigh."

Susan grabbed her purse and ran out the door. She knew Mr. Monroe was always late for work. She should have enough time to drive to the hardware store and return before he arrived. Her car shot out of the parking lot. Within minutes, she was in the store and made a purchase. Quickly, she returned to the school, parked, and ran to the building.

Mr. Monroe was not at school.

Susan entered the office and smiled. Kenny politely returned the smile when he saw her. He sat at the same place. She pulled the desk drawer open, grabbed a black permanent marker, and dug into the flimsy, plastic sack from the hardware store. Sitting down in her office chair, she carefully wrote Kenny's first and last name on a pair of extra-large welding gloves.

"Here." She handed them to the young man, and his eyes opened wider at the sight of the heavy, thick gloves. Susan watched his face light up.

"For me?" He looked up at her.

"Yes Kenny, and I wrote your name on them so no one can steal them from you. Wear them every night

119

when you chop firewood, and it will help your hands, okay?"

"Okay, and thank you, Mrs. Penleigh."

"You are welcome, Kenny. Now keep them in your pocket and come back every day. I want to see your hands get better."

"I will, Mrs. Penleigh."

The bell rang for the first period class, and Kenny jumped up from his chair.

She followed him out in the hallway and watched him walk off in a hurry. She saw how quickly he blended in with the other kids. Some of them slapped him on his back, others called out to him, and gave him a high five in exuberant happiness.

Susan's eyes watered over, and she blinked as she thought about him. This young man, Kenny, was just trying to make a go of life with no idea what he was up against. *I will have to ask Izabella about his family.*

A buzzer went off from the intercom unit in the office, she turned from the bustling hallway and went back into her office.

She flipped the switch of the intercom and heard the loud ruckus of a fight happening inside that classroom. Students yelled, and a teacher hollered even louder over their noise.

"Mrs. Penleigh, call 9-1-1. I need help in Room #857, immediately."

"I'll call now." Susan flipped the switch back into place, pressed a speed dial number on her telephone, and gave the dispatcher the request. She then buzzed the vice principals office on the intercom and gave a sigh of relief when he answered.

"Yes?"

"Mr. Tillman, I notified the dispatcher, a deputy is coming. You need to help the teacher in Room #857. Sounds like several are fighting."

"Thank you, Mrs. Penleigh. Notify Coach Ramsey and have him meet me there also."

"Yes sir."

Coach Ramsey walked into the office from the break room, standing with his hand clutching a bundle of mail.

"I heard him, Mrs. Penleigh, and I am on my way."

Susan left the office behind him and locked the door. Making the rounds to collect attendance slips, it crossed her mind, again, how helpful it would be to have a student aide complete this task. Several students needing only two credits to graduate this term spent their extra time sitting in the library. *Maybe it is selfish of me to want their help. The school district could well afford to hire an office aide.* She sighed and walked faster. Within ten minutes, she approached the troubled Room #857. The door was shut, and thankfully, the teacher had attached her roll sheet slips on a clip outside in the hall near her door. Susan grabbed it, and sounds of a turmoil continued coming from the room. As she left the door, Mr. Tillman and Mr. Ramsey could still be heard. Demanding order, their voices rose high above the shouting students. Something crashed inside the room, and Susan hurried away.

Her office beckoned invitingly while she slipped through the vacant halls.

121

The constant shrill ring of the phone could be heard, and thoughts of a quiet refuge vanished as she unlocked the door, and entered her office.

Nerves all a jitter she sat in her chair, and with a shaky hand, grabbed the phone.

"River Town High School."

"Mrs. Penleigh?"

"Yes."

"This is Mrs. Harris, I have a doctor appointment today, and you have Mrs. Dawson for the substitute in my class. Is she there?"

"Yes ma'am. She arrived and has your lesson plans for each period, your attendance sheets, and schedule for lunch. I give the subs a copy of that information when they sign in at my office."

"Well, I think I mixed up my fourth period lesson plans with my sixth period class. Could you straighten that out for me, Mrs. Penleigh?"

"I will try, Mrs. Harris. I will write her a note explaining your message, walk to that particular wing of classrooms, and hand it to her, so as not to disturb the class. I am not allowed to use the intercom when a class is in session."

"Thank you, Mrs. Penleigh."

Susan hung up the phone. A dull throbbing pain began across her forehead.

She wrote the note, locked her office, walked to the other wing of classrooms, and hand delivered the note to the substitute. She flopped into her chair upon returning and tried to line the day out with priorities.

Glancing at her open doorway, she saw a deputy standing in the hall. Mr. Tillman soon approached him with a male student in tow. After much discussion, Susan could only hear as low, muffled conversation; the deputy handcuffed the student, and they left.

Earl Tillman walked to her door and stood with one eyebrow raised. "Has Mr. Monroe arrived yet?" He looked at Susan.

"No sir, he has not."

"Well, tell him his prize student, Larry Baker, the basketball phenomenal of River Town High, threw a desk across a classroom, and the teacher has filed charges against him. There will be a hearing, and there is a safety issue."

"Yes sir."

Tillman made rapid strides down the hallway, and the phone rang at the same time. Susan took a message for Mr. Monroe and hung up the phone. It rang again immediately, another message was taken as the intercom buzzed.

Susan hung up the phone and clicked the switch on the intercom.

"River Town High School." Susan heard snickers and giggles from students while her voice boomed out inside that classroom.

"We know it is, Mrs. Penleigh." The teacher laughed.

Susan flushed with embarrassment and laughed with them. "I am going to move the telephone to the other side of my desk, as far away from that intercom unit as I can. Maybe that will help."

"We all have our moments, Mrs. Penleigh." The teacher laughed again and buzzed off without telling Susan what she wanted.

◆ ◆ ◆ ◆

Principal Rex Monroe arrived, and Susan's day took on an even faster pace. Looking forward to lunch, she finally sat exhausted in the cafeteria with a small taco salad. The fresh greens, mixed with chopped onions, shredded cheddar cheese; dotted with white scoops of sour crème, and green guacamole sat inside of a crispy shell with the spicy tantalizing smell of taco flavored meat. *Who said cafeteria food was bad?* Aroma drifted to her nostrils, and Susan blinked her eyes looking at it, and could not wait to dig in. *Umm!* She inhaled another promise of flavor, as the steam off the warm meat drifted up from her plate.

"Hey girl."

Susan glanced up to see Izabella.

"Have a seat. It is nice to hear a perky voice, and not someone fighting, or complaining."

"Sounds like a rough day." Izabella set her tray of food down and pulled out a chair.

"Not so much rough, less of that, and more nonstop busy." Susan chuckled.

"Think you will feel like attending FBLA today? It will be held in my classroom, as soon as school is out."

"I would love to, Izabella."

"Good. We are going to nominate officers this evening, and that will help you get familiar with the group."

"I will enjoy getting acquainted. Do I bring anything?" Susan poured a small amount of ranch dressing over her salad.

"No, I picked up some snacks and drinks. Susan, you can have your turn next time."

"Okay, I will. Oh, I met a student today I wanted to ask you about."

"Really? Who is it?" Izabella cut into her lasagna with the side of her fork and lifted the tasty morsel to her mouth. As threads of melted cheese oozed out, she twirled her fork around, and never lost a bite.

"Kendrick Vargas."

"Oh, you mean Kenny? Great kid, and great lasagna."

"I could not help but notice." Susan nodded. "What about his family, any moral support there?" Susan opened the napkin from her set of eating utensils.

"He has a lovely family, and Kenny adores all of them. Why?"

"I was concerned when he came into my office with blisters popped open and bleeding. He said he chops firewood for his dad." Susan dove into her taco salad.

"You know, that sounds just like Kenny. Always helping his dad. They are very close."

"Hmm, okay, I won't be so worried about his welfare, but I will keep an eye on his hands. Until they heal, anyway."

"Mother hen."

Susan laughed, and they finished their lunch; each parting, going off in different directions.

◆◆◆◆

The last bell rang for the day, and Susan braved the crowded hallways with teenagers hurrying to get outside. Someone turned and crossed her path, nearly knocking her down. She caught herself, and the student stopped briefly, glancing back at her. "My bad," he yelled and dashed for the open double doors.

My bad, ha, I have to remember that.

She made her way to Izabella's classroom and gratefully entered.

"Hi, come on in," Izabella called out, and motioned for Susan to sit next to her. Several rows of desks were being used, and Susan slid into one quickly. About twelve students walked around a table, busy rearranging items, or so it appeared. One of them nodded at Izabella, and turned to the group of twelve. "Everyone please be seated."

Izabella then stood and addressed the group.

"We are here today to vote for officers. Our past president will lead us in the process. I want to welcome all of you here today, and I would like to announce a new member. Mrs. Susan Penleigh has joined our organization." Applause erupted momentarily.

"I will now turn the meeting over to our President, Robert Frasier." More polite applause scattered throughout the room.

Robert Frasier stood erect and carried himself in a professional manner.

"I want to lead us in prayer, before we begin this meeting. Will you please bow your heads in respect?" He paused and continued. "Dear Heavenly Father, We thank You for Your guidance and the blessings You have bestowed upon us. We ask Your forgiveness where we have failed You, and pray for strength to move forward. In Jesus name we pray. Amen."

He walked to the table, reached for a stack of papers, and a cluster of pencils. "Our voting will commence at this time." He passed a page and pencil to everyone in the room.

"We will make our selections and return these to Mrs. Izabella Contrell. Results will be reported during eight o'clock morning announcements from our school office tomorrow. Please listen at that time and ask your friends to join."

Students looked over the voting page. Susan noticed how quickly some students made their check marks by each name on the list, got up, and handed it to Izabella.

Everyone was so well behaved.

After the last voting page was turned in to Izabella, she encouraged all to enjoy the snacks placed on the table.

"Mrs. Penleigh, please join us." Robert gave Susan a paper plate. "Help yourself." He motioned towards the refreshments.

"The cupcakes are delicious. Try one, they are lemon crème." A girl told her.

"Thanks. What is your name?"

"Regina Burke, and I saw you in church last Sunday."

"You did? I do not see how." Susan laughed. "That is one huge church."

"It is. A few of us go there, but not too often."

"Really? Hmm, I am curious, why not often?"

"Well, it is kind of embarrassing, and yes, I know it does not matter what you wear to church, but my friends and I have one thing we can wear, and we wear it over and over. Some kids poke fun at us. So sometimes we do not go."

"Well, with the economy like it is, and a lot of people out of work; clothes are the last thing some families can buy. I grew up with a younger sister, and she wore my hand-me-downs for a few years," Susan admitted.

"Oh, I like used clothes. There is a place we went to last year, and they had a large variety."

"Where is that, Regina?" Susan took a bite of cupcake.

"It is in a town a long ways from here. Have you ever heard of Mount Pleasant?"

"I have now. Tell me about the place."

"It has a Goodwill Store, and they are real friendly there."

"Regina, are you talking about the Goodwill Store, again? I want to go." Another teen squealed out in excitement and wiggled her fists about.

"Izabella , could we take these kids there?"

"As a FBLA group?"

"No, the school will not be involved, we will go on a shopping trip."

"I don't see why not."

Regina looked at Izabella. "Mrs. Contrell, they have t-shirts, and blue jeans, and sometimes even a dress in my size."

Robert walked near Susan. "Mrs. Penleigh, is this shopping trip just for girls?"

"No, but we cannot take the whole school. How about FBLA members and you must have a permission slip signed from parents, to release liability issues."

"Okay, but would a grandparent work, or an aunt, if parents are not here?" His concern was obvious.

Izabella spoke up quickly. "Of course."

Susan glanced at her new friend. "I think with both of us driving, we will have room for the whole group. What do you think?"

"Well, we would have room for them but not if they bought much." Izabella frowned.

"Oh, that's right, but this is no ordinary trip. We will shop. I have a neighbor who may volunteer his time and another vehicle. Guys, let me ask him, and if all goes well, we will leave this Saturday." Susan looked at Izabella, "That is if Saturday will work for you?"

"I am open, sounds like fun."

"Robert, as President, will you make copies of our standard permission forms, but leave the school out of it. Put Mrs. Penleigh's name and mine as sponsors, and leave room for her neighbor's name."

"Yes Ma'am."

Regina grabbed Robert by his arm. "Come on, we can use the copy machine in the library."

"Let's all go. Thank you sponsors." The teens were exuberant and left the room.

"Get some rest, girl." Izabella winked at Susan.

"Rest?" Susan laughed. "Now or later?"

Chapter Twelve
August 27, 2011
8:30 AM

Content, but determined not to let his guard down, Rick was relieved to have moved home. An early morning appointment put him in high gear and full of confidence. Happy to show property, the Realtor organized folders in his briefcase, and left.

Punctual, he arrived at the downtown historical section, and parallel parked on the tree lined street. He strolled to the bustling sidewalk café, ordered coffee, and waited for his clients.

A people watcher, Rick, spotted an intense couple in the midst of a crowd, checking out the area. Only a true tourist would pay attention to any detail. Locals would walk by briskly, in a hurry to get to their destination, and often miss the storefront flowering window boxes in full bloom, or the birds taking advantage of the enormous bird bath in the courtyard.

The couple approached his table.

Rick's smile was genuine as he rose from his chair and extended his hand to the man.

"Rick Yeager. I think we talked yesterday about a building for sale."

The stranger shook Rick's hand. "Yes, we did. I'm Darrell Oliver, and this is my wife, Sharon. Thanks for wearing the black Stetson hat. I told Sharon that must be you."

"Nice to meet you."

"Rick, I like this development. Most towns attempt to revive a downtown of abandoned buildings with paint. River Town wove charm into every corner. This reminds me of the wrought iron courtyards in New Orleans with all the plants and shrubs."

Sharon chimed in. "The sounds and smells are equal to the quaint shops and eateries of the River Walk in San Antonio, without the river actually being here in downtown. Perfect setting for my art studio, I am impressed."

"Well, let's check out the rest of it." Rick led the way and showed the Oliver's a building with enough space, and eighteen century grace, to suit their needs. The transaction was finalized at a nearby bank by a local notary. Rick gave Darrell and Sharon Oliver the name of a reputable construction contractor. The Oliver's left ecstatic and in a hurry.

"Rick, Rick Yeager." A voice called as he neared the exit door. Rick turned and saw one of the loan officers approach.

"Matt Whaley, good to see you," Rick greeted his friend. "How in the world are you doing?"

"Can't complain. What's that old saying? If I was any better I'd be twins." Matt laughed at his own joke, and Rick joined him with a belly laugh.

"You old rascal, you haven't changed a bit."

"No, but that's what I wanted to talk to you about. I don't like what I've been hearing; don't like what's going on around town, lately. Come in my office where we can talk."

Rick nodded and followed the older gentleman to a glass enclosed office. They sat in padded, brown leather chairs, and Matt came to the point fast.

"I heard your home was vandalized and your truck, too. Sorry you experienced that ordeal, Rick."

"Thank you, Matt. I'm more careful now, and almost paranoid, truth be known."

"I understand. Uh Rick…" Matt hesitated.

"What is it, Matt?"

"I don't like gossip, but you need to be warned. Other houses along the river have been broken into this past week. A sudden rash of burglaries is scary, makes you not trust anyone. The law enforcement doubled their patrol in that area." Matt sighed loudly and squinted at Rick. "I might as well tell you, your daughter is rumored to be back in town. I haven't seen her, though, but that's the talk being passed around."

"Tessa? She is supposed to be in rehab. I'll have to call and verify she is still there. What a shock, Matt. Thanks for telling me."

"You needed to know."

"I appreciate the information." Rick stood, shook hands with his old friend, and quietly walked out of the bank with a frown on his forehead. *Tessa, um, um, um. Are you the one stealing?*

His stomach knotted up, and he drove home. Rick scrambled some eggs and popped two slices of bread in the toaster. He carried his breakfast and a glass of milk to the patio in the back yard. He sat, and nibbled at the food, all the while looking out across the river at the woods on the other side. *Are you over there, Tessa? Are the thugs I saw your friends?* Rick's mind was racing

132

with scenarios when he realized his heart was racing also. *Got to calm down.*

He finished eating, and picked up his plate and glass. On the way to the house, he noticed a funky smell drifting towards him. *What is that?* Rick nearly choked as the smell grew stronger, reminding him of toxic chemicals. *Could be a meth lab. I've read reports on how bad the smell is, and how the illegal drug is made in remote areas.* He hurried inside, shut the door, and sucked in a deep breath of clean air.

Chapter Thirteen
August 27, 2011
9:00AM

Logan Wakefield backed his Chevy Silverado truck into the parking lot at the empty Tall Pines Marina. Guaranteed to be a convenient, central location; he waited, and looked in all directions for Susan, Izabella, and twelve teenagers to arrive.

Not being one to merely sit, he left the vehicle and meandered to the massive thirty foot pier. *Hard to believe.* He gazed down at acres of dried up lake bed. Boat ramps and docks stood isolated in cracked dry ground. *Never seen a drought this bad.*

"It's not only our area that's dried up. Lake Palestine is almost gone, and that is southwest of us. You would think we'd all get more rain from the gulf, but it ain't happening."

Logan, startled by the old timer, gave the man a courteous tip of his Stetson hat.

"I've been hearing reports of burn bans getting close to us." Logan looked directly into the man's weathered face.

"Yes sir, and this heat is bad on everything. More folks are having blown tires, unless they are brand new. The roads are too hot to drive on. Showed on television, a man put a thermometer to the road, and it was over one hundred and seventy degrees. Railroad repairs are up, the rails are warping in the heat. Foundations are cracking right under solid built homes…I tell you, speaking for myself, I do not know

134

how a farmer can bounce back when everything he plants gets burnt up. Cows don't have anything to eat, either, and now wildfires are popping up."

The old man took his stained, straw hat off and wiped the sweat from his brow with the back of his hand. "Folks need to get right with the Lord. Too many thinking bad is good." He raised his head to look at Logan. "Been nice visiting with you."

"You too, sir."

Logan watched the old man depart as smoke shot out from behind the noisy old truck. *His words will weigh heavy on anyone's mind.* Sweat ran into his stinging eyes, and he dabbed a handkerchief across the moisture on his face. A quick jaunt back to the Silverado, Logan basked in the air conditioner, and poured water from a plastic disposable bottle onto a napkin. Laying it across his eyes, he almost moaned with immediate relief, the stinging was gone.

So what would Susan think if she could see me now, ha. Well, knowing her, I would not be the one to put the wet napkin over my eyes. He smiled and glanced into his rear view mirror. Susan was turning into the parking lot. *Oh, lady, we have to talk…*

◆ ◆ ◆ ◆

Oh…Logan is already here. How nice…oh no, he backed up. Well, I know I cannot back up that close to another vehicle. Susan waved and pulled in next to him. He climbed out of his truck and opened her car door.

"Susan, sit in my truck with me. I have got it ice cold in there."

"Sure, and thanks for coming, Logan. I'm glad you are early. We can spend some time together before the kids and Izabella arrive."

135

He helped her up into the truck. "I would like that. Hey, did you see an older man just leave from here in a truck?"

"The one making chugging sounds?" Susan cocked her head to the side.

"Has to be the same one. We talked about the drought and wildfires. First time it's ever been this bad. Gets you to thinking about precaution."

"This is all new to me; the wildfires are a brand new fear to overcome. I was raised around Seattle. We had earthquakes and Mt. Rainier erupting to worry about. One day I'll never forget. I was at school in P.E. class. We were all lying on our backs doing leg exercises, when the overhead, hanging florescent lights started swinging back and forth. The teacher instructed us to form a line and file outside as was procedure. Kids yelled, some cried, and no one could remain calm.

"I'll always remember feeling the ground beneath me trembling. We immediately looked at Mt. Rainier and smoke was coming out of the top. Would lava be next? We would be directly in its path. That was fear like I'd never experienced. Later, when the ground quit shaking, we went back inside, and saw a huge crack in the concrete wall of our school."

"I've never been in an earthquake. Don't want to be either." Logan shook his head.

"Well, I finally overcame that fear and now it looks like I have a new one. I'm not used to wildfires. They terrify me. Gives me a sensation of helplessness."

"Susan, we have measures in place to take against wildfires. I want to tell you something, and it will help you overcome this fear."

"What?"

"The words fear and faith do not belong together."

"Thanks, Logan. I needed reminding."

"Well, okay. Are you good with that, now?"

"I'm good. I'm focused in the right direction; faith."

"We can all get sidetracked sometimes. So, back to the kids, how many do we each transport, and what is the game plan?"

"Well, they do not know it, but I want to take them to eat at the El Chico's Restaurant across the street from the Goodwill Store. I drove there one day this past week and checked everything out after school."

"I wondered why you were home so late the other night." Logan looked perplexed and frowned.

"Well, I have to admit, I did not see any lights on at your house when I got in."

"Well, duh, no. You cannot look at your neighbor's house with your own lights on."

Susan chuckled. "So *my* neighbor did not just happen to be awake at that hour?" She raised an eyebrow.

"No, as a matter of fact, I was concerned that *my* neighbor might have had car trouble, or needed my help with something, and did not have my phone number at the time." Logan winced.

"Well, I certainly am proud of my neighbor, and that I now have the phone number."

"Susan, do not mention it. That is the least I can do."

"Least you can do?"

"Yes, it's a new jingle. *Like a good neighbor, Logan Wakefield is here.*"

"Oh, please. I did not know you could sing, too. This *is* my lucky day." Susan leaned her head to the left and extended her arm out in a fake swoon.

Logan winked. "Now that is what I am talking about."

Susan grabbed her purse and threw it at him. He ducked as it sailed toward him, and someone knocked on the truck window.

"Izabella." Susan's face flushed, and Logan got out of the truck in a hurry.

"Good morning, you two."

"Climb aboard, ma'am." Logan retrieved a folded handle inside the truck for Izabella to grab onto and helped her into the back seat.

"Glad we can talk before the kids get here," Izabella stated.

"Yes, I agree, and I was telling Logan that I want to treat the kids with lunch at El Chico's Restaurant. There is one across the street from the Goodwill Store."

"Oh, they will love that. Susan, I am so excited. I intend to help pay for the clothes they pick out. It will be *my* surprise."

"Sounds like we all have the same idea, I'm helping out too, and it is going to be awesome to spring this on them." Logan looked at both women.

"Oh, here they come." Susan glanced at the cars entering the parking lot. "How are we going to drive them? How many in each vehicle?"

"Logan can take the boys, and Susan, you and I could divide the girls up, but I can get more in my van. How about six girls with me, three girls with Susan, and Logan you get the three boys." Izabella took a deep breath.

"Sounds good to me." Susan nodded.

"Okay, let's do it." Izabella agreed.

"Come on, let's get out and meet everyone, give them a big welcome." Logan helped Susan and Izabella climb down from the truck.

Smiling faces greeted them, and the kids all but bounced with excitement. Izabella collected the signed parental permission forms. Seating arrangements were made, kids piled into the correct vehicle, and were driven off. A group decision placed Izabella to lead, Susan was positioned in the middle, and Logan would bring up the rear.

Plans were to stop, eat a light breakfast in Daingerfield, and arrive in Mount Pleasant near nine o'clock. Chatter was nonstop, and Susan listened as the girls rattled on and on. Not about to interrupt them, she kept her eyes on the road.

Driving through Jefferson, Avinger and Hughes Springs, brought each girl to a window, peeping out at the cute shops they passed. The girls pointed at places they wanted to check out on the way back.

"Many towns along the way have great shops, too." Susan relaxed her posture.

"Oh, look it's a Pittsburg Hot Links Restaurant." One girl pointed again as all three teens quick glanced. On and on it went, a fun trip had by all.

Izabella pulled in at the Brookshire's Grocery Store parking lot in Daingerfield.

Susan followed behind her, exited the car, and stretched. She glanced around for Logan, and he was not far behind her.

"Where do you guys want to eat? It is too early for lunch." Izabella climbed out of her van and looked at Susan.

"I know. I could run into Brookshire's, buy orange juice or chocolate milk, a few boxes of muffins, and handy wipes, of course. It would take too long if we all went in somewhere and ordered."

A Silverado truck turned into the parking lot. Logan turned off the ignition and got out.

"Ladies, how is it going?"

Susan walked to him and laughed. "My head is roaring for clarity. I've never heard bits and pieces of so many stories in my life."

"It's been fun, and I have renewed respect for school bus drivers." Izabella rubbed the back of her neck..

Logan stifled a yawn. "Excuse me, but my guys have aced this trip. We are buddies now. It has been nonstop man talk."

"Oh, so now they are your guys?" Susan opened her mouth in mock surprise.

"Hey, we have bonded. What can I say?"

"Well, that just confirms what we knew. We have got a great group of kids." Susan sighed and glanced back at the parked vehicles.

"Agreed." Logan cleared his throat. "I want to share this expense, so breakfast is on me."

"Thanks Logan. We were discussing bottled juice or milk and boxes of muffins, instead of stopping somewhere and everyone piling out. They can eat while we drive."

"That will work. Tell you what, you ladies count heads and supervise all the kids with a restroom run while I go buy the stuff."

"Good idea. Let's do it." Izabella went to her van. "Out, everyone get out and shake a leg, stretch those arms." She looked at the other vehicles and waved at the occupants.

The kids rushed from the car and truck. Susan quickly retrieved a small spiral notebook and pen from her vehicle.

"Okay, your choice of orange juice, milk or chocolate milk. I need a raise of hands now. How many for orange juice?" Scanning the group she saw four hands wave wildly into the air. She quickly wrote four next to orange juice. "Okay, milk? Three. Got it. Chocolate milk? Five... Here, Logan." She ripped the page off the notebook and gave it to him.

"Line forms for the restroom, come on, let's hurry and get this done. Maybe we can all return before Logan has to wait on us." Izabella gathered the kids. A bit noisy, they walked in the store single file.

Susan and Izabella stood near the restrooms as the teens took their turn among volumes of chatter. Progress was made swiftly, and the line began to shorten.

"I am so proud of them, they are such an orderly group, loud but orderly." Susan laughed at Izabella.

"Well, if they keep this up, they might fool around and get another trip somewhere else, later." Izabella looked the kids over as she talked quietly to Susan.

141

"That would go over big."

"I will take half of them back to the truck and cars. We have six of them standing around ready to go eat. You watch the other six, and it should not take long for them to finish." Izabella offered.

Susan nodded solemnly, Izabella gathered her group, and they left the store.

Logan approached the remaining group carrying bags in both hands. "I will be outside. As soon as everyone returns to their seat, I will start passing this stuff out."

"Did you get handy wipes? I forgot to mention those." Susan glanced at Logan.

"Yes ma'am." He turned, and two more kids left with him. Within minutes, the last four kids followed Susan outside, and all were accounted for.

◆◆◆◆

Logan passed the food and drinks out, making sure to give everyone plenty of handy wipes. He patiently went to each vehicle and got everyone's drink request correct.

Weary, Logan finally climbed into his truck, and Robert Frasier, FBLA president, yelled. "Hey, man I got a Diet Coke."

"What?" Logan turned, and looked at the young men drinking milk and orange juice in the back seat.

"I was joking, Mr. Logan. I wanted to get you riled." He beamed at Logan.

"Hey, I have been known to have Senior Moments, now."

"You rock, Mr. Logan."

"Thanks, man." Logan took a bite of muffin, and the kids joined him in a comfortable silence.

♦ ♦ ♦ ♦

Someone knocked on the truck window, and Logan lowered it a few inches.

Susan spoke first. "Izabella and I are going to run to the restroom, will you watch everyone?"

"Sure." He called out while the two women walked back to the store.

"I wish all the ladies at our school were as nice as those two are." One of the students said.

"Darrell? Did I get your name right?"

"Yes sir."

"Well, Darrell, we cannot always pick the people we want to be around, but we can control how we act around them. I guess the saying 'Silence is Golden' would apply there."

"I can see where that might come in handy. If someone in authority is having a bad day, the best thing to do is keep quiet, and keep out of their way."

"Hey, you got it. That will also apply to a job situation, as well. None of us are perfect, but we can all try to treat others as we would like to be treated." Logan passed another box of muffins around, and each teenager grabbed another one. "So," Logan continued, "have you guys lived in River Town long?"

"Me, I live with my Granny." Robert took a swallow from his bottle of orange juice. "I moved here from Atlanta, Georgia when my mom got a job offer in New York. Her career was sky rocketing, and she did not know any baby sitters, so Granny agreed to take me in. Mom wants me to stay with family while she works, and she calls us all the time. Maybe you have heard of her? My mom's name is Cee Cee Beckham."

Logan choked on his muffin, and small chunks of food flew out of his mouth as his eyes widened, and he blushed. Robert beat on Logan's back furiously.

"You okay, Mr. Logan?" A chorus of concerned voices rose inside the truck while the other teens rushed from their seats to help beat on his back, also.

"Stop. Stop, I am okay. I just lost my breath, is all. Thanks guys." He turned and gave Robert an incredible look of surprise with his eyes still widened. He glanced again at Robert and shook his head back and forth several times.

"Seriously, your Mother is Cee Cee Beckham? *The* Cee Cee Beckham who got her start in Broadway Musical plays? Man, she has one fantastic voice range of any singer I know of. She is known the world over."

Robert looked at his friends Darrell and Keegan, who were now seated again in their seats inside the truck, equally wide eyed, and amazingly silent in the back row of seats. Robert sat in the front seat next to Logan.

"I got him again." He yelled exuberantly, and raised a fist up into the air.

"Robert…" Logan's smile faded.

"Hey man, I will be straight. I do not even remember my mama. My Granny raised me at her house when my daddy got incarcerated. I do not remember him either. I was three years old when it happened. I still do not know what he did, but he will be out when I am thirty five years old, and my Granny will not even *talk* about my mama."

144

"I am sorry, Robert. I had no right asking you about your private life."

"I cannot change what my parents did, or did not do. I am responsible for myself, for my own decisions, and my own actions. All I can do is try to have a better life, and I do that by looking to Jesus Christ for my salvation. I can assure you, Mr. Logan, I do not want to spend eternity burning in hell. My God in heaven is a loving Father, a forgiving Father, and I pray earnestly for His Will to be done in my life, and I pray often to Him about anything I consider doing in my life, so His work will continue through me. No, I am not perfect, but I pray to live a life that all others can see Jesus love through me, I pray to have all my sins forgiven, and I profess publicly that Jesus Christ is my Savior."

"Where do you go to church, Robert?"

"I don't go. I watch church services on Sunday morning television."

"It's great to hear more of God's Word, to apply it to our own life, but Robert; you are missing the fellowship, and encouragement members give each other. I attend Chapel of Christ in River Town. Why don't you to join me next Sunday?"

Robert leaned forward. "Hey, Mr. Logan, my main man; I like what you are saying. Proud to meet you there and sit beside you. We can learn together."

"Keegan, Darrell, you guys are welcome too. I do not want to pressure you, but we are not promised tomorrow. No man knows when he will be called from this life and stand before Him on judgment day. It is never too late to change our ways. I hope you choose salvation. Think about eternity, and where you want to be. It is either Christ or the Antichrist. Read Psalms1:6, "For the Lord knows the way of the righteous, but the way of the ungodly shall perish."

"Mr. Logan, I live with my girlfriend and her baby. We are our own family. I took her in because she was alone and needed help with her child." Keegan sat upright and spoke in a sincere manner.

"Keegan, I am sure that makes you feel like the man you think you are, but you cannot compromise the Word of God. You are not married. You cannot live in sin, and think it is pleasing to God. I do not care if everyone is living together. It is not the way of a Christian. If your peers act like it is an okay lifestyle, then you are in the counsel of sinners. Go back, and read Psalms 1:1. "Blessed is the man who walks not in the counsel of the ungodly, nor stands in the way of sinners, nor sits in the seat of the scornful."

"Keegan, to me that means the person who lives according to the Word of God, who does not trod the evil path of sin, but rather evidences faith in God. I had to share that with you. A Bible based church usually has a Wednesday night in-depth Bible study. I have learned so much there on scripture."

"It would be a mistake to not look up scripture, right, Mr. Logan? We all need guidance."

"Right, and guys, I make mistakes every day. Sometimes I think bad of someone because of what they have done. Say they try to get people to think bad of you; when they are really the bad guy. That is a tough situation, but you have to avoid those people. Forgive them, yes, but stay away from them, or it will only get worse. Read Proverbs 15: 1. 'A soft answer

146

turns away wrath: but grievous words stir up anger.' My problem is that I want to tell these people I know what they are doing, and they are not fooling me. That is wrong. So, I go on my happy way, and stay away from them, and I don't let them see a reaction if they try to anger me. That is tough to do, also, but you will be the better man."

Susan and Izabella returned to their vehicles, and the group departed Brookshire's Grocery.

"Hold on guys, we are leaving Daingerfield." Logan was the last to leave. He turned his truck towards their main destination and headed out of town.

"Mr. Logan. Look, it's a donut shop."

"Where?"

"On the right, across from the Dollar Store. Can we stop there on our way back?"

"Sounds like a plan, remind me, okay?"

"Okay."

Logan listened to the boys ramble about what they were going to buy at the Goodwill Store. When they entered the town of Mount Pleasant, Logan kept on driving.

"Mr. Logan, this sure is a long town. How much father is it, Mr. Logan?"

"A few more minutes, and it's on the left side of the street."

Each boy strained to spot the place, until it finally came in view. Izabella, and Susan parked near the front door, and Logan joined them. All of the kids hopped out, went inside, and grabbed a shopping buggy. Aisles and aisles of clothing hung from racks, and the teens took their time to make their choice. They bought for their families first, and themselves last.

When they got in line to pay for their purchases, the three sponsors paid for everything the teens selected. It was truly a great moment shared by all. Huge Goodwill bags were packed into the vehicles, and a meal of their choice was enjoyed at El Chico's Mexican Restaurant. Susan paid the ticket as twelve stuffed and happy teens crawled back in the truck and cars.

Yes, they did stop for donuts on the way back through Daingerfield. Night had fallen, and due to the late hour, the cute shops in other towns would definitely be visited on the next trip.

Chapter Fourteen

September 5, 2011, Labor Day
6:30 AM

Rick jumped out of bed, shocked to see the room flooded with bright sunshine. *Might as well enjoy my morning coffee, don't have any appointments today.* He dressed, strolled outside, and retrieved the newspaper from the front lawn. At first, it appeared like a typical day. Quiet. He glanced around. *A few neighbors still have to work today, Labor Day or not. Course it's way too early for them to leave.* Rick frowned as he noticed the foul smell had returned. He was almost at the door when he heard a thunderous explosion from behind his house. He ran fast and gasped at the sight of a gigantic fireball as it erupted in the woods, and the stench plummeted across the river towards him.

Rick called 911.

Fire department and law enforcement personnel took immediate lifesaving action. Alarms blared from strategically placed weather warning speakers. Police scanners squawked, and thankfully, volunteers responded throughout the county.

Rick watched in amazement while the Texas Forestry Service helicopters buzzed overhead dumping tons of water as the fire spread. Smoke billowed from the woods across the river and surrounded the entire neighborhood. Strangers arrived, helping hose down houses.

KWAT-TV News Team from Channel 3 unloaded equipment and filmed live along the riverbank.

Someone banged on Rick's front door, and he raced to answer it.

A deputy stood erect while smoke thickened in the air. "Sir, you have five minutes to evacuate."

"Evacuate?"

"Yes sir. Do you need assistance? This is escalating into a dangerous situation. Other fires have started nearby in Harrison County, one on FM 1793, and another on FM 9. Gregg County is battling one they call the Moore Fire. Wildfires are starting all over the area; up and down Interstate 20, Kilgore, and Gladewater. Two summers of drought have caught up with us. High winds and low humidity are hurting us. Do you need any help? "

"Uh, no. I don't need assistance. I'll leave now. Thank you."

Rick's heart pounded in his chest. For the first time, the seriousness hit him. *Dangerous situation indeed.* He raced into the bedroom, grabbed his hat and wallet, and dashed outside. Thick, white smoke blinded him, and he tripped over a dog. Rick pushed himself off the ground and headed to his truck. The dog followed and whined.

"Okay fellow, you belong to someone out here. Come on with me." He opened the truck door, and the animal jumped inside. Rick backed out of the driveway and waited as neighbor's cars rushed by. He darted his truck onto the road. *Look at the traffic. Everyone is leaving at the same time.* He noticed fire trucks parked near houses and other vehicles parked at random along the road's edge. Rick dodged a few cars driving back to the evacuation area and shook his head.

150

He swerved the truck again, and the dog fell to the floorboard.

"Sorry little buddy. Hold on, we're getting out of here."

Rick's hands shook on the steering wheel with each mile of progress. Sweat drenched clothes clung to him, and he realized he forgot to turn the air conditioner on. He sighed deeply when the animal shelter came in view.

Rick glanced at the dog's red collar. "I saw you roaming last week. Who's your owner?" *I'll drop him off, and hopefully, they will look for him there.*

Chapter Fifteen

September 6, 2011
7:30 AM

Students scattered in the hallway at the intrusion of sirens. The unexpected noise blared constantly. Startled, Susan's office chair fell while she lunged and ran to look out the window. *Bad weather? Awful thunder storm approaching?* A quick glance at the sky, and she trembled. Smoke rose high and covered a wide area across the horizon. Still trembling, she ran to answer the sudden ringing phone.

"River Town High School."

"Susan, I didn't notice you being home yesterday. A woods fire jumped the river and spread to parts of our neighborhood. We ran for our lives. Authorities evacuated us. Stay where you are, it's safer there."

"I was at Izabella's. Rick, I can't sit here and work. Not with that going on. I can't, I just can't."

"Nothing can be done here. The road is blocked off. No one can enter. I have to go."

Susan heard a click, and the call ended. She stared at the phone as Ricks' words kept repeating in her mind. The sirens stopped.

A scream brought her to her senses. Susan followed the sound to the hallway where a young girl struggled to remove herself from the hold Rex Monroe had on her arms. Slightly overweight, the tall girl's blond hair hung halfway down her back, and it was flying in all directions. She bent over, and tried to twist away from him. Rex Monroe flung her into the double row of

152

metal lockers, and the banging impact brought even louder anguish from the girl.

I can't stand this. I won't let this treatment continue. Susan briefly stood in the office doorway with her mouth open in shock, and one white-knuckled hand gripping the door frame. The instant she rushed to the girl, Mr. Monroe glanced toward her.

"Mrs. Penleigh, take this student to your office. Call, and tell the parent to get here fast." He reached out and dug his fingers into the girls hand while he pushed her at Susan.

Crying, the girl clung to Susan. She rubbed the girl's back and glared at her boss.

"Let's go." As they entered the office, Susan turned and noticed Rex Monroe breathing heavily. She watched him open a door to a classroom further down the hallway and disappear inside.

"What's your name?"

"Ma..Ma ..Mary Beth." Her voice shook.

"Well, Mary Beth, he is gone. We have a phone call to make."

The phone sat on the nearby counter, and Mary Beth snatched at the receiver, whimpering as she dialed.

"Mom, co ..come and get me." She managed to say in between sobs. "Hurry."

Susan glanced at the girl's hand still holding the receiver. She saw half-moon indentations where the end of Rex Monroe's thumbnails left their mark and drew blood from the girl.

"Mary Beth, sit here. I'll get some peroxide and antibiotic cream."

Susan ran to the closet and retrieved the first aid kit when a fellow student darted into the open doorway and looked at Mary Beth.

"Here, stand up, Mary Beth. I'm taking pictures with my cell phone."

"Thanks, Rusty." The girl inhaled in a jerking manner, and her shoulders shook.

Susan glanced at him. "Get the marks on her hand."

He took several close-up pictures, and Mary Beth quickly raised the bottom of her shirt to expose red whelps around her waist where Rex Monroe had grabbed her side. Rusty held the cell phone high and clicked fast. Seconds later, he stuck the phone in his pants pocket and rushed out of the office.

Mary Beth collapsed in a chair, and her whole body shook. She wrapped her arms around herself and continued to shake.

Susan opened a bottle of peroxide and nearly dropped it when a female voice yelled from the hallway.

"Where is my daughter?" The woman barged into the office, glaring at Susan.

Mary Beth jumped from the chair, ran to her mother, and burst out crying again.

"I'm Loretta Jordan, Mary Beth's mother. I happened to be a few blocks away when she called. What is this about?" She held her daughter in her arms and addressed Susan.

Rex Monroe's voice boomed in reply as he entered the office. "What's this about? She was caught in a classroom with a cell phone. That's what this is about, and she would not give it to me. They are prohibited on campus, and I took it away from her."

"Mom, everyone in school carries a cell phone. I got caught with mine, and he hurt me."

"I hurt *you?* Young lady, please describe your actions to *me*."

"I defended myself."

"No, you displayed how anxious you are to leave this school permanently." Rex Monroe whirled toward Loretta Jordan and pointed a finger at her.

"I want your daughter withdrawn from my school, I will not allow the behavior she displayed today to happen on my campus."

"Mr. Monroe, you can't make me withdraw her. This is her senior year." Loretta Jordan widened her eyes at him.

"Yes, and she's a senior for the second time. Ms. Jordan, your daughter does not attend school often. We have a truancy issue. It's time she left, or you will pay the $200.00 fine."

"But, you can't do that. You don't understand, I'm a single parent, I only have a part time job."

"No, *you* don't understand, Ms. Jordan. She is bringing my attendance report down. I *will* report her to the truant officer, and you *will* pay a fine of $200.00; or you can withdraw her right now. Home school her, write it down on the withdrawal form. No one ever checks to see if anyone is being home schooled. I want her out of here, before she decides to quit, and I will not have her increase my drop-out rate."

He rushed to a filing cabinet, pulled a drawer open, retrieved a form, and waved it in the air.

"I don't play games, Ms. Jordan." Rex threw the typed page on the counter, scribbled on it, and shoved it at Loretta Jordan.

"This is the withdrawal form, sign on the bottom line, and write where she is going to continue her education."

Silence flooded the room as Loretta Jordan lowered her eyes to gaze at the page. She reached for the ball point pen and slowly tapped it against the counter.

Susan leaned towards her and frowned. "Ms. Jordan, I… "

Rex stopped her in mid-sentence. "Mrs. Penleigh, stay out of my business."

Loretta Jordan raised her head and looked at Susan. A wrinkled brow met Susan's stare. Quietly, she signed the paperwork, and nodded at Mary Beth. Rex Monroe snatched the form, made a copy of it, and handed the original to Susan. Loretta and her daughter walked out of the office without speaking.

Rex suddenly grabbed the copy and bolted out the door.

Susan did not move, but could hear him out in the hallway.

"Ms. Jordan, here is your copy."

He returned to the office, and Susan looked at him, curious. *How can he do that? What kind of person is he?*

"Mrs. Penleigh, I have a conference with two teachers in a few minutes. When they arrive, send them to my office," he spoke briskly and ducked into his adjoining office.

I cannot concentrate. How can he act like nothing has happened?

"Mrs. Penleigh?"

Susan glanced at the doorway to see the teachers solemnly standing side by side.

"Please go in Mr. Monroe's office. He is waiting for you." She managed a smile while a dull, pounding grew in her temples. She rubbed the sides of her forehead with both hands, and the headache worsened.

Thin walls were not enough to keep Rex Monroe's thunderous voice confined to his office. Susan could hear each word he shouted. The stress shot her blood pressure sky high as the sudden cold, wet sensation of a light nose bleed trickled from a nostril. Susan grabbed a tissue and dabbed at it, and the pounding inside her head roared.

"So you are tutoring students on your free time? I will fire you if you do not stop. You do not have authority to be in charge of public students. Who do you think you are?"

Susan heard enough. She walked to the principal's office door, knocked on it, and entered at the same time.

"They are volunteers, that is who they are, and so am I."

Rex stood from his chair and pointed a finger at Susan.

"You are fired."

Susan turned and left his office while he poured his rage out at the two teachers.

As she gathered personal belongings, her head quit pounding, and Susan realized true relief.

Hmm. Philippians 4:7 "And the Peace of God which surpasses all understanding shall keep your hearts and minds through Christ Jesus."

So, this is the peace that surpasses all understanding. Thank you, Lord. I know you have other plans for me.

She threw her set of school keys upon the desk, walked out, and left the job.

The fire...I must return home and check on it...so thankful I wasn't home then...and so thankful Rex Monroe is no longer my boss...

Chapter Sixteen

September 6, 2011
10:00 AM

Barricades blocked both lanes of the road into Rick's neighborhood. The black and white deputy's patrol car, parked directly in front, seemed to emphasize the severity of the situation. Rick eased the Toyota Tundra truck onto the shoulder, and climbed out. He lifted his head and scanned the immediate area for billowing smoke. Rick gently bit his lip. Relived no smoke could be found, he strolled to the deputy.

"I'm Rick Yeager. Nice to see you protecting us, looks like the fires are out." He extended his hand for a handshake, and the deputy obliged.

"Deputy Acker. Thank you, sir, and for the most part, yes, the fires are out. Crews are still watching a few small hot spots smoldering in the surrounding woods. Do you live here?"

"Sure do, I want to check on my house."

"I have orders to keep everyone out except the residents. May I see your identification?"

Rick gave the deputy his driver's license and squinted in the blazing sunlight.

Upon careful examination, he handed it back to Rick. "Everything seems to be in order. I would advise you to collect photo albums, any valuables, insurance policies, anything that can't be replaced, and lock them in your truck. We may have to suddenly evacuate again."

"I thought it was okay to come back."

River Town

"It is for now. A fire engine will be on standby in the neighborhood as a precaution. We will all be patrolling tonight. Most people don't realize how dry it is. Wildfires are popping up all over Cass and Marion County, even in Bowie County." Deputy Acker wiped sweat from his brow.

"Must have just happened. I've been watching the news about the horrendous wildfires in the central part of the state, around Bastrop, Texas. Winds aren't helping matters any."

"No, but thankfully, crews are coming in from everywhere to fight the fire. Several homes, and a lot of acreage have already been lost, and it's still not under control. Lightning may have started it."

"That reminds me. I need to report what I saw when the fire started here. I am the one who called 911 about the fire, but something wasn't right prior to that."

"What do you mean?"

"I smelled a strange odor in the air a few times before the explosion. It was like a burst of chemicals appeared in the air and lingered. It didn't go away quickly, and nearly gagged me. I ran inside the house to breathe."

"Anyone else notice it?"

"I don't know… most of my neighbors were at work. Later, I observed two men across the river walking through the woods. When they saw me both men halfway hid themselves behind trees. Strange."

"I'll put it in my report, anything else?"

"No. They acted suspicious, really weird with the odd smell, too."

Deputy Acker wrote Rick's name, address and phone number. Another vehicle neared the barricade. He and Rick glanced at the slow approach of the car.

"It's Susan. She is a neighbor, I can vouch for her," Rick stammered at the deputy, and they walked to Susan's Chevy Equinox.

She idled her engine and lowered the window.

"Hey girl, I didn't mean to scare you when I called this morning. The neighborhood fires are out now."

"Listen, I appreciate you warning me. Thanks, Rick."

"You can go on back to work, Susan, things are fine."

"It's a long story but, I won't be going back to work. Is it safe to stay at home?"

"Well, yes, for the time being, but what's going on?' He frowned.

"Later. We will talk later, okay."

"Okay."

"Ma'am, it is safe now, but we may have to evacuate at any time." Deputy Acker hastened to mention.

"Thank you, officer. Ten o'clock news on the radio announced wildfires have just sprung up again in Gregg, Panola, Marion, Harrison, and Cass County. They are scattered all over. It's frightening."

"Yes, ma'am. A judge declared this an emergency and officially activated the Emergency Operations Center. We now have state and federal assistance available. The U.S. Fish and Wildlife Service providing personnel along with planes and helicopters equipped to scoop water from Cherokee Lake. Maude Cobb Convention and Activity Center in Longview is bustling with firefighters coming and going. Get photo albums, deeds, insurance papers, anything valuable or irreplaceable, and lock them in your car. We never know when a fire might break out again, and it's best to be prepared. A unit from the River Town Fire Department will be stationed here tonight in case hot spots grow out of control. We'll be patrolling, also. Drive around the side of the barricade, and you can return home." He tipped his hat at her.

She nodded at both men, put her car in gear, and carefully drove around the barricade.

"I'm heading home myself. It's too hot to be outside." Rick returned to the truck and followed Susan for over a mile.

She pulled into her driveway, and Rick kept driving to his own house while he glanced in amazement at the nearby fire damage. Tall burnt trees stood like black silhouettes in a Halloween picture, bleak and ghostly. Many homes were surrounded by black charred lawns that crept too close to their exterior walls. *Thank God for all firefighters.* The deputy flashed through his mind. *And thank God for all law enforcement personnel.*

Rick arrived home and parked the vehicle. He opened the truck door and stepped onto the concrete driveway. Lingering smoke remained in the air, similar to extremely low lying clouds. Not a breeze blew, and Rick marveled at the blanket of smoke only a few feet off the ground. A deep cough progressed quickly, until he went in the house, where the cough lessened. Inside, everything reeked of the strong smoke smell. Rick shook his head at this discovery. *Thank God I still have a house. Wonder what the back yard looks like?*

A brisk walk through the house, and he opened the back door. Deep in thought, he stared straight ahead when a slight movement against the outside wall caught his attention. Rick quickly turned his head towards the sound.

"Daddy."

Rick blinked at his daughter in disbelief. Soot covered her arms, and her hair was in disarray.

"Tessa." Shocked, he stood stiff.

"Oh, Daddy," she gushed, and embraced him in an instant hug.

"How did you get here?"

"My boyfriend got me out, and…and…I didn't know it, but he…he is best friends with that dirty ole' man, Cotton."

"You don't need to be involved with thugs. You need to go back to the drug treatment center."

"I'm scared, Daddy."

Rick melted as fast as a piece of chocolate in the heat of summer. *And she knows it.*

He held her close and slowly patted the top of her head while years of pain returned in full force. He fought back tears while his heart ached.

"Baby girl, I can't help you. You have to want to help yourself."

Tessa sobbed and held on to her father.

"I have to ask you something, Tessa, listen to me. Were you across the river from me a few days ago?"

The crying abruptly stopped, and a meek answer is heard by Rick.

"Yes, Daddy."

"What were you doing there?"

"It was a meth lab. It exploded."

"You know you have to go back to the center."

Tessa glared at him. "Like this? You want to drop me off at the center like this?" She spread her filthy arms wide apart.

"Go wash up, and we are going to talk to a new friend of mine. Then, see about getting you some clothes at Wal-Mart."

Tessa cleaned quickly, and Rick drove her to talk to Deputy Acker, still parked up the road. The boyfriend's description was given and all other pertinent information. Clothes were bought, fast food was eaten, and arrangements were made for Tessa to return the next day to the drug treatment center a hundred miles away.

Both exhausted, Father and daughter settled in for the night. About four o'clock in the morning, Rick awoke to glass shattering from the double windows in the living room.

Tessa's boyfriend broke into the home and demanded Tessa leave with him.

Numb with sleep, Rick managed to call 911 and hold a shotgun on the intruder. Deputies arrived and escorted the shouting drug addict out in handcuffs.

Rick drove a sullen Tessa back to the center after breakfast. He silently prayed for her and thought about the break-ins of his house and truck. He tried even harder to forgive what a drug addict will do for drugs.

Rick couldn't look at her. She sat rigid and angry. He blinked his watery eyes several times and sighed deeply. *What is she, twenty three years old now?*

Chapter Seventeen

September 7, 2011
7:00 AM

This seems surreal. Standing inside the house, Susan scanned each room for more articles to pack and filled several boxes. It was automatic to look out each window she passed, and Susan constantly searched the horizon for smoke.

Satisfied with her efforts, she packed even more into the trunk and back seat of her vehicle. She placed a sheet over her belongings in the car and went back into the house for a light breakfast of fruit and a granola bar. In between bites, she spotted the Bible she'd left on the counter earlier, and grabbed it. She chuckled to herself. *Don't think I can wake up and have coffee without my Bible.* She finished eating and carried the Bible to her car.

"Susan, hey Susan, wait up."

A glance across the road showed Logan Wakefield making long strides into her front lawn.

"Be ready to evacuate, fires are scattered all over many counties. I'm gone to help."

"I am ready, Logan, I didn't know you were a fireman."

"Yes, ma'am, a trained volunteer. Got to go."

"Be safe," Susan called out to Logan as he ran back to his truck. She watched him drive down the road and shuddered. She checked her surroundings and noticed her neighbors still at home, judging by all the parked cars and trucks in driveways. For the first time, Susan gasped at seeing how close the fires came to her house. *Guess I looked at the broad picture and not the details, yesterday.* The once clean neighborhood displayed charred lawns and the fire must have jumped from treetop to treetop, through the tall pines. Trees were burnt and some of the tops were gone.

Sweat ran down her spine, and her hair stuck to her forehead. *It's already hot. How do the firefighters stand the intense heat of a fire?* Susan lifted them up in prayer and heard a loud motor approach. *A helicopter?*

Rick drove into her driveway at the same time, killed the engine, and jumped out.

"Do you see that?" He cupped his hand over his eyes and glanced up. "They are looking for fires. A tremendous one is spreading around Avinger, Jefferson, and Linden; the Bear Creek Fire. The command post is set up in Linden, and I'm going there to relieve volunteers and help coordinate. If an evacuation is necessary, deputies will inform neighborhoods."

"I know, and I appreciate you telling me. My neighbor, Logan Wakefield is a volunteer fireman, and he left a few minutes ago."

"Tall skinny guy?"

"Uh, yes."

"I've seen him before but never did meet him." Rick shifted his weigh and coughed. "The civic center in Marshall is being prepared with cots and food to shelter any evacuees. Keep that in mind, Susan."

"I will, and thanks for stopping by, Rick."

"Oh, I wanted to. Take care." He waved and left fast.

166

Susan thought she saw smoke in the northern sky, and at first, she passed it off as a light yellowish cloud. *Light yellowish cloud? No such thing.* She jerked her head back to the same area in the sky and to her horror the 'cloud' turned dark grey and black, rolling higher and wider in the sky. *Fire.* Sirens blasted out across the neighborhood. Susan ran inside the house to get her car keys and purse. She snatched them up, locked the door, and hurried to the Chevy.

A deputy pulled up behind her in his patrol car. He jumped out and sprinted to her.

"Ma'am, you have five minutes to evacuate. Fires are closing in. You need to leave immediately. Drive to the Civic Center in Marshall for shelter."

"I'm on my way now. Thank you," she breathed.

He drove to the next house, and Susan waited for other cars to exit past her house before she could get out of her driveway. Finally, her turn to get on the road, she accelerated too fast, and the car squealed as she left the driveway burning rubber. Once again, she dodged the barricade at the beginning of the road. Trucks pulling travel trailers slowed her progress, and the thought crossed her mind; she couldn't imagine so many people lived along the river. Susan drove nonstop to her destination.

Total chaos ascended on the civic center. Over eighty people arrived at the same time.

Susan parked her car and stood in the parking lot, watching the sky. She could hear parts of conversation while many people meandered about.

"It's already burned down," one woman announced to the crowd.

"Excuse me, ma'am, but what burned down?" Susan approached her.

"River Town High School, it's a total loss."

Susan's mouth flew open in shock, and she gasped as others moaned aloud.

"Look, a new billow of smoke is reaching the sky fast. It's all black smoke," someone from the far side of the parking lot yelled. Another person raised his voice for all to hear. "Black smoke means houses."

"Where is that coming from?" Susan yelled back.

"The houses along the river."

Chapter Eighteen

September 9, 2011
7:30 AM

Ash and embers fell from the sky as wildfires burned hundreds of acres and countless homes along the way. Planes swooped down to nearby lakes obtaining water and dumped massive amounts on blazing areas. Rick stood outside the command post, an empty office building in East Texas, near the town of Linden. Squinting, he watched chemicals sprayed from airplanes leave a red mark on its downward path to the burning forests.

"I've never seen anything like this," Rick remarked to volunteers from a Lions Club.

The members brought cases of bottled water and snacks for the firemen, bringing the goods into the building assembly line style.

A van from a church backed up to the site. Two older ladies scooted out the front seat and hastened towards Rick. "We have cases of gator-aid drinks and the use of our emergency generator."

"Thank you, kindly. Do come inside and fill out paperwork. We'll return the machine, later." Rick ushered them inside the building.

"I'm Virginia, and this is Sylvia. We've been watching the news and keeping up with the fires. Thought this might come in handy." Virginia turned to look at Rick.

"Yes, ma'am, we appreciate your support."

Sylvia jumped when a woman manning the phones slammed a receiver down and yelled, "Yea! Fire fighters are on their way from California and Oklahoma."

"For our Bear Creek Fire?" Rick made long strides to another volunteer.

"Yes, and some are going to Bastrop. Fires are still raging and spreading in central Texas."

"We're blessed with help from many states."

The door burst open, and a man entered in sweat soaked clothing. "Heard you could use a backhoe to clear land for a fire-break, I brought you mine. Where do you want it unloaded?"

"Leave it on the trailer, if you can. We'll haul it to an area in need. Nice to meet you, I'm Rick Yeager." He approached the man and extended his hand.

"Dennis Monroe."

They shook hands and Rick frowned. "Monroe. I know I've heard that name before."

"Well, if you live anywhere close to River Town, you have surely heard about my brother, *Rex* Monroe. That rascal is the principal of the high school."

"I'm a Realtor in River Town, and I guess the best thing I can say about Rex is that now I know his brother, Dennis."

"You are old school, so am I. If you can't say something nice about somebody, don't say anything at all." Dennis looked straight at Rick.

"Yes sir, enough said." Rick glanced at each person near him and beamed. "I am so proud of your help. Mr. Monroe, I'd like for you to go with Mrs. Bobbie.

She'll show you the forms to fill out so we can return the equipment."

Bobbie peeped out the window. "How do I list it… tractor, backhoe, or loader?"

The owner spoke rapidly. "Backhoe, and I've got the serial number."

"If you'll excuse me, I'm going to unload the generator." Rick nodded at the group. "Ladies, sir, thank you all for coming." He hurried out the door and gasped; the generator sat on a wooden pallet near the building.

One man from the Lions Club called out upon seeing Rick exit the building. "You want to leave this here?"

"No, I hope we can transport it with the backhoe."

A fast inspection proved it was possible. Four men slowly carried the heavy generator to the backhoe trailer and set it in a corner.

"That will run flood lights tonight. The Texas Forrest Service is working with our local fire chief. They will determine where it goes. Maybe around Avinger, I don't know. Thanks, guys." Rick shook hands with the men, and they left.

Vehicles in the parking lot suddenly departed, and others arrived. The intense heat should have zapped any promise of energy, yet firemen climbed onto trucks, headed for the fields, and waved.

"Shift change," Rick mumbled to himself, and waved back.

A loud rattle only a diesel truck can make caught his attention, and he quickened his step as he read the advertising on the side panel. "Big Pines Lodge… Best Catfish in East Texas."

The driver stopped the vehicle, lowered his window, and the idling engine clanged in noisy rhythm.

"I can't believe my eyes. What are you doing here?" Rick looked at the two passengers and shook his head at Jason and Cindy Lou. "You are supposed to be at work at the Dairy Queen."

Jason spoke over the loud motor. "It's gone. Wind blew a woods fire onto the roof two days ago, and the Dairy Queen burned to the ground. We work for Big Pines Lodge, now."

Cindy Lou leaned past Jason to look at Rick. "The owner is coming with more help. He wants to feed all the law enforcement and firefighters here at the command post. We'll set up, and they will fry catfish outside."

"River Town lost the Dairy Queen. It won't be the same without it." Rick looked down at the ground and glanced away. "I didn't know… but what about Big Pines Lodge? They don't do catering. How are they cooking, here?"

Jason coughed at the light smell of smoke in the air. "The Elks Lodge in Marshall loaned them everything to cook with, and they are helping with the meal, too. This is Wednesday, so Big Pines is open today. Couldn't take away many employees from there. You know it will be busy."

"It always is." Rick nodded. "Are they doing the French fries and jalapeño hush puppies here with the catfish?"

"Yes, and they almost didn't have enough catfish. Cotton Taylor was in and out of Big Pines kitchen because he hauled the trash off. Well, come to find out, he was stealing and placing whole bags of fish inside a trash can. He was peddling bags of fish out of his truck in several neighborhoods late last night for twenty-five dollars a bag. Deputy Lodi followed him in an unmarked patrol car and arrested Cotton in someone's driveway." Cindy Lou raised an eyebrow and sighed.

"That's Cotton. I'm glad he got caught."

"The high school burned, too, Mr. Yeager," Jason began. "And some houses."

"Tragic. Hard to comprehend. I just heard fires are breaking out along Interstate Twenty, near Longview and Gladewater. I am in and out so much; I only catch bits and pieces from the scanner."

"Watch the news. The fires are being covered on television, nationally."

Chapter Nineteen

September 12, 2011
5:00 AM

Except for a few exit signs glowing bright red, it was dark. Susan tried to lie still. The narrow cot offered relief, but the small of her back throbbed, and she stuck a pillow under it for elevation. One arm dangled off the side of the bed, and her shoulder ached from all the attempts of flopping over to sleep on her side. *I may not have a job, or a home, but thank God I am in this shelter, and thank God, I have a car. The town of Marshall, Texas is super, even helped in previous years with Hurricane Katrina victims.*

She glanced at row after row of refugees sprawled on their own cots. By the looks of each person, they were equally uncomfortable. Many tossed and turned, a few whimpered. One man lay flat on his back with his arms folded under the back of his head. His breathing was labored, and he snored at intervals, oblivious to the room full of strangers. *I have to get up.* Susan sighed deeply and jerked at a sudden leg cramp. She bit her bottom lip and gently rubbed the calf area until the pain subsided. *Tonic water will stop leg cramps. I remember a doctor told my mother it works because of the small amount of quinine in it. I'll have to go to the store.*

Sliding her feet off the cot, Susan slowly stood. She grabbed her purse and carefully meandered to the dimly-lit, front, sign-in desk without disturbing anyone.

"Sir." Susan addressed the male volunteer. "I'm Susan Penleigh, and I am going to the store, and I'll be right back."

"Mrs. Penleigh, if you will wait a while breakfast will be served."

"Thank you, but I'm not hungry, and I thank God for all the local area churches taking turns feeding us here. That speaks volumes for this community."

The volunteer nodded. Susan grabbed a ballpoint pen, wrote her signature on the sign out form, and walked outside.

Not a breeze blew, and the heat was stifling. The Chevy was easy to find among the few vehicles scattered across the huge parking lot. Once again, Susan realized how blessed she was to have her car. She started the motor, and 5:10 a.m. displayed on the dashboard. The streets were empty of local traffic. Occasionally, an eighteen wheeler passed her on Highway 59 with out-of-state license plates. The town sported blinking red lights at this hour, and Susan cautiously drove to the all night grocery store near the main intersection of Highway 59 and Highway 80.

Parking near the entrance, Susan walked to the automatic doors and nodded at the few customers that were leaving.

"Susan. Susan Penleigh. Is that you?"

Susan pivoted, and came to face to face with a woman who entered the store behind her.

"Bernice Cooper. It's great to see you." The two women hugged each other and quickly stepped back in silence. Susan grimaced, as Bernice, clearly overcome by emotion, experienced a trembling chin.

"Are you okay?" Bernice's voice broke.

"Yes. I am. How are you and your family?" Susan raised an eyebrow.

"I am still shaken from the fires, but with God's help, we survived."

"Good. They have booths here in the deli. Let's get something to drink and talk. Do you have time?"

"Definitely." Bernice followed Susan through the store and swiftly arrived at the deli. Coffee was ordered, and they relaxed in a booth.

"I heard the school burned. Your job is gone. I am so sorry."

"Bernice, my job was gone before the school burned. Mr. Monroe fired me."

"What? He is an evil man, him and his control. What does he have to control now?"

"Not me, those days are over."

"I thought our days were over, too. The wildfires came so close to our house. It's been two weeks since it happened, and I still have nightmares. I cannot get a full night's sleep. Oh Susan, the fires were terrifying. Let me tell you about it." Bernice frowned and glanced pleadingly at Susan.

"Go on, Bernice, I'm here to listen."

"The smoke was too thick to see through. A deputy knocked at our door and told us to be out within five minutes. He left and went to warn the neighbors. I looked at the grim expression on my husband's face. 'No, he said. We are not leaving. We will save our house.'

"I was shocked. He ran outside and began hosing our house down. He began on the roof and let the water run until it collected in puddles on the ground. We were alone. All rescue workers were gone. The smoke quickly grew surrounding our property from the woods around us until flames abruptly appeared and shot sixty feet in the air into the tall pine trees across the road.

"That sound haunts me now. The raging fire sounded like a demon roaring from hell. It was so loud. It was horrible to hear the fire. I heard the roar. Live ashes settled on our dead grass and fire ignited, racing across the front and sides of the lawn. I could not breathe without choking. My husband kept watering, and the fire came within inches all around our house, but it was saved. Everything reeks of burnt timber and heavy smoke. The smell will gag you from inside my home, but I have a home. We are one of the fortunate few."

"I will pray for you to have peace. It is over now, Bernice."

"Thank you, and what of your home? Did the fires come close?"

"My whole neighborhood is gone. I did manage to save some things I packed earlier in my car. I do have a car." Susan smiled.

Bernice reached across the table and patted Susan's hand. "You are strong and brave."

"No, my faith is strong. God has other plans for me." Susan gave a tired little smile and rose from the bench. "I am glad you and your family are safe. I need to make my purchase here and go. Let's leave with prayer."

Bernice nodded and also stood. They held hands and each prayed. Both women parted and went their own way. Susan bought three bottles of tonic water and returned to the shelter.

People were waking and activity increased as lines were formed to restrooms. Many voices carried across the room, and babies cried from disturbed routines.

Susan walked past the endless cots lined into straight rows all across the civic center. A new home indeed for one and all; rich and poor, young and old alike. Suddenly, their lives were thrown together in mass confusion. The glares of the down trodden, the pitiful glances of hope on a face as a person strolled by; each with their own story of wildfire encounters. Susan mulled it over and decided to help as many as possible. Even if all she could do was a small gesture of kindness to give them some degree of comfort, she would.

Then, she noticed Lisa. The petite brunette teenager was huddled next to a big, burly guy that was a good six to eight years older than she was. It reminded Susan of a lost, orphaned kitten that crept up against someone who fell asleep nearby. Hair tangled, and make-up smeared; she sat in a heap next to the guy, who in all appearance was not in much better shape.

When one considers the circumstances these people came from, it was no wonder that everyone accepted their situation and were too weary to demand anything. They were simply exhausted and wanted a place to lie down.

Susan heard all about Lisa and saw her around town. Alone and pregnant, Lisa placed her baby for adoption last year and tried to stay in school. She ran with an older group that were into drugs and displayed loose morals. Eventually, Lisa came to school less and less until in her tenth grade she quit school. Lisa moved in with the older boyfriend, promptly got pregnant again, and decided to keep this baby.

Her younger sister, Tonya, followed in Lisa's footsteps, and also, moved in with a known local drug dealer. Ryan would strut around, flashing money to young girls. Several of them actually fought over him. Two girls bragged about carrying his baby at the same time and acted like it was an honor. Ryan ended up getting Lisa's younger sister pregnant, also. An emotionally distraught Lisa soon got on drugs herself. A neighbor raised her baby when she became too dopey to care for the infant, and Lisa tried to talk her sister into moving out of town before she got into the same trap that Lisa now found herself in.

But no, it did not work. The younger sister, Tonya, stayed and birthed a son. The father of her baby continued to flirt with other younger girls. Tonya was stressed and argued with him constantly. He left her one night and took off with two of his male friends to party with them. They wrecked the car, and all died at the scene of the crash.

Tonya was hysterical when she was told about Ryan and finally did move away. She gave her baby a chance to be around a more uplifting group of people that wanted a better future. She got her GED and a steady job. *Good for Tonya.*

Lisa raised her head and watched Susan from the side of the guy's chest. Her face was spotty with sores, her teeth were rotted, and many were missing. Her eyes appeared dull when they were open, and she was skinny as a rail.

Susan tried not to stare at the girl. Lisa was drifting in and out of sleep and clung to her boyfriend. Susan watched as he took his shoes off and rubbed his filthy feet over Lisa's legs.

He has no respect for her at all.

"Psst! Mrs. Penleigh, over here."

Susan abruptly turned and recognized Coach Ramsey's wife, Willa. She rushed to Willa, and they walked to a row of chairs against the wall.

"I didn't know you were here." Susan eased herself into a chair.

"Oh yes, we arrived during the night, and I can't sleep. My husband is one of the men snoring." Willa smiled. "I couldn't help but see you noticed Lisa."

"Sad."

"Yes, and that's the guy who helped destroy her future. Of course, it was her choice. I knew Lisa well. With a high IQ, she was a computer whiz. He made failing grades the years he attended River Town High. Typical tough guy at school. Number one bully to his more intelligent peers."

"So he tried to pull everyone down to his level, didn't want them to be better than he was, or smarter." Susan frowned.

"Exactly. When his friends thought he was "cool" he won, and they didn't know it, but at that moment they were the losers. He began selling drugs to them, and

180

soon, the smartest kids had failing grades like he did. The big difference: they had the brains to pass him up, and yet didn't, and let *him* lead them like cows going to a supposedly greener pasture. The so called friends of his did not realize that without *them*, he was nothing. He had to have "them" as a crowd of admirers. He tried the cocky struts and went after lonesome girls. Unfortunately, it worked."

"So those leeches are still waiting to destroy someone else they want to be in control of. Someone they can have look up to them for a change. So, if they get kids on drugs, then they have something that the others will come to them for. That is why the drug dealers laugh and act so cocky. It is all a game with the drug dealers. They only care about themselves and the glittery life they see themselves in. I get the picture now." Susan nodded.

Pitiful, how Lisa clings to him…

Chapter Twenty

September 13, 2011
9:30 AM

Logan Wakefield shifted his weight and leaned toward his right side for balance. The dozer he was driving hit a stump and threw the track off. He climbed down, pulled a handkerchief from a pocket, and wiped sweat from his sun-tanned face.

"Yep, so much for that." He stood and looked at the dozer.

Reaching for the long, portable radio, he made contact with the command post in Linden, Texas.

"Logan Wakefield here. I'm in zone four on the map and need assistance with the dozer, it's thrown a track. I lack a quarter of a mile to complete a plow line around this neighborhood. The structures to the north are safe for now. Over."

He waited as the weak static signal came through the air waves, and a voice responded.

"Rick Yeager here. Hey buddy; you must be the volunteer fireman my neighbor Susan mentioned. Sorry to meet you under these circumstances, but hang on. Help will arrive shortly. A crew is working three miles away. Over."

Logan heard a crackling sound, and in a split second, a dead pine tree tumbled to the ground in record speed. Logan ran from its path but the long branches brushed against him. Tangled in the massive tree, Logan fell, quickly pressing the button, and calling on the radio. "Rick, Rick, Rick..." until he passed out.

"Rick Yeager here. Over"

Silence prevailed.

"Rick Yeager here, come on Logan, speak to me. Over."

◆◆◆◆

Logan was aware of muffled voices in the distance, but he couldn't open his heavy eyelids. He couldn't get his mouth to cooperate and talk, either.

Hands lifted him onto a gurney, and the sensation of being in the air overwhelmed him.

Someone called his name and told him to wake up. Logan thought he heard the squawk of an EMS radio, but he concentrated on how peaceful it was to be...floating. *That's it, I must be floating...*

He floated higher and looked down at a snow bird. *How strange for it to be here.*

The snow bird flew in circles before resting in the warmth of an empty shoe box, abandoned amongst the decaying ruins of the smelly garbage dump of River Town, Texas. Flies buzzed around and darted back and forth from the thrown bags of trash that burst open on impact. Logan watched as cars passed through the area, dumping more into the pink, topless railroad cars. An eighteen wheeler arrived and attached the railroad car to its front loader. Fascinated, Logan listened for the big rig to change gears. It screeched, carried the pink container off, and emptied it into a distant landfill. Logan tried not to gag when he pictured this scene again in his mind. *No, don't do it over and over...not...over and over...*

He tried to wake up and lifted an eyebrow, straining ever so hard to open just one eye. No luck. *Luck?* Logan did not believe in luck. *I am not going to lie here and slide downhill in my strong convictions. The word luck has no place in my life. I reap what I sow.*

In his mind's eye, he willed the garbage dump to disappear and a different scene materialized.

◆◆◆◆

Crows cawed with a robust loudness. Growing in numbers, their range expanded as the piercing calls echoed through the valley of scattered trees and over grown bushes. Logan wandered on a small trail that seemed to beg him to go further into the woods. He could smell the fresh scent of a spring rain, and his fingers lightly touched the dew covered sprig of a long, green, leaf of fern. Remembering the thrill of being a child, and carefully slipping his fingers down a fern leaf, he grabbed one and tore it off the plant. He clutched it to his face and felt the soft wisp of tiny leaves gently brush against his cheek. *Dare I remove the tiny leaves from both sides of the stem? One fast pull with my fingers and the leaves slide off.*

Wait, this is not the plant I remember…with a long pod on it. What was that plant? Oh, I remember now. It was not a plant…it was a tree. Yes, that is exactly what it was, and I could reach up and strip entire sections of leaves off, and they would remain all gathered into a clump inside the palm of my hand, after I pulled the switch through my hand. Then, I did indeed have a switch. It was great to poke at things with a semi limp switch. You could dream up all sorts of uses for it, especially as the child I was back then…I was entertaining myself…I think I was about eight years old at the time…

184

"Logan, Logan, wake up. Logan, can you hear me?"

Logan rolled over, now actually in a hospital bed, and felt warm and cozy. He clutched the covers near his neck and could not speak to whoever was talking to him.

I do not want to speak. I am dreaming, and, it is a good dream, but I do not remember what it is about. I will walk in the forest and enjoy nature. Yes, that is the dream. I hear birds on tree branches.

He drifted off into another dream, oblivious of those trying to wake him.

The new nature trail he took in this dream wound around the trees, similar to a maze, among sunshine filtering on the leaves. He set a leisurely pace and enjoyed the peace and solitude of the area. Logan wandered further and caught sight of a white-tailed deer leaping across the trail and into a field of wildflowers. *Wildflowers, what a breath taking site to behold.* His senses were suddenly filled to capacity with the mingled fragrances of many flowers. It was beyond imagination how soothing the aroma was, and it immediately made him dizzy.

He continued to drift in his dream and noticed he was no longer walking. He seemed to linger slightly above the ground. A passing breeze pushed him along, and the forest vanished. Miles of ocean appeared before him, and he hovered over a narrow strip of beach. The fresh smell of the salty sea assaulted his nostrils. The gentle breezes grew instantly into stronger, more forceful winds. Sea gulls darted about, swooped on to the shore line, and quickly flew off again with ear-piercing calls. Turning to face the ocean waves, he noticed the urgency they now took to rush faster onto the shore. He looked in surprise at all the many white capping waves coming from as far away as he could see. They were even on the actual horizon, rising up and hurrying to the shore, all at the same time; waves so tall it made him tremble.

His hair blew in the wind, and he marveled that his hair was long and flowing. It danced about in the air as the wind grew even stronger. *A squall line, that's what they say on T.V. about a fast moving storm. This is a squall line.* Logan glanced behind him and gasped. The path that brought him here was now gone. White-cap waves covered it up, but he did see a small house a mile down the beach. There was no litter to be found, no people either.

This must be an island.

A quick look out at sea again, and Logan spotted a huge boat full of people. He watched as their boat was tossed amidst gigantic waves, and no one appeared frightened. They held on to the boat, and their faces were expressionless. Sometimes the boat rose to the top of the monster waves and then darted down as the waves dropped and crashed, surging past the vessel. The boat went deeper out to sea, until it became a tiny speck, and disappeared from the horizon.

Logan had a brief mental picture of being stuck here, and decided he was really on a peninsula, and relaxed.

He willed himself to the house. It was a two story, rambling home that desperately needed painting. The house had many windows, each with a matching pair of shiny black vinyl shutters. The new shutters with their new vinyl material, stood out like a sore thumb on the shabby, large, old home. This was so unusual. Someone should have painted the worn, wooden siding on the outside of the house first, and added the new shutters last. *Who did the improvements?*

"Who did that?" Logan sat up in bed and repeated his question to a room full of concerned family and friends. "Who did that?" He looked wide eyed at his surroundings.

"Hey, bud, you had us all worried. Welcome back." His brother, Ben, bolted to approach the bed. He stared at Logan with concern.

Logan's head cleared and a wide smile swept over his face. "Man, what a dream. Glad I am here." He laughed and felt the warmth of his face blush. "Wow."

Chapter Twenty-One
September 14, 2011
8:00 AM

Aromas escaped oblong serving dishes mounded high with a variety of breakfast food. Savory smells of bacon, eggs, and hash-browns sprinkled with lightly-sautéed, diced onions, mingled deliciously. Sausage tantalized stronger, promising the best choice for anyone's taste buds. The scent from stacks of pancakes and dozens of homemade yeast rolls wafted through the ceiling fans, and the smell lingered over the cots. Activity bustled in the civic center simultaneously; feet shoved into shoes, hair brushed fast, and people got in each other's way.

Bubbly and bright-eyed, three younger children scrambled to get in line, eager to eat.

"Hurry, Granny." One boy couldn't contain his excitement and jumped up and down.

"I'm coming, child, settle down, you're making me nervous." The old woman hobbled to the buffet tables and looked weary.

"Here." He handed her an empty plate and bounced as she shook her head at him.

Susan, at the end of the buffet line, glanced at the women servers.

"Thank you for the meal. Please tell your church members we are grateful."

"Oh, it's our pleasure. We want to help any way we can."

Susan ate while seated on her cot. Savoring her breakfast made time to reflect on the other evacuees. *What can I do to help?* She swallowed her last bite and giggled at the funny antics of so many restless children. *That's it; I'll give their parents and grandparents a break.*

Abruptly signing out, Susan drove to the Marshall Public Library with a plan guaranteed to be enjoyable. Several children's books were carefully selected and checked out. In a flash, her next destination was TSC: Tractor's Supply Company. Susan found the item she needed and returned to the shelter.

"May I section off an area and read to the children?" Susan made her request to the civic center coordinator who worked with many local churches and organizations.

"Certainly. Announce it over the microphone when you are ready."

"Thanks." Susan dodged people and veered to the farthest corner from the sleeping area.

*The roll of lime green surveyors tape will stretch taunt. Thank you Tractor's Supply. S*usan tied one end to a chair that wound through a circle of chairs creating a carnival atmosphere. The gaily roped off area drew immediate attention.

"Good morning everyone. If you need to take a shower, or go back to sleep or just have some quiet time; please send your children to me. I'll be in the lime green corner to your right and it is… story time. We will be play acting to the stories I read. Please let your children participate. I promise it will be fun."

At least fifty kids ascended on Susan; squealing and hyper.

"Okay, sit on the floor, and I will start reading. Remember, when I say, 'they did what?' I want you to stand up and show me what happened. Are you ready?"

"Yes," a loud chorus answered.

Susan opened the first book and read about four puppies who wanted to dance. As the puppies practiced, she would loudly comment, 'they did what?' and every child would stick out an arm or hop on one foot. Within twenty minutes, Susan had the children rolling on the floor in laughter.

"We need four feet to do this like a puppy. Everyone get a partner and hold hands. Here we go. If you need a partner, come see me."

Twenty minutes turned into an hour as Susan slowed the pace and read another book that required intense listening

"When I say, 'did the bird do that?' please be very quiet, stand up, and flap your arms like a bird. If I say, 'did the kangaroo do that?' please be very quiet, stand up, and hop like a kangaroo. Remember no one can talk."

Susan read to the children who clearly displayed they focused on the story. So many solemn faces watched her as she read every word, and at the appropriate time, they acted out their response.

The next book came with a message. This one was about a little airplane that would fly around and be helpful. Susan instructed all the children to lie on the floor and close their eyes while she read the story. They were to imagine it was them helping others.

Before the story ended, parents and grandparents approached the area, each sporting a rested face…all frowns gone.

Willa Ramsey gave a 'thumbs up' sign, entered the story area, and settled in a chair next to her friend.

"Let's take turns, Susan, and make story time a daily routine."

"Sounds like fun." Susan raised her head and addressed the group collecting their children. "What do you think, same time, same place tomorrow?"

People nodded enthusiastically, and the kids cheered.

"We'll see you then." Susan watched them leave, each family strolling back to their cots.

Willa handed Susan ice cold bottled water. "Girl, take this, thought you could use it."

Susan took a long swallow. "Thanks, didn't realize how dry I am. How long did I read?"

"Two hours."

"Those kids loved acting it out. Reminded me of my school days, and a group playing 'Simon Says' with the teacher."

"How about Red Rover, Red Rover, let Susan come over? Do you remember that one?"

"Yes, of course. I guess that ages us, but I don't care. We were all so active in school then."

Willa glanced sideways at Susan. "Shall we try to add some games to story time?"

"Why not, some of the adults might join in." Susan fell silent.

Willa made no attempt to answer.

Susan took another long swallow of water. "I heard insurance adjusters are coming this evening, along with other agencies to offer assistance. A lot of evacuees didn't have time to bring their medicine. The challenges facing us here just keep growing."

"We're all in the same boat. That's why we have to try and cheer the kids up. They are even more scared by what has happened. Also gives the adults time to sort things out." Willa glanced across the vast open room and pulled her chair close to Susan's.

"Oh, there is Gwendolyn. Do you know her?" Willa waved at a young woman who returned the gesture.

"No, I don't."

"She is an inspiration. I have to tell you about her. She was the oldest girl at the high school and tried to hide her age. She made fairly good grades but struggled with the scores of her TAKS test. It was one of the most important requirements needed to pass for graduation.

"Her mother had died at child birth. She was raised by her father and sometimes with her stepmother. The stepmother was not the type of woman who wanted a child, or wanted to be at home, cooking and cleaning. She preferred to be an aspiring business person. So, she left Gwendolyn's father regularly, once a year, to continue her career.

"I remember Gwendolyn as the quiet girl with a quick, pretty smile, so loving and so considerate. I worked at the high school then as computer technician assistant for the whole school."

"Excuse me, but where can we find clothes? Is clothing being donated here?" A middle-aged woman and a teenage girl both ran to Susan with worn, tired expressions on their faces. The girl stifled a yawn.

"Yes, clothing in all sizes are against the back wall. You'll see a sign over the tables stating what size and gender." Susan pointed to the area.

"Thanks." The woman grabbed the girls arm and hurried through the chattering crowd.

Willa glanced at Susan. "Now, where was I? Oh, yes, Gwendolyn. One day she came into my office and showed me a piece of jewelry that belonged to her real mother. It was a small pinky ring that Gwendolyn wore on her right little pinky finger constantly. Its opal stone shined and sparkled. I thought I had a pair of ear rings that were a perfect match. I went home and dug through my jewelry box until I found the small dainty opal ear rings. It was the same color just like Gwendolyn's ring.

"I could not stand it; I wanted to give the ear rings to the shy quiet girl. So what if others thought I was giving Gwendolyn special treatment, well in my own mind, I thought it was past time for Gwendolyn to be treated special.

"Long story short, I called the willowy young girl into my office, and presented the pair of ear rings to her before school let out one afternoon.

"Gwendolyn was so taken back by the gesture; she could not believe she now owned a pair of opal earrings that were a perfect match to the opal ring. She hugged me, and then Gwendolyn's father walked into the office looking for her. He was her transportation

193

every day as she didn't like riding the rowdy school bus. He immediately shook my hand when Gwendolyn showed him what I had done. They both thanked me. Gwendolyn put the ear rings on and a sudden, wide grin appeared. 'What a happy girl' I thought, as the father and daughter left my office all smiles.

"Who would ever think, a few days later, that Gwendolyn would fail her TAKS test again? Too old to stay in school any longer, she was so hurt, she cried. In tears, she told me she would get a GED, because she wanted to finish her education, and get a good job. She did get her GED plus training and skills to help for the rest of her life. She can be independent and not have to rely on some 'guy' like Lisa does.

"Oh, and the age Gwendolyn was about to turn in a few days after school was out…she turned twenty one years old. She tried that long and that hard to graduate.

"Yes, if anyone deserved the ear rings I gave away, Gwendolyn certainly did, with or without the matching opal pinky ring, her real mother passed down to her through her father."

"Willa, I want to meet her. She is an inspiration," Susan stammered.

"Oh, you might. I see the stepmother has returned since the wildfires have passed through the area. That means she is now totally dependent upon Gwendolyn, and Gwendolyn's father. Their cots are in a corner near a back wall, together."

"Together? That tells a lot about them in one word. So they are a family?"

"Yes. It's a shame Gwendolyn never had a mother growing up. Now, she is taking care of one."

"I recognize a Christian." Susan drew her mouth tight and nodded.

"She is, and she was raised by one."

"I think that's why the stepmother returned, she recognized their strong faith."

"Life goes on, Susan. We all grow. Did you notice the McKinley brothers? Matt and Mead?"

"No, and I've never heard of them."

"Locals call them M&M."

"Are they inside this shelter?"

"Most certainly. Can you spot the two young men still sleeping near the middle of the room?"

"Hard to miss, they are sprawled all over the narrow cots."

"They are totally exhausted. The boys took snacks and water to the command center, and helped out at the fire lines last night. Matt is the oldest brother and spent his senior year of high school at River Town in the county jail for burglary. He called my office each day of school at straight up nine o'clock."

"'Why are they not giving me my schooling? No one is letting me finish my senior year, Mrs. Willa. I want to graduate with my friends, and it is the law. Mrs. Willa, the county has to let me study for my exams while I sit in jail waiting for my trial to get on the docket.'

"Susan, I would tell him the same thing every time. 'I do not understand it, Matt, I know they are supposed to do that, but I cannot make them do it. I am not in charge, Matt; the presiding judge in the county has the

195

authority and will not listen to anything I say. It could be because you are eighteen years old. I don't know. I am so sorry, Matt.'

"They kept the eighteen year old in jail for the remainder of his second semester, and he did not graduate. He did not get to look at one book while he was in jail. He sat and contemplated why he was involved in the stupid car burglary in the first place. He had broken into a parked car, tore out the car radio and C.D. player, and got arrested.

"Now, not only did he have a criminal record, but he lost his chance to study, and finish his last year at River Town High School. He was one disappointed young man.

"I wondered if anyone in our county could have helped Matt. The school district where Matt was incarcerated, by law, is supposed to send a teacher to continue his education. It is the law, and no, it was not up to Matt to get it all arranged. So, yes, I took another kid under my wing."

"Ladies, pardon me for interrupting your conversation, but we are passing out cold bottled water. Do you care for some?" A burly man stopped and raised his eyebrows at them.

"Yes, thanks." Willa took two and passed one to Susan as the man walked toward others.

Willa took a drink and continued. "I discovered the boys did not have a mother at their home, and their father was in jail, for what, I don't know. Matt was sentenced to spend more time in jail. I gave a Christian book to his younger brother, Mead. I told him to read it and requested he give it to Matt to also read while he completed doing his time in jail. He did.

"I watched out for both boys as best I could without being allowed to visit Matt in jail. When Matt got released, it was a great day. That young man was no longer incarcerated, but he lost his senior year in high school. He was too old to return and learned a valuable lesson, as well. The choice he made to break into a car nearly destroyed his life. No, he never got his GED. He was bitter and did return to jail twice for burglary. The younger brother graduated and does not have a criminal record. Now, their home has burnt to the ground, and they are helping the firefighters."

"I am struck with the fact that they are probably not even twenty-one years old and have experienced so much. I want to meet them, later, if you think it's possible," Susan blurted.

"It's possible."

Chapter Twenty-Two

September 15, 2011
10:00AM

Fires in River Town were out. The infamous Bear Creek Fire was finally contained, after starting on September 4, 2011. It claimed 41,050 acres in Cass and Marion counties, numerous structures, and 92 homes were lost. The counties timber industry was scorched for $349 million. No longer needed, the command post in Linden; devoid of supplies, equipment, and volunteers, closed within the next week.

Rick returned to the old neighborhood on the river. Sight-seers congested the area, driving the roads through burnt forests of black trees, while small flames still leapt among the charred remains. Strange objects of metal, melted beyond recognition, lay scattered in the ruins of former homes.

Rick gazed at the tall fireplace standing alone in the midst of black, smoldering ground, littered with rubble from brick and concrete.

My home…

He kicked his boot into a pile of ash covered debris, soot shot upward, adding to the smoky haze in the air, and a hacking cough ensued. The unpleasant singed smell got into his lungs, and he could taste it in his mouth. He spit, took one last look at the area, and fled to the Toyota Tundra truck.

Time to go, and go forward…no, I'll be running forward...

Rick climbed into his vehicle and headed for the Civic Center in Marshall, Texas.

Options and priorities…no home, no job, no property in River Town left to sell. Makes life more precious each day. Think I'll move closer to Tessa…start visiting her…

Winding roads, up and over hills, took him past years of good memories. The trip to Marshall blended with the personalities of new friends he'd met and sold property to. Each person stood out in his mind.

Consider the ten acres to the couple from Daingerfield, who wanted a private retreat in Woodlawn with a pond. *Happy couple.* He drove past vast acres of cleared land, and smiled, remembering a woman from Winnsboro. If ever he met a cowgirl with a big heart…she was it. Determined to have a working ranch, this 'Willowy Wonder' wore her boots like a pro …and made a profit.

Good people.

Lost in thought, Rick arrived in Marshall and concentrated on the positive.

Susan Penleigh, new friend. I am needed elsewhere. Will our paths cross again?

Pulling right, off Highway 59, he made a left turn into the circle drive at the civic center. *She has to be here.*

He saw school buses, travel trailers, trucks, cars, the Red Cross mobile, several church vans, Channel 3 News, and Channel 12; both mobile units were on standby, as well as Fox 51. Rick weaved his truck to a parking space through a maze of vehicles coming and going in the worse drought…worse heat wave… in Texas history. Steam vibrated off the pavement, 114 degrees displayed on his dashboard for the outside temperature, and not a breeze blew.

River Town

He strode to the entrance and opened the door. The fact that the civic center was now a refugee shelter hit him like a double-barreled shotgun accidently dislodging. Rick reeled at the sight of numerous cots strung across a vast open area, and hundreds of people milling about.

A nearby six foot long table with signs above it, informed all visitors and evacuees to either sign in or out. Three people dutifully sat in attendance, obviously busy, as people came and left.

Rick spotted their microphone and approached the table.

"I'm trying to locate a Mrs. Susan Penleigh. Is she listed here?"

"Let me check the registry, sir." The volunteer scanned over several typed pages and looked at Rick. "Yes, the woman you are looking for is here. I can announce she has a visitor, if you'd like."

"Please do."

"Mrs. Susan Penleigh, you are needed at the sign-in table, you have a visitor." The loud speaker boomed out over many levels of conversation scattered throughout the center.

Rick glanced around, anxious to see her, and noticed her from a far corner.

Wide-eyed, Susan stood upon hearing the message, and briskly made her way to the entrance. She recognized a few people, nodded in their direction, and kept scurrying through the crowd. Focused on the entrance area, she spotted Rick.

A slow smile crept across his face as he lightly embraced her.

"Susan. You are safe."

"Yes, and thanks for coming." She squeezed his hand. "I've been concerned about you."

"I'm okay. The fires are contained. I'm done. You have been on my mind. I decided to stop in and check on you."

"Stop in?"

"Yes, I'm leaving. Thought I should be closer to my daughter, Tessa."

"Tessa?'

"She is at a rehabilitation center in Tyler, Texas."

"Oh, well… I hope everything works out for you and your daughter."

"So do I, Susan. This is something I have to do. I'd never forgive myself if I didn't try to help her again."

"I'll keep you both in my prayers."

"Thanks, we'll need them. Let's stay in touch. I'll call you when I can. Same cell number?"

"Same number." She blinked.

"Bye, Susan." Rick grimaced and turned from her.

"Bye, Rick," Susan spoke softly as he walked away.

Chapter Twenty-Three
September 16, 2011
3:00 PM

"Mrs. Penleigh…I'm over here."

Susan wheeled around, her heart quickly pounded in excitement, while she tried to place the voice. Arms waving high, the tall teenager got her attention. Caught up in a moment of nostalgia, she blinked back tears. It was Kenny.

Long legs loped as steady as a quarter horse gaining ground across a grassy meadow. It would be difficult not to spot him. Kenny, in an over-sized, bright red Texas Rangers baseball jersey, and blue jeans; whooped so loud, refugees stared wide-eyed, astonished.

"Mrs. Penleigh, I'm so glad to see you."

He grabbed both her hands and pumped them up and down. Susan beamed at him. Energy exuberated from Kenny. He released her. An impromptu break dance ensued, and he raised one foot at a time to perform, while jerked arm movements fell in place with the rhythm.

A flood of bright lights startled Susan as a camera man focused on her and Kenny. A reporter spoke into a microphone and approached.

"Live from Marshall, Texas; this is Jayne Sehlke with KWAT, Channel 3 News. The civic center is home for hundreds of evacuees escaping Texas wildfires. This shelter provides food, clothing, counseling, and other emergency assistance. Many volunteers are here to help. I'm standing beside a happy young man, in spite of dire circumstances. May I have your name?" She held the microphone close to his face.

"Yes ma'am, I'm Kenny Vargas, I live here."

"I watched the vigorous hand shaking and the fast break dance you performed. Care to share your exuberance with the viewing audience?"

"Oh, I'm thrilled to see Mrs. Penleigh from River Town High School. She has helped a lot of us students there…before it burned, I mean."

"Wildfires erupted in countless towns in the East Texas area. Mrs. Penleigh, were you affected by this catastrophe?"

"Yes I, along with many, lost my home. I lived in River Town, and the high school is totally destroyed. I was able to save some belongings due to the advance warning by local law enforcement, and I have my car. I am thankful for that, and to have this shelter available for us is a blessing. Local churches are taking turns feeding us, and it is remarkable to see entire congregations bringing meals. This community needs to be commended for their volunteer efforts."

"With folks like you, Mrs. Penleigh, the community *is* well aware of the thankful refugees." The reporter glanced at the teenager and continued.

"I'm sorry your school is gone, Kenny, but memories will always continue. How nice to connect to someone who treasures them also. With KWAT-TV, Channel 3, this is Jayne Sehlke. Back to you, Roy."

Lights went dim; Susan and Kenny blinked rapidly, and Jayne gave the microphone to the camera man. He packed it with other equipment and gathered extension cords.

"Good interview. It will air on the six o'clock news this evening. I do need you both to sign this release." Jayne pulled a form and a ball point pen from her folder and watched as they scribbled their names.

"Done, and thank you." Susan handed her the page.

While the reporter and crew made their way to the exit doors, Susan glanced at Kenny.

"Well, that was fun."

"And we're going to be on TV." Kenny chuckled.

"Yes, and are any school buddies around to visit?"

"A few live here. We hang out whenever we can. Mostly, we try to stay busy and help out."

"Help out?"

"You know, the older ones need a strong arm to guide them to places inside the shelter, so they don't get bumped into. We try to protect them."

"Kenny, that is wonderful. I'm proud of you."

"Hey man, come on." Another teen yelled at Kenny.

"Coming." Kenny looked at Susan. "Got to go, Mrs. Penleigh."

"Great to see you again."

"You too." Kenny, with a slight smile, took off to join his friend.

Susan wandered through a congested area of strangers and flopped in a chair near a wall sporting an enormous bulletin board. She scanned the large print notices, when something in her line of vision moved.

Distracted, Susan observed a young woman sleeping on the floor, oblivious to the notices above her. She was barely stretching and seemed to be pushing away from her mate.

It's Lisa. Susan gasped. The girl rose at the sound to look Susan straight in the face. *How forlorn can an expression be?* Lisa screwed her face up in an attempt not to cry. Tears slipped from her blood-shot eyes, and she jerked slightly, as if in pain.

Susan ran to her, and the boyfriend awoke at the same instant.

A rough voice boomed from deep inside the boyfriend. "Sit down, Lisa." He rolled over and glared at her. "Sit down...*now*," he thundered.

"I want to talk to her." Susan raised one eyebrow, stared at him, and squared her jaw.

"You don't say." He tried to spit at Susan and missed. The gruff manner didn't intimidate Susan, and she kept eye contact.

"Jake, leave her alone," Lisa muttered and swayed.

A doubled-up fist shot out and landed in the middle of Lisa's right leg.

"Ouch. Stop it, Jake." Lisa appeared dizzy. She stumbled to Susan and clung to her.

Susan's anger took control, and she let out a yell a Comanche Indian from the 18th century would have been proud of.

"Don't you dare," Susan roared, and her face burned from anger. "Leave now, or I'm calling 911." Chest rising in heavy breaths; Susan trembled, pushed Lisa behind her and stood facing Jake. He lashed a fist out at Susan, and an off-duty deputy, working security at the shelter, lifted Jake up off the ground.

The deputy held Jake by force with both hands and spoke in a calming manner. "Real men do not hit women." He never took his eyes off Jake and continued. "Is anyone going to file charges against this person, or do I release him?"

"I will," Lisa stammered.

Jake squirmed in the grip of the deputy who handcuffed him immediately.

"Ladies, I'll escort him out to the patrol car and return to write my report."

Lisa visibly shook, and Susan's blood pressure raced through her veins in lightning speed.

"I can't take anymore," Lisa whimpered.

"It's okay, Lisa. I'll stand by you." Susan's demeanor calmed, and she realized, as a Christian, this was the path the Lord had for her.

"You don't understand, I'm an addict. I need help." Lisa focused on Susan and squinted.

"Lisa, if you want help, I know of an excellent rehab facility in Tyler. A friend of mine has a daughter there. I can drive you there for treatment whenever you are ready."

Choking back sobs, Lisa couldn't stop shaking. "I…I'm ready."

Chapter Twenty-Four

September 17, 2011
Greenville, Washington

Susan's daughter Molly lifted her voice in light-hearted amusement the instant her older sister answered the telephone. "Karen, are you ready for this?"

"I don't know, try me."

"I saw Mother on TV. She was on the six o'clock news."

"Molly, excuse me, but what did she do?" Karen sucked in her breath and choked.

"Shame on you. She was with people in a refugee shelter."

"Oh no. I suppose she gave her name on national television."

"What's with you, Karen? Where is your heart?"

"My heart? You are the one who's been keeping up with her. You are the one with *the heart*."

Molly fell silent.

"Look." Karen paused. "I've been helping Dad organize a golf tournament at the country club. I know I should have talked to Mom, but I am so close to working out the details for the club's charity event. I want it to go smooth, and I want it to be enjoyable. Is that so wrong?"

"Did she call you?"

"Yes, but it was brief, I couldn't talk long." Karen cleared her throat. "She was working at River Town High School and seemed to like it."

"The school was destroyed by the Texas wildfires."

"What?"

"I was in the other room when the news came on. I ran to the TV the second I heard her name, but I missed some of it. Anyway, she appeared okay. I was happy to see her."

"Molly, why are you calling me? Why don't you hurry and call her?"

"I never wrote her new phone number down. She called and left it on the answering machine, and when the power went out, I lost all my messages."

"So… you haven't kept up with her, either?"

"I was hoping you knew her new number." Using her shoulder, Molly pressed the cordless phone closer to her ear, and grabbed a notebook and pen in anticipation.

Karen made no attempt to hide her annoyance and exhaled loud. "No, I do not have it. This is ridiculous. I can't believe we have not kept in touch with our own Mother."

The pen slipped from Molly's grasp and bounced off the floor. "I thought we agreed we wouldn't show preference to either parent. I thought because of the divorce, we would spend equal time with both of them."

"Look, Molly, Dad needs my support…"

"I hate to interrupt you, but my cell phone is ringing, it's Scott. Maybe our brother has heard something. *We will* finish this later, *Karen*."

"We will finish this… *now*." Karen's voice was cut off as Molly slammed the receiver down.

Chapter Twenty-Five
September 18, 2011
9:00 AM

Susan stood sweltering outside the car at the gas station. A quick swipe of the card, and she waited for the acceptance. Beads of moisture formed immediately; her clothes were damp with sweat. Words finally flashed instructing to proceed, and she hurried to pump a full tank of gas.

Heat shimmered off the pavement. A brief peep in the window to the back seat confirmed Lisa was still asleep. *Thank God that so called boyfriend, or drug dealer or, whatever label he claims, is no longer in control of Lisa. Such a fragile person, I can't imagine what she has endured because of his rage.* The automatic shut-off valve clicked. Susan returned the nozzle to the lever and pulled the receipt from the slot. Grateful to slide inside the cooled vehicle, she turned the ignition key and drove off.

Two hour drive to Tyler, here we come.

Traffic usually flowed smooth on Interstate Twenty, east bound side, and west bound. Not today, though. Both lanes in front of her were blocked by several eighteen wheeler trucks traveling together. Eventually, those in the left lane signaled to the right lane, and Susan sped to pass all of them.

Lisa popped up. "Wow, this car can take off and go."

"It's a Chevy. You can count on it to get you through a tight spot every time."

"Mrs. Penleigh, I thank you for getting *me* out of a tight spot. It's like I didn't have a mind of my own while I was with Jake."

"Lisa, I am a firm believer that God had me in the shelter to meet you. I am the vessel He is using to bring you help."

"Mrs. Penleigh, what was that… a vessel? I remember something about a potter and clay."

"Good memory, Lisa. The scripture is Isaiah 64:8, "But now, O Lord, You are our Father; we are the clay and You our potter; And all we, are the work of Your hand."

"I like that. I know the choice I made to stay with Jake was wrong, and I am ready to be shaped and molded by our Father." Lisa grabbed her stomach and moaned.

"Are you okay?" Susan quickly glanced in the rear view mirror at the young woman.

"My stomach is churning, and I'm starting to shake and sweat."

"They will have medication for you as soon as we arrive. Try taking slow breaths to calm yourself."

"I'm afraid Jake will find me when he gets out of jail. I don't know if I will ever be safe."

"Grab your purse, Lisa, and find something to write on. It's the National Domestic Violence Hotline phone number; 1-800-799-7233. Keep it with you at all times."

"Thanks. I wrote it down, and I think I can memorize it too."

"Try it, Lisa."

"1-800-799-7233."

"Good girl. They are confidential and open 24 hours a day. Lisa, it *will* get better."

"That's a relief. I'm not used to being on my own with Jake possibly stalking me."

Susan darted a quick look at her. "Lisa, pray with me."

"All right."

"Lord, we pray for Your protection on Lisa. Wherever she goes surround her with ministering angels and bless her with a peace that surpasses all understanding. Lord, we pray for forgiveness, and for her to want a relationship with You, and draw closer to You by reading Your Word and through prayer. Guide her in Your Ways, Lord, in Jesus Holy name we pray, Amen."

"Amen."

"Lisa, I will be coming to visit you at rehab. Don't think I'm dropping you off to never return."

"Oh, I know I'll see you. I heard they don't allow visitors for a while though."

"I got the same information. Why don't you lay back and rest. I'll wake you when we get to Tyler."

"Okay, but what kind of place is it?"

"A four story brick building with a built in swimming pool and a bowling alley."

"You are kidding."

"Nope."

Lisa yawned. "Well, in that case, I better rest quick. Think I'll stretch out for a while."

Susan remained silent as she heard sounds of movement from the back seat. Her passenger was lightly snoring within minutes.

211

River Town

She drove the remainder of the way reminiscing about recent turn of events. Harsh reality of the recent wildfires flooded her mind. *How can a poor economic county start over? Such gentle people facing total destruction. Voters couldn't pass a bond to rebuild the school, it couldn't be paid back.* Susan tried not to cry, but tears fell as she considered the school kids and their plight. *And what about Lisa? How could she endure that brute of a man in charge of her? How many others like Lisa are suffering somewhere?* Susan said a silent prayer and wiped her tears away. She turned her attention back to driving, but the situation continued to nag at her. *I may be one person, but at least I can try to help.* She sighed.

Thanks to the GPS, she arrived at her destination with no problem.

"Hey, we're here."

Lisa sat up and glanced around the new area. She combed her hair and nodded at Susan. "Let's do this."

Susan parked the car near a grove of trees and barely lowered her windows. They both left the car at the same time, and before reaching the entrance, an attendant approached with a legal-size, yellow envelope.

"Welcome. Which one of you will be staying with us? I am expecting someone named Lisa." The employee beamed.

"I'm Lisa, and this is Mrs. Susan Penleigh."

The attendant handed the envelope to Susan. "Here is a package of visitor instructions. Please read them carefully. You will need to sign several statements and return them later." She glanced at Lisa. "So, according to our records, Lisa, you are from River Town?"

"Yes ma'am."

"Sorry to hear the town suffered from the wildfires. It was all over the news." She put her hand on the young girl's shoulder, and Lisa grimaced.

"A lot of people are starting over," Susan chimed in.

"And so are we. Ladies, say your goodbyes. Susan can return in two weeks."

A quick hug with Susan, and Lisa walked away with the attendant.

Susan overheard their conversation as she strolled toward the parked vehicle.

"We're going to relax by the pool, if you'd like."

"Oh, I would love that." Lisa continued, "But I don't have a swim suit."

"We have some you can use."

Lisa and Susan turned to look at each other.

Smiles appeared quickly. With a wave, they resumed walking in opposite directions.

Susan eased in the car and noticed her cell phone vibrating in a circle on the front seat. She grabbed and placed it to her ear, while she bent to start the motor.

"Hello? Wait a minute; let me put you on speaker phone." Susan hurried and made the adjustment.

"Okay, hello?"

"Susan, it's me, Izabella. Where in the world are you?"

"I'm in Tyler."

"I was watching the news and saw you. I was stunned and drove straight to the shelter. They said you were gone, but would return. My nerves are a jumbled mess thinking about you. Susan, I want you safe at my house, there's plenty of room. Please move

213

in with me until this situation has a chance to improve."

"Yes, Izabella, I'd love to. Thanks for offering."

"You are most welcome. Do you need my help gathering your belongings?"

"Only a few items are at the shelter, the rest are in the trunk of my car. I'll get them, tell some friends where I'll be staying, and drive on over."

"Fine. I'll expect you for dinner."

"I'm looking forwards to it. I'm heading back to Marshall now." Susan clicked the phone off and backed out of the shady parking space. The glare from the blazing sun made her blink. She noticed a man ambling to the main entrance, but dismissed him from her thoughts. Pulling out onto the road, she glanced again at the back of the man. *Sure looks like Rick.* He opened the door on the building, and Susan realized it was not Rick. *Hmm, and what if it was? I'd leave him alone, that's what. He needs his time with his daughter.*

Susan shifted her weight in the seat and drove two hours to Marshall, relishing the quiet.

◆◆◆◆

At least plans are being made to find homes for the refugees. I would feel guilty, otherwise.

Susan finally arrived and was overwhelmed at all the commotion. A steady stream of people entered as others left the front doors at the temporary shelter. The Civic Center was filled to capacity, and it was difficult to distinguish volunteers from refugees. Susan's eyes watered as she thought of the serious teens assisting others, and she knew she would miss all of them. *I have to come back and help. That is my number one priority.*

She took several steps inside and melted into the crowd. Vaguely, she heard someone call her name, but couldn't recognize anyone nearby. A light touch on her back, and Susan whirled, face to face with Willa Ramsey.

"Come on, Ms. Gad-A-Bout, it's time for the M&M boys." She seized Susan's arm, and they trekked deeper into the room, dodging people until Susan noted the back wall looming ahead. Lost in a sea of strangers, all seeming to talk at once, Susan was relieved to hear her friend yell above the noise. "Guys, over here." Willa waved at two young men who made steady strides toward her. Both thin, and sun-burned, a slight smile grew wider as they glanced from Willa to Susan.

"Here is Mrs. Susan Penleigh, she's the one I mentioned at breakfast."

"Nice to meet you, ma'am," one replied, as the other nodded.

Susan shook hands with them.

"Matt is the oldest, and Mead McKinley is the tallest." Willa gasped as a burly man fell into her side.

"Excuse me, lady," he mumbled, and made no attempt to leave.

M & M scowled and showed a noticeable aversion to his company.

The intruder belched and stood on first one foot, and then the other. Susan whispered to Willa, "This is nonsense. We can't visit. Let's all leave."

She glanced at the boys and motioned for them to follow. Willa and Susan pushed their way to a nearby exit door, and the four burst outside laughing.

215

"That dude was out of it. I'm standing guard at the door." Matt raised an eyebrow.

"Maybe he is lonesome," Susan reflected.

"I don't think so, Susan. He seemed indifferent." Willa leaned against the brick wall.

"His presence confirmed all of you need some privacy, and more important, a home. Matt, Mead, I heard you helped fight the wildfires. That is how you can leave the shelter, find work. I'll call a friend of mine, if you'd like. He may know of someone that needs help."

"Sure, it won't hurt to try. What do you say, Mead?" Matt remained by the door.

"Okay by me." Mead stifled a yawn.

Susan retrieved the cell phone from her purse and dialed fast.

"Rick? Hi, it's me, Susan. Hope I didn't call at a bad time."

She paused and drummed her fingers on the side of the purse as she listened.

"Hmm. Well, congratulations. I'm glad you bought an old farm house. Yes, it sounds like a great deal. Being a Realtor you can repair and keep it, or…"

Matt cleared his throat.

"Rick, I called to see if you could help two young men find some work. They are in the shelter here in Marshall, and are hard workers … of course … uh, why don't you talk to them yourself? I'll give the phone to Matt." She handed the phone to the older brother.

Hearing bits of a one sided conversation encouraged Susan that plans were proceeding. Matt suddenly took a deep breath and pitched the phone to Mead. The seriousness of the situation sunk into Susan's being, like a tremendous weight was laid on her. She silently prayed for the boys and everyone else in the shelter. Time crawled by. Mead returned the phone to Matt. Rick kept talking to each boy. The heat was unbearable, but the alternative was worse. At least it was quiet enough to talk on a cell phone outside.

Willa frowned. She wiped sweat from the back of her neck and appeared anxious.

"Yes sir, and we won't let you down. Thank you, Mr. Yeager for everything. Okay, we will see you in the morning, ready to go. Ask for us at the main entrance. Yes sir, can't wait. Thank you again. Goodbye." Matt handed the cell phone to Susan.

"We got a job. Thank the Lord, brother." Matt gave Mead a direct look.

"I already have." Mead's face broke into a broad smile, and he lightly punched his balled fist at Matt's arm.

Willa threw her head back and yelled, "Yee-Haw!" The infectious yell exploded as Susan and M&M joined in.

"Talk about relieved. I was getting nervous," Willa announced.

"Me too." Matt exhaled loudly.

"You can relax, Matt. Rick Yeager is a good man. He will treat you right as long as you do the same for him." Susan sighed. "I thanked the Lord, too."

"Mrs. Susan, it turned out more than just a job. He wants us to live at the farm house with him. We will all three be doing the remodeling on it. He said the house

217

was two stories high and included eight bedrooms. After that, he wants to buy another house and repair it to sell. Just think, this is our last night at the shelter. Glad you thought about calling Mr. Yeager."

"Don't give me the credit, give God the Glory. That is how He works through us. He had me here to help you meet Rick."

Willa chimed in. "When a plan falls in place, it is of God. It is His Will. I can assure you, *this* is His Will." She raised her voice, "Group hug." The four of them formed a circle, squeezed heartily, and cheered before parting.

"I'm leaving now," Susan stated. "I will be staying with a teacher I met in River Town. What about you and your husband, Willa?"

"We are leaving at the end of the week. My husband's sister insists we relocate to Dallas and live with her. She will be driving here to get us Friday evening."

"That's great. Let's keep in touch." Susan struggled to keep a straight face and not start crying. *Such a dear friend. No telling when we will see each other.* She hugged Willa again and gave M&M a thumbs up sign.

"Go get your stuff, Susan." Willa's mouth quivered. She edged to the boys, and they all waved.

One last smile, and Susan turned, making her way through the mob of people while the welled up tears slipped gently down. *Lord, take care of them.* She rubbed her hand across her eyes and veered to the sleeping area. A final rest on her cot, and she dug her belongings out from under it. Susan wrapped the items in a towel, signed out at the entrance, and glanced around. She saw expressions of hope in a smile, some expressions were unreadable...totally blank, others cried...clearly showing grief and misery; all were evident on so many refugee faces. *It is difficult to leave.* Susan bit her lip and stepped out the main door.

A brisk walk through the parking lot, and she unlocked the car. Emptying the front seat of several boxes, Susan carried them to the trunk and added the towel bundle. She slammed the lid on the trunk, slid in the car, and reached to close the door.

"Mrs. Penleigh. Mrs. Penleigh, wait up."

Robert ran to the vehicle, out of breath. "I saw Mr. Logan on television this morning. He is at Good Shepherd Medical Center."

"Logan? Is he okay?"

"I think so. A dead tree fell on top of him. He's bruised with lacerations, but alert and talking."

"Thanks Robert. I'll have to run by and check on him. How are you doing?"

"Well, since our county was declared a disaster area, my folks decided to stay and rebuild. I'll be with my friends, after all." Robert's eyes glistened. Not able to contain his excitement, he looked up at the sky and hollered, "Thank You, Lord Jesus." Robert nearly bounced off the ground.

Susan jumped out of the car and waved both hands high in the air. "Yaaa," she yelled and looked at a gleeful Robert. "I'm so happy for you and your family."

"Thank you, Mrs. Penleigh."

"I'm leaving to stay with Mrs. Izabella, but I'll return to help." Susan hugged Robert and got back into

219

her car. *Waving bye to Robert is such a good step in the right direction for both of us…I am lighthearted…that heavy burden is gone….I gave it over to God.* She nodded at the President of the Future Business Leaders of America, started the engine, and drove away whistling.

Traffic flowed and Susan pondered what Robert mentioned. *Hmm, he saw Logan interviewed on television. Izabella saw me earlier, interviewed also. Maybe, I should phone my kids in case they saw it on the news and let them know I am okay. I need to call them.*

She pulled into a shopping center and idled the Chevy in a parking space near a deli. Susan dialed each of her three grown children, and no one was home. *They lead such busy lives.* She left a message on their answering machines, told them she was fine, and said goodbye. *Seems like I'm always telling someone goodbye, lately. Well, I am...I am going forward with my life…no, I'm running forward.* She sighed, and got out of the car. The sun blazed down on her, and she immediately became engulfed in humid heat. Susan hurried inside the store. *I'll get a salad to take to Izabella's. It should go well with whatever she is preparing for dinner.*

"Broccoli salad, please, one pint." Susan placed her order, facing the counter, and heard a jingle as the front door opened behind her.

A deep, male voice spoke so close she could feel his breath on her neck. "I thought that was you."

Susan frowned. *Rex Monroe? It can't be.* She jerked her head around for a look.

It was.

"Hello, Mr. Monroe."

His anger and habit of yelling flooded her mind, yet she remained calm. No emotion, no hate, no nothing.

220

Lord, this is my enemy, I am praying for him, please have him behave…I never know what to expect from him…

"I was hoping I'd run into you someday. Remember the red prayer book you left in my office? Well, I finally took it home, and it didn't get destroyed in the school fire. I did read some of it."

"That is good to know." *And that prayer book was planting seeds…*

"I guess I was kind of hard on you…didn't think about it until I read some of those prayers."

"I hope you are led to *say* some of those prayers one day." Susan briefly smiled.

"You think that would help?" Rex Monroe continued standing close to Susan.

"Honestly, yes… and if I may be blunt with you, I'd also recommend counseling."

"You mean like taking an anger management course?"

"Like that, only more personal, more one on one." Susan stood erect and professional.

"Well, that's an idea but I won't travel to large cities for counseling."

"You don't have to. The Soda Lake Baptist Association has counseling, along with other services for the community. It's right here in Marshall."

"Thanks, I'll check it out."

"Ma'am your salad is ready. That will be $4.59."

Susan handed a five dollar bill to the clerk and smiled. "Keep the change." She snatched the package off the counter and turned to Rex Monroe. "Maybe we'll run into each other again." Susan extended her arm and shook hands with him.

Rex spoke in a solemn manner. "I'm sure we will."

Susan walked out of the deli and dashed to her car. Plopping inside, she let her guard down and slouched in the seat. *Wow…*

Chapter Twenty-Six
September 18, 2011
5:30 PM

The trip to Izabella's brought the degree of destruction full force to Susan's senses. Tall, charred-black trees stood like broken sticks on either side of the road. A grey, burnt car still parked on the driveway of a missing home, its contents a mere mound of black soot and rubble.

Startled, she identified the stench that penetrated into her vehicle. Susan shuddered as she drove over the winding hills and viewed acres of black soot-covered ground. Eerily silent, the entire area was devoid of any birds or wildlife; their fate unknown. The strong smell of smoke saturated everything...it would all be a memory hard to remove from anyone's mind.

Arriving at Izabella's house gave Susan a moment of true relief. She observed the home most would take for granted. Overwhelmed with sudden joy, Susan giggled out loud. *Reminds me of a child waiting patiently and finally shouting, 'My turn...Hey , it's my turn'. Hmm, if there was a huge neon sign across it...and thankfully it's not... flashing the message, Welcome Weary Work-a-holic, I could not be any happier...*

The brick home itself wasn't anything spectacular, pretty standard, but it was a *home*.

Susan parked the car near the double garage, honked the horn twice, and glanced at the house. Draperies parted at the front window and fluttered back together, instantly. Izabella's vigilance was apparent. She bounded out of the door.

"Let's get you moved in." Izabella marched straight to the car. "Load me up."

Susan popped the hood on the trunk. Clothes, still on hangers were draped over a few boxes. These were placed on Izabella's outstretched arms. Susan grabbed the suitcase, two shoe boxes, and closed the trunk. "I'll get the rest later. Are you sure you're ready for this?"

"Yes ma'am. I'll enjoy the company." Izabella clicked a small remote and huge double doors opened. "This way." She nodded. They entered the house through the garage entrance, and Izabella increased her pace.

Once again a house guest, Susan rushed to catch up with Izabella. She followed her down a hallway, and around a corner, into what was the guest bedroom.

It was massive. Nothing could ever prepare her for the enormous room. She glanced at the sitting area with a reading lamp at each chair, plus a matching ottoman. *How inviting…*

Cool colors of peacock blue and shamrock green popped from the furniture, matching the Fiesta dishes set about the coffee table for refreshments. Gleaming white walls brought the accents out even further. *Unbelievable.* Susan reached to touch the shiny green leaves on a pot plant over five feet tall. *It's real.*

Izabella opened a set of doors to reveal a walk in closet complete with two, red velvet, French provincial benches, and one wall tiled in mirror squares.

"I've made room for your clothes on this wall. If you need the ceiling fan, the remote is on a bench. Of course, you remember that." Izabella nodded.

"Of course." Susan smiled.

The room was L-shaped, and off to the end of the hook of the "L" was the king size bed. A two-step foot stool sat near one side, obviously needed for climbing. The bed itself was four feet tall, just with mattresses. A cushy soft, calico-print cover lay over it, trimmed in eyelet material, and Susan gasped when she recognized what it was. *A biscuit quilt.* She ran her hands over each row of "biscuit" size puffy mounds, and could only imagine the labor that went into this undertaking. *What a project…what a handmade quilt…*

Susan dashed about placing her shoes and clothing where they belonged.

"Izabella, what a lovely home. Thanks again for inviting me. I loved staying here with you during Labor Day. The tutoring lessons were great."

"Yes, they were. Susan, enjoy the Jacuzzi in the bathroom. Talk about relaxing. I promise it's a well-deserved treat."

"Don't tempt me, after all those showers at the shelter; I know I'll be shriveled up like a prune."

They made another trip outside, finished unloading the car, and locked up. Susan handed Izabella the container of salad.

"I love this. I'll add it to the dinner I prepared earlier. Let's clean up and fill a plate."

"Lead the way." Susan's voice rose, delighted with expectation.

Hands were washed and dried in the kitchen, and Izabella began pulling dishes out from the oven and refrigerator. Aroma attacked Susan, and her mouth watered abruptly. Izabella placed the hot pan on top of the stove and removed the lid from the cold bowl. Susan stared at the contents. "What is the white ingredient? It looks like a corn desert."

"It could be. I get two cans of whole kernel corn and drain the juice. Fill a large size microwave bowl with the corn. Add one half stick of butter, and an eight ounce package of low fat cream cheese. Heat until cream cheese is easy to mix with the corn. Put the entire bowl in the freezer. Take it out in ten minutes to stir. Depending on your freezer, you may have to return it again. When the mixture is thick and the yellow corn is covered in cream cheese, it is ready to serve cold. Oh girl, you can't quit eating it." Izabella stirred the corn mixture and set it aside.

She removed a layer of foil from the oblong pan and a rich, garlic smell assaulted Susan's nostrils. Susan peeped and saw pieces of skinless chicken baked in the pan.

"I can't stand it. I have to get a bite." Susan grabbed a knife and fork, cut off a section, and dipped it in the garlic sauce.

"Umm. This is too good. How do you fix this?"

"It's easy. Take your favorite pieces of chicken, remove the skin; that is pure cholesterol you know, and dot the chicken with butter. Sprinkle enough granulated garlic to cover all of it, and just a few dashes of black pepper. I bake it at 325 degrees, adding water if necessary. Every thirty minutes I turn the pieces over, and re-sprinkle. When the meat is done, at least an hour and a half, two hours if the chicken is thick; I dip the juice over it, and cover the pan with foil until served. You don't want to dry it out too much, and the garlic is good for you. Oh, and I don't cook with salt."

"Well, it is delicious." Susan nodded.

They filled their plates, and both ate hungrily.

"Izabella, I try not to eat so much at one time, but it was an exceptional meal. Well done, my friend. I will cook the next dinner, and let you sit back and enjoy."

"You've got a deal." Izabella raised both eyebrows.

◆◆◆◆

It was after dark, and Susan did indeed resemble a shriveled prune from remaining too long in the tub. Belly full, body pelted by Jacuzzi jets of water, Susan yawned, and climbed into the enormous bed, sinking deep into it. She was sleepy and briefly wondered if she was actually experiencing dizziness. The thought left her as fast as it came. *I have to cook something great for Izabella. I have to go to the grocery store tomorrow…tomorrow…*

Susan decided she must have fallen to the floor. Looking around, she got her bearings and found herself sitting in aisle eight inside a modern grocery store.

"I am in the produce section." Susan glanced around and saw no one. She did hear the canned music that is always played at grocery stores. A melody that you can never remember, and it is always a tune you know while it's played, yet it seems to just fade away. Presently, it is in the stage of simply going on and on, a soundtrack for shoppers.

227

Susan stood up and raised her head as she distinctly heard the sound of water being sprayed.

There it was… she found the source. A fine mist of water sprayed over the iceberg, romaine, and loose leaf lettuce; both red and green.

"Must be on automation. Has to have a timer somewhere, but who set it, and how did I get here?"

Susan looked at her surroundings and did not see one door anywhere.

"How do I get out of here?" She walked to the end of the aisle and found more counters loaded with other produce, all fresh and in mint condition, but still no door and no exit sign. "Hmm." Susan walked in the opposite direction and considered the fact that she could easily be in a maze. "Something has to give."

Susan peeled a banana, took a small bite, and puckered her mouth.

"Euww."

It was unlike any banana she ever tasted, with a flavor that resembled wheat germ. Even worse than that, it left a bad after taste that was more like a dry powdery film. It clung to the back of her throat and made her gag. She choked, and coughed, and nearly lost her breath.

The mist of water turned itself off, and Susan wanted a drink more than anything. It sounded refreshing, and most of all it would be wet. Anything wet would do. She searched the aisles and yes, they grew in number. Still no exit doors, no windows, not even a restroom. Just more and more aisles of delicious looking produce.

She walked at a leisurely pace, carefully examining each new area of fruit.

Red cherries looked promising, but no, she didn't want to chance selecting ones that could have a tart flavor. She strolled past them and spotted red seedless grapes. "Now, that looks great." With one tiny bite, she tried a grape. "Ugh." It was horrible. Drier than the banana, she spit it out and wiped her mouth with the back of her hand.

"Susan, Susan can you hear me? Susan, wake up," Izabella demanded.

"What? Not another bite, I cannot do it. I have to get out of here. Let me out of here." Susan tried to rise out of her bed and into a sitting position, yawned, and sank back into the comfort of the bed.

"Susan, come on, wake up. It is me, your friend, Izabella."

"Izabella, how do we get out of here?" Her mind was still stuck in the produce aisles. She got excited that Izabella must have come to get her out. "Was it a maze, or did you find a hidden exit door I did not know about? Oh, I do not care, I am simply relieved to get out."

Susan opened her eyes and saw the jolly face of her friend from River Town High School. "Izabella, I am glad to see you."

She finally woke up.

"You were talking in your sleep. You sounded distressed."

"Remind me to tell you how you saved me from aisle eight in a strange grocery store." Susan laughed and bent over to straighten the covers.

229

"Aisle eight at a grocery store?"

"Yes, and you are a lifesaver...in and out of dreams."

"Susan you are worn out. No one should have to try and sleep on a narrow cot at a crowded refugee shelter."

Chapter Twenty-Seven
September 19, 2011
7:00 AM

Breakfast was over, and Susan stood at the counter refilling her coffee cup from the carafe. She considered her host.

"We are going to be living in close quarters. I think it would be a good start to get better acquainted. Make sure we are on the same page, you know, view the same things as like-minded people. Care to hear my story?"

"Of course, and I'm enjoying our girl time. I've got the perfect place to get comfortable. Come on." Izabella leaped from the stool and took off. Susan followed her into the den and down a long, winding hallway. "We'll sit near the back of the house in the glass room with all the plants. I call it my sunshine room. It is cool in this heat wave." Izabella talked as fast as she walked, and Susan hurried to keep up.

Abruptly, they veered into the glass room. Susan looked at the ceiling and saw billowing clouds gently shifting across the sky. Landscaped grounds, burnt and dry, were stark against the lush greenery filling the room.

Both eased into plush, chaise lounge chairs with three inches of padding to lie on. Susan re-positioned her chair to a sitting position. She gazed at the sky between the leaves of a cascading, variegated ivy plant.

"I haven't seen this room before. Your ivy must have runners twenty feet long," Susan marveled.

Izabella squinted. "At least."

A sharp intake of breath erupted as she bolted and approached a six foot tall tree. "What? A kumquat tree inside here?" She fingered the tiny balls of green fruit growing in its early stage. "Do you know I once found kumquats at a grocery store for $12.99 a pound? When these turn yellow, I would love one. I even eat the peeling, it is so tangy."

"Only if you save the seeds."

"Hey, they have to be spit out anyway. No problem. Tell me what the others are." Susan glanced at the equally tall, green trees against the side glass wall.

"These are my experiments: self-pollinating cherry, nectarine, lemon, and lime trees. I trim back their height to fit the room. Notice the larger trunks. They also have large root systems that I fertilize every six months. I don't dare plant any outside; this Texas heat would kill all of them within a week. The rest are an assortment of house plants."

Susan strolled back to her chair. "Reminds me of the peace and quiet I treasured in the rose garden I used to have." She sat and stretched out her legs.

"Used to have?"

Susan smiled. "I used to have a rose garden with a bench in the middle of it. I enjoyed having my morning coffee there. I would pray, and plan my day; it was such an inviting place. Guess you could say it was my retreat."

"What happened to it?"

"My divorce happened. It was a bad one. Most divorces are, but mine was *awful*. I'm glad it's over.

232

The only good thing about the marriage was our three children. They have been a blessing and continue to be, even now."

"So where are they, Susan? How come I have not seen any of them? And how many are girls and how many are boys?" Izabella fired off one question after another.

"Whoa, slow down, girl. There are two daughters, and one son. Scott is the oldest, next is Karen, and Molly is the baby. All happily married and super busy."

"Do they live close by?"

"No. The girls live in Seattle, Washington near their father. Scott's in the service and stationed in Virginia." Susan glanced outside.

"My ex-husband brainwashed the kids into thinking I was divorcing them and not him. Dave never spent time with the kids. So, during the divorce he bonded with them, and to this day they are catching up on the father they didn't get attention from earlier. I knew about his roving eye, and I'm still discovering his affairs with different women. He finally got a wealthy girlfriend and married her soon after the divorce. Dave and his wife are manipulative and pretentious people.

"It can be difficult to forgive," Izabella stated.

"I did my share of forgiving, but it's not healthy to remain in a stressful situation. You can turn the other cheek just so many times. After a while, I refused to be slapped in the face, so to speak, by the same person, over and over. The couple was a thorn in my side..." Susan paused and rubbed the back of her neck.

"For years I tried to work and live there. I even dated. When the girls were married and Scott joined the service, I made my decision. I'd had enough of Dave and Marta trying to keep the kids involved with them and their activities. They seemed determined to remove me from the lives of my kids. That, along with everything else, is why it was time to leave. I went online and checked out different areas. I liked Texas the best. Who would ever think this year would be the worst drought in Texas history and have terrifying wildfires? I still enjoy Texas and the friendly people."

"I'm glad you are here, Susan. Drought and wildfires come and go. It's not a constant part of our lives, though. Stress should not be constant in anyone's life."

"My comfort and strength came from the Bible, still does."

"Susan, I understand what you are saying, and I also noticed how much of yourself went to the kids here at River Town High School. You are such a 'Mother Hen.' I see that as a big part of your character. It is a big part of you. I did not know you have children. I realize how much you love them…you didn't disturb their time with their father."

"No, I didn't. What about you and the school kids, Izabella?" I have to say that you looked out for the best interest of the kids at the high school, too." Susan leaned forward and looked her friend straight in the eye. "I still can't believe the high school has burnt to the ground. It's hard to imagine it gone with so many houses and businesses destroyed, as well."

"I know, Susan, and it's rotten for the principal to have fired you."

"Everything happens for a reason. Mr. Rex Monroe was in the habit of starting an argument with me, over anything, at any time. I always tried to be kind and reasonable with him, but some people you simply cannot please. He was one of them. I even tried hard to complete my work accurately, and in a timely manner, but it didn't matter. Did you know I was not allowed in his office?"

"You're kidding."

"No ma'am, I am not kidding. No matter how important a telephone message was that he received, I was not to buzz his office or ever interrupt him. He instructed me to write and tape it to the door of his office. Nor was I allowed to have his cell phone number for emergency use. Mr. Monroe did give that private number to two young, attractive, single female teachers, though." Susan's voice reached a higher tone as she spoke. "Once, there was a scare about a rival school's tough teenager coming to fight one of ours during school hours, Mr. Monroe could not be found. A sheriff's deputy patrol car drove around the high school, keeping guard, and it was one of those young female teachers who finally called Mr. Monroe. He was not on campus, but visiting a relative, at the time. When he did return, he did his best to yell at me and try to get me involved in an argument." Susan shuddered and clamped her mouth shut.

"You are not the first secretary to have trouble with him, you know."

"Yes, I know. On my first day of work, he told me he recently lost a secretary. I was originally hired to be a teacher's aide, and he decided to make me his secretary."

"Well, I wasn't aware of that. I could have warned you earlier. Like I told you before, I worked there for years. I saw how he treated his other secretaries. He even tried to ruin their work records."

Susan did a double take at Izabella. "What? Are you serious?"

"Sure am, and you are better off away from him. Not having a job may seem like a lot on you right now, but at least we are in it together, and we do have a place to stay."

"I am thankful, Izabella. Oh, that reminds me. Did I tell you about the red prayer book I left in his office?"

"No, girlfriend, you didn't."

"I tried to give him a prayer book when I first went to work. He did not want it, but I left it anyway. Mr. Monroe told me he did not pray and mentioned something about how some people do have other religions. Well, I realize now he was not a Christian, and my being verbally attacked by him, so often, must have been spiritual. You know…good versus evil. I say this because he was so strongly *against me*, on everything.

"I said he *was* not a Christian then, because I ran into him yesterday. He was civil to me, said the prayer book was at his home, and he did read some of them. So, it didn't burn in the school fire, and he is making an effort to read it. I pray he continues to change."

"Amen to that. Wouldn't he be in a great position to mentor as a Christian working at a school?"

"Look how many he could influence by having good traits, everything else would be a bonus. Izabella, let's remember to pray daily for him. He needs to be on our side."

"Will do. Now enough about him. Let's get back to you. Susan, you mentioned dating since your divorce. What happened?"

"Here? Yes, a time or two, nothing serious, though."

"No, I mean after your divorce, when you still lived in the state of Washington."

Suddenly silent, Susan stood, shoulders slouched.

"Uh… yes." She frowned. "The first one I dated, Dillon, was a scam. I know my ex-husband was involved in it. All I got was angry." Susan paused. "After that, there was someone I enjoyed being with, but…much to my surprise things crumbled apart."

"Well, let's talk about the second one, then. Still painful?"

"No, I simply never saw the end coming. His name is Mark Shackelford. He ran a shelter for abused women. Mark did this because his own daughter turned to a lifestyle of drugs and a boyfriend who was a user, also. It was because his daughter died of a drug overdose that he got her child, Lucy. Until his daughter's death, he did not even know there *was* a Lucy. So you can imagine how he treasured that little girl who suddenly came into his life. Mark went through the courts and has legal custody of her. You can get an idea of the ordeal he experienced alone. His wife died years earlier."

"Tragic." Izabella listened intently.

"Mark spent the rest of his life raising Lucy and working at the shelter. I met him at church, and we did date. My girls were younger then, and they got along fine with Lucy. Mark was a perfect gentleman, and we worked together well, whenever I helped out at the shelter."

Susan paused and hung her head in thought. "He really was like a knight in shining armor to each woman there, and no, there was no ulterior motive. He was not aware of his charming effect on them. They called him day and night for advice, for encouragement, for help in some form or another. He treated them all like the daughter that he missed. I brought it to his attention one evening when he and I were eating dinner at a local restaurant. We were interrupted by yet another phone call, from one of the younger women. He actually stopped eating, laid down his fork, and listened with an intensity that he displayed at the first sign of a problem. He sounded sincere.

"The phone call went on and on. I was not hungry after that. I sat still and listened to him give someone suggestions."

"Susan, was he the least bit attractive?"

"Yes, he was. Mark was tall and slender, hair beginning to turn grey at the temples. He dressed well and spoke in an articulate manner."

"No wonder they flocked around him." Izabella nodded.

"I told him at the dinner table he needed to separate work from his personal life. That was a bad choice of words on my part, I guess, because he jumped at it. I was surprised, to say the least. So, it was a good thing it happened when it did, and everything came out into the open. I could not go through life with him constantly helping them day and night."

"What did he say?"

"Izabella, he leaned forward across the table from me and spoke quietly. 'Separate we will, Susan.' He said. 'For I have devoted my life to helping abused women, and I will help them whenever they need me.' I just sat there a moment, stunned, and I slowly stood from my chair, reached down and grabbed my purse. He quickly stood and stared at me. 'Goodbye, Mark. I wish you well.' I told him and walked out of the restaurant. I called a taxi and waited on the sidewalk for it to arrive. I remember the ache inside as I tried to deal with his cold, shocking announcement. He cut me out of his life as fast as someone turns a water faucet on and off." Susan grimaced.

"Mark didn't try to stop you from leaving that day?"

"He did stand at the table without saying another word, waiting for me to leave."

"Susan, it was all for the best. You did the right thing."

"It was the only thing I could do."

Chapter Twenty-Eight

September 19, 2011
9:00 AM

Quietly, Izabella ducked her head and glanced away from Susan. Her voice sounded strained as she finally spoke.

"Oh girl, I don't know what to say. You opened up some wounds I thought were buried and gone. It's funny how we can get wrapped up in work, even with years going by, and then something can happen and trigger those old feelings again."

"They resurface." Susan drew her mouth in a tight line.

"My heart goes out to you, Susan, and I am compelled to tell you *my* story." A single tear trickled down her face, instantly followed by several more.

"Izabella, you don't have to say anything."

"Well, I am, and it may take a while." Izabella wiped her tears.

"I'll listen as long as it takes." Susan smiled, and stretched out on the plush cushions of the chaise lounge chair. Izabella began her story.

◆◆◆◆

"I was born in Biloxi, Mississippi and grew up in that wonderful gulf coast city. I loved it there: the people, the food, the ocean, everything. It was really special to me. My aunts and uncles lived nearby and so did one of my favorite teachers. She taught me the correct way to construct a sentence, told me all about verbs, and I was intrigued at what she knew. I tried copying her because I was impressed with the generosity of her wise skills. We would sit for hours. I was intrigued at her fun process of writing a short story.

"Eventually, I did write several short stories, and she encouraged my attempts…but I am getting ahead of myself.

"It was in the spring of nineteen hundred and forty-eight that she wrote her best seller novel, and at the time, she did not know it. She let the whole manuscript sit in a box on a shelf for years, while she went about her business, and obtained a job as a teacher in our local school.

"I grew up in her shadow, fascinated by her words, and the writing she did. My parents moved to River Town, and I went away to school at Steven F. Austin University in Nacogdoches, Texas. I received my teacher's certificate and returned to River Town to teach.

"Both of my parents were active in the local church, and always donated their time and energy to different projects helping others less fortunate. This was a regular part of my life. I still practice it today."

Izabella glanced at Susan, made eye contact, and continued.

"It was in the year of nineteen hundred seventy when I fell in love. My parents did not approve of him. Myself, I thought he was rather dashing. He really did sweep me off my feet. His name was Theodore Hilton, and I accepted his invitation to lunch one day after church. Theodore was new in town, and I didn't have any time for romance in my life, up until then, anyway.

241

River Town

"We went to eat at a little café with home cooked comfort food. He kept me laughing, and I got caught up in the stories he told, he was such a great story teller. Anyway, I sat on the edge of my seat and listened to each word he spoke, and I was impressed with the way he would carefully pronounce each word to further heighten the suspense of that particular story. It was all new to me, and yes, Susan, I was very vulnerable at that point in my life.

"He held the chair for me when I was seated at a restaurant, and again, when we got ready to leave. A perfect gentleman, he was always so kind and always so complimentary towards me. I was not used to that treatment.

"Today, if that happened to me, I would think twice about it. If I ever encounter, or experience anything similar with another man, I can assure you I would be quite leery, and I'd be put off by that. It would be a red flag for me: what is he up to, why is he doing this, what is he after, or what is in it for him?

"At this time, all I saw was his beautiful smile, how gracious he was, and how happy he made me feel. Never did I question his motives about being with me, at all. I should have wondered about the fact that here I was, slightly overweight, and this gorgeous hunk of a man was fascinated by me. I should have thought that was odd in itself, but oh no. I was so busy enjoying all his attention, I never saw beyond the facial expressions he flashed around with perfect timing, at whatever he said.

"I thought this was all about me, and he honestly was impressed with me. Theodore Hilton enjoyed spending time *with me...* just being in my *presence*...anywhere; restaurants, church, movies, etc."

Izabella took a deep breath and resumed her story.

"It was not long, and we became an item about town. Everyone assumed we would eventually marry, as we were almost inseparable. He moved into the apartment over the office of the Cooper & Cooper Law firm. I still lived at home, and he began questioning me about my family's finances. 'Your family certainly has a parcel of prime property here in River Town. Have they ever thought about developing it? Have *you* ever thought about developing it, Izabella? After all, you are an only child; I am sure all of it will belong to you one day. Surely, you do not want to just sit on it and let it waste away?' He would look amused at me and raise both eyebrows in mock surprise. A real suave and debonair type of man.

"Later, I found out he was also very calculating and manipulative. He was even shrewd concerning whom he associated with; in private or public.

"I became pregnant, much to my parents dismay, and Theodore was immediately summoned to the home of my parents.

"When Theodore arrived, my father was red in the face from being upset and angry with both me and Theodore. Mother had Theodore sit in the living room, and then, she went to get Father. I was still upstairs at the time.

"I heard them arguing downstairs, and my father actually yelled. I was shocked because my father was always so level headed and calm. He was the type of person who thought an issue over and discussed it thoroughly before voicing an opinion. His eyes looked tired, and his whole appearance seemed wilted and old.

"Theo, on the other hand, looked fresh and vibrant, full of spunk, like a race horse rearing to go, rearing to take charge of a race and finish as an eager winner.

"I heard my mother call for me to come down to the living room, and I slowly walked to where they were all seated. All except for my father, that is, he was pacing the floor.

"I sat across the room from all of them, alone on a love seat. Theo rushed to my side, grabbed my left hand, and squeezed it slightly in a loving manner. He smiled at me and looked deep into my eyes.

"Theo glanced at my father, and with the nerve of a true smart-aleck, mentioned my child would not want for anything, due to my father's wealth in River Town.

"My father rushed to where Theo sat with a smirk on his face. My father drew his fist back and hit Theo square in the jaw. Theo's smirk was gone. I heard a bone crack, and Theo grabbed his jaw in shock and pain also, I am sure it must have hurt tremendously.

"'How dare you insult not only my daughter, but the integrity of our entire family, as well?' Father was outraged.

"Theo stood up then and walked away from the love seat.

"'And what do you propose to happen, sir? You have a daughter who will be giving birth right here in this town. I dare say she will be a disgrace to many. It is just a matter of time.' Theo looked me straight in the

244

face, threw his head back, and gave me a big, belly laugh.

"Tears formed quickly in my eyes and spilled out streaming down my checks. I jumped up and ran to the stairs, away from everyone. My mother stood and came to me as Theo yelled.

"'All you have to do, my dear Izabella, is have your father deed me the riverfront property he owns, and I will take you away from here, baby and all.'

"'You rascal.' My mother turned and yelled at the smooth talking man.

"'You scoundrel.' Father walked towards him as red in the face as I've ever seen him and breathing rather hard.

"I ran half-way up the stairs, terribly hurt by what he said, stopped and looked at him. 'So that was your plans all along, was it Theo?'

"Theo dashed to me and held me in his arms. 'I do love you, my dear Izabella, I can assure you there is none other like you anywhere in my entire life.'

"I looked tearfully into his face and tried to stop sobbing.

"My father yelled out into the now silent living room, 'Then why do you not marry her and make an honest woman out of her, Theo?'

"Still holding me in his arms, Theo started laughing and held me tightly while he replied to my father.

"'Because sir, I am already quite married, and therefore, cannot marry another. I will take Izabella with me and she can live with me and my wife. We will raise the baby ourselves, unless you want to hand over the deed to your river property.'

"I saw the pain in the eyes of both my parents, as they both emitted an audible gasp, clearly shocked.

"Heart racing, I turned in Theo's arms and yelled, 'No, that will never happen. Let go of me, I have some say in what happens in my life. I will never go anywhere with you again.'

"Theo pulled a gun out of his coat pocket. 'Oh, yes you will, my dear.'

"He opened his eyes wide. They bulged and gleamed like a mad man while he cocked his head to the side and sneered. He shoved the gun barrel against my side.

"I was shocked again, and a great strength came over me. I moved my head ever so slightly and decided to catch him off guard with a smile…and yes, it did work. He relaxed his grip on me, and I immediately snatched the gun out of his hand, and he fought me for the gun. My parents watched in horror, helpless to do anything.

"The gun went off in a loud pop that crackled through the room. Theo slumped over, and I fell tangled with him, down the stairs.

"Blood was everywhere, and at first no one knew if Theo would jump up after his fall, or remain lying on the floor. I hurt so bad I could not move. My body was twisted, and I moaned. Theo lay quiet and still with blood gushing from his side. Finally, he stirred, ever so slowly, and moved his arm out from his body.

"'Doctor, I need a doctor.' He thrust the words out of his mouth in between gasping for air.

"I began bleeding and wouldn't let anyone touch me. I hurt deep inside and cried if my parents tried to lift me.

"Father called the River Town Police Department and advised a shooting had occurred. He said he was going to press charges for extortion and harassment, and an ambulance was needed for Theo and me.

"I required immediate surgery and there was not a skilled surgeon on call that evening in the tiny hospital. Another doctor, a young intern, tried to save my life. There was no time to transport me to a distant, larger hospital. It was touch and go for a while, as I lost a lot of blood, and yes, I lost the baby. Not only did the tragic episode shake my entire family then, but it continued as I was told I could no longer have other children.

"All because of a smooth talking, good looking, con man. I was so lonesome, I fell for every word of his well-planned schemes. So, I hold myself accountable, and I did pray for my sins and yes, I asked God to forgive me."

Izabella glanced at Susan.

"Let me tell you about sin. First, a thief comes to steal, kill, and destroy. Read John 10:10. Theodore Hilton was my thief. The devil wants to break you down and beat you up with sin. When you confess your sins and name each one to God, He will forgive you. It's important to then turn from that sin. The devil will keep bringing it up that you did sin, but remember, God forgave you.

"After you deal with your sins, you get an inner peace and joy, and you can receive the blessings that God wants to give us.

"None of us are perfect, Susan. Sin is destructive, it blurs the point between right and wrong.

"Have you ever left church stirred but not changed? Confession without turning from sin is no good. I try to pattern my life after the Bible. Read Joshua 1:8 and also read 1 John 2: 15-17. Those scriptures have helped me a lot.

"Now you know why I am a jolly person, Susan. The devil cannot beat me up over my sin with Theo and my baby. I have been forgiven."

"Izabella, I can't imagine living through that, much less alone. I see more clearly how a relationship with our Heavenly Father is so important. I do pray for His Will in every area in my life before I try any new endeavor."

Susan stood up from the window seat and stretched her arms.

"I don't like to pry in others private business, or personal lives, but…what happened to Theodore Hilton?" Susan frowned and meekly looked at Izabella.

"Our local Police Department arrested him because he was wanted in another county for other crimes. He lived, and the gunshot wound left him with a disfiguring limp. I heard he got life without parole for one of his other episodes. Theo had pulled a gun on someone. He shot and killed the man." Izabella shook her head and sighed deeply.

"Do you mean he did the same thing to another woman and her family that he did to you and your parents?" Susan's hand flew to her mouth.

"Yes, Susan, he did. I think it goes without saying why I never married. I realize all men are not like Theo, yet I feel like I don't need a husband. Maybe someday a man will enter my life, and my decision will change, but until then, I am happy with myself and my life. I do not have enough hours in the day to do all I want to do.

"I treasure my peace and joy in the Lord, and I am grateful to be able to help others who are not as fortunate as I. It is truly a blessing, and Theo did not ruin my family like he thought he would. The old devil is in prison even today, as we speak.

"I am so blessed not to have been compromised into a life with the likes of him. Can you imagine how horrible it would have been?

"Naturally, I can see how some young girl can be tempted, and that is why you have to be strong in God's Word. His Word has been there for me, time after time." Izabella cocked her head to the side and smiled at Susan.

"Izabella you are a blessing to be around. Thanks for sharing your story."

"Thank you for listening to me ramble. Always remember, a saved man feels dirty when he sins, and an unsaved man jumps into sin and loves it."

"That pretty well sums it up."

Chapter Twenty-Nine
September 20, 2011
12:30 AM

Susan heard pots and pans rattling. She rolled on her side and stuck her arm under the pillow. *What a racket…*The insistent noise developed a rhythm. She sat up in bed, and listened…*oh, it's the phone.*

Who could be calling at this hour? She squinted at the time displayed on the alarm clock…*12:30 AM…midnight?* Susan blinked a few times, rubbed her eyes, and grabbed the phone off the bedside table.

She spoke in a gravelly voice, "Hello…" and sat waiting.

"Mom, did I wake you?"

"Molly? Is that you?" Still groggy, Susan turned on a reading light attached to her bed.

"Yes, I lost your number, but Scott had it. I forgot the time change. Sorry I woke you. It's 10:30 here."

"That's okay. Are you all right?"

"I am. How about you? Texas wildfires are all over the news." Her voice broke. "I caught the interview with you in a shelter… Mom, I've made arrangements, and I'm driving there to get you."

"Oh no, it's not necessary. Molly, how thoughtful, but really, I am fine here. A friend invited me to share her home, and I couldn't be doing any better."

"Who is she? How did you meet her?"

"I met Izabella at school; she was a teacher there before it was destroyed by fire."

"Oh, Mom, so neither of you have a job. Let me come and get you."

"No, when things settle down, I assure you, we will actively seek employment. Molly, I only moved in with her two days ago. We help each other here. Don't worry about me. Did you get the message I left on your answering machine? I called you, Karen, and Scott; couldn't get anyone. Figured you'd see me on TV and wanted to tell you I was okay."

"Yes. In fact, that's what made me think about you. The 10:30 news went off, and I hurried to call you, before I got distracted again. Mom, I stay so busy, you would not believe."

"It can get hectic. When I was your age, there weren't enough hours in the day to accomplish anything. It only gets worse as you get older. I think that's because we cram too much into our schedule."

"I agree, Mom. I knew you would understand."

"Well, anything important going on, besides being busy?"

"No, routine stuff, wait, I do have something to tell you," Molly gushed. "Remember my friend, Tee Tommy and his Uncle Dillon? Well, it turns out his uncle has a twin."

"Really? Dillon Tavish … hmm, I was right. So I *was* dating two different people. The mole on his neck disappeared at times, and then suddenly reappeared. When I noticed it, I remembered my camera. You know how I love to take pictures. Anyway, I printed several pictures that proved one "Dillon" was slack faced; the other one was a bit chubby faced. I told "him" to leave. I was appalled. I have reason to believe

251

your father sent "him" my way, based on some of your father's remarks."

"Dad often ate lunch with Dillon. I saw them together on numerous occasions. Anyway, Dillon and his twin were involved in a big scam. They tricked another woman by doing the same thing to her that they did to you. She pressed charges, and it was splashed all over the front page of the *Seattle Times*. I asked Dad about Dillon, and he didn't want to talk about it. Dad did say he used to have an employee who also worked at a radio station, and *that* person was a friend of Dillon's."

"I know."

"Dad doesn't talk at all about his time in prison. He jumped back into his social activities and is still going strong."

"I figured he would keep a low profile. Oh, well, that is his business, not mine. Have you heard from Karen or Scott, lately?" Susan yawned.

"Oh yes. I hear from Karen all the time. She is usually going to a meeting, stuck in one, or leaving one. She calls me when she is in transit. Scott is another story. We talk about cooking, or the weather, or politics. He's given me some great recipes, and he has the uncanny ability to recognize the true character of a politician. Makes for in depth discussions that can go on and on. So, there you have it, conversation I can count on, always interesting. I love our talks. It's part of who they are, part of them."

"We are all unique in our own way. I'm glad you keep up with each other."

"Mother, I'm rambling, and I woke you up. It's a big relief you are out of that shelter and at Izabella's. Go back to sleep, we'll talk later. I love you, good night."

"Love you too, good night."

Chapter Thirty

September 21, 2011
6:30 AM

"Let's try for an early start today." Susan sighed.

"Early start where?" Izabella poured another cup of coffee. "I'm content on a lazy morning in my pajamas."

"I need to check on Robert and Willa at the shelter, and Logan in the hospital, and I want you out of this house and with me, and..."

"Okay, okay, count me in."

"Super." Unable to contain the excitement, Susan blurted. "We'll have a busy day, might even swing by the Texas Workforce and see if any jobs are available."

Izabella burst out laughing and spilled coffee over the table. "Where is this energy coming from?" She cocked her head at Susan. "We better hurry before it's too hot outside. I can't take the heat. Give me thirty minutes and I'll be ready." She ripped a paper towel off a roll and wiped the mess.

"Same here. Thirty minutes will work for me." Susan darted out the kitchen.

◆◆◆◆

It didn't take long to arrive at the shelter. The women entered and gasped. Less than fifty refugees remained in the massive civic center.

"Where is everyone?" Susan scanned the room.

A man approached with a large 'Volunteer' tag on his shirt. "They've been moving out. Many left with out of town family members. Others are staying with friends in the community."

254

"Exactly like me at Izabella's. Well, I'm happy for those who are gone. I don't recognize anyone, except…" Susan cupped both hands to her mouth, and yelled, "Robert."

The young man turned from watching television and saw Susan. "Hey," he hollered, and rushed to her from the back of the room, dodging a few empty cots in his path. A quick hug by all three, and Robert shook his head. "Sure is good to see you ladies, again. Reminds me of my school days."

"School can't be put on hold. A meeting is scheduled here at 9 o'clock Saturday morning. Any students left in the district will soon be attending school. Don't know all the details. Well, people are coming in, I have to go. Enjoy your visit." The volunteer called out as he walked to the sign-in table.

Susan nodded and glanced quickly at Robert. "Great to see you, too. "

Izabella joined in. "Our days at River Town High School will always be remembered, and students like you bring pleasant memories to mind."

"Thank you, that means a lot to me." Robert beamed.

"I'm excited about the school news, sounds like progress." Susan strolled to a sitting area and flopped in a chair. Robert and Izabella followed suit.

"We heard rumors about it, but I won't be affected. I also have news." Robert raised an eyebrow and paused.

"Come on, we're waiting," Susan coaxed.

"Spit it out," Izabella demanded, rising from her chair.

"All right, already." Robert laughed holding his hands out toward Izabella. "We are moving in with an older couple who attends our church. They live past the county line in another school district." He placed his right hand over his heart. "I will actively pursue my education by this time next week."

"Excellent. I'm so happy for you. Are your parents here? Can I meet them?" Susan leaned forward.

"That is the rest of my news. They are working at a nursing home."

"Well, things *are* improving."

"It couldn't have happened at a better time. The shelter will close in two weeks, so everyone is scrambling to get out of here. All of the local churches are helping relocate the refugees. It's overwhelming, such a blessing. Reminds me of my talk with Mr. Logan when he drove us guys to Mount Pleasant."

Susan frowned. "Don't tell me you heard his ghost stories during the entire trip."

"From Mr. Logan? Oh, no, ma'am. He never told us any ghost stories. Mr. Logan knows the Lord. He talked to us like we were his own sons, even gave us advice. I respect him, Mrs. Penleigh."

"Really? Hmm, that's a side of him I didn't know well. Thanks for sharing; it pleases me to know how you feel about him."

"All of us got into discussions with him. He is a good man."

"I'll keep that in mind. We are going to visit him next, at the hospital."

"Tell him to hurry and get out of there."

"I will, and tell your parents I'm proud for them, and especially for their son." Susan smiled.

"Yes ma'am."

Izabella looked at her watch and stood. "We need to be going."

Susan jumped from her chair. "Let's pray." They held hands while Susan gave a short prayer, and then, turned to leave.

"Oh." She stopped. "Write the name of the church you will be attending, and we'll see you there, sometime." Susan dug in her purse and handed Robert a small, spiral notebook and pen. He scribbled on her notebook and shoved it at her. They smiled at Robert and went on their way.

◆◆◆◆

Within ten minutes they arrived at the hospital.

Sauntering down the hallway, Susan strained her ear at the distant sound of a woman talking. As they approached Logan's room, it intensified and became obnoxious. The high-pitched nasal voice irritated Susan's nerves. She glanced at Izabella and opened the door.

"Behave now, and swallow your meds." The blonde spoke in a shrill manner. She sparkled and wiggled in her matching scrub ensemble with several shades of pink hearts.

Susan glared at her, trying not to show emotion.

Lord, help me remember Matthew 7:1 and not judge her.

Susan and Izabella entered, and Logan's face lit up.

"Come on in." Excitement generated as his voice boomed out." Susan, meet my cousin, Mary Jane. Mary Jane, my friend, Susan." He pointed to the nurse. "…and *you* behave."

257

She gazed at Susan a moment before bubbling with exuberance. "Oh my. You bear a remarkable resemblance to my other cousins; Connie, and Donna."

"Can't be possible," Susan stated coolly. "I'm from the State of Washington."

"Pardon me for speculating." She flitted toward Susan and pouted.

"No problem, Mary Jane."

"Well, I have an aunt in Lufkin, Texas. You look like her daughters."

"Sorry." Susan shrugged her shoulders and sped to the other side of Logan's bed.

He snatched her hand and squeezed it, giving her a wink and a smile. Swallowing pills immediately and gulping water from a light grey container; he frowned at Mary Jane. "Pills are gone. You can leave now. I have company."

Mary Jane smiled and fled the room.

"My cousin is an eccentric, please overlook her."

"Honestly, I don't know what's worse…she is your cousin or she is your friendly nurse."

Logan threw his head back and belted out a vigorous belly laugh. "Ha, ha, ha, ha … Susan … you amaze me." He grabbed his side and laughed louder.

"Excuse me, but some of Logan's relatives are not admitting to any acquaintance with Mary Jane, at all."

Susan jerked her head when a man barged into the room.

His hand extended toward Susan. "I'm .."

Logan's laughter halted, and he interrupted the man. "Susan, may I present my brother, Ben, to you?"

"Of course."

"Ben, this is Susan; she is *my* friend."

Susan shook Ben's hand and displayed a brief, tiny smile as she made eye contact with him. *What a family…*

Izabella took that moment to clear her throat, and Susan quickly introduced her.

"Ben, Logan, meet Izabella. She's been wonderful to invite me into her home."

"Well, I'll have to get her address. My doctor discharges me this afternoon." He raised an eyebrow. "Susan, we have a lot of catching up to do. How about dinner tomorrow evening?"

"Sure, what time?"

"Is seven too late?"

"No." Susan grabbed a napkin off a tray, retrieved a pen from her purse, and wrote the address. "Here you go. I'll look forward to it."

Abruptly, Susan noticed how quiet Izabella and Ben were. She turned to look at them and suppressed a smile.

Ben focused on Izabella and nodded at her. "Izabella, my pleasure." He reached to shake her hand.

Izabella seemed mesmerized by him and stood with a silly half smile on her face. As they shook hands, both looked startled, and immediately dropped their hands.

"Wow, static electricity, what a shock." Izabella's eyes darted towards Ben.

"Not like any static electricity I've ever encountered. More like powerful energy, crackling on contact." He shook his head. "Incredible."

"Yes, it was." Izabella chuckled.

"Well, we can't let this connection pass. Izabella, if you'll give me your phone number, I'd enjoy getting acquainted. "

"I must admit, I'd like that. Here, take my business card." She pulled one from her billfold and gave it to Ben.

"Hold on, now," Logan sputtered. "I'm not saying he is harmless. I'm not…"

Ben sprang at Logan. "I object. Stop, or I tell Susan everything you did wrong during your entire life."

Suddenly quiet, the two brothers stared at each other with raised eyebrows.

Izabella broke the silence. "Gentlemen, we have errands to attend and must leave."

Brief smiles were exchanged by all four as Susan and Izabella escaped out of the room. Susan heard Izabella giggle as they raced down the hallway and bolted out an exit door.

"You are giddy." Susan laughed at Izabella. "How can we look for work in this frame of mind?"

"We aren't. We'll go tomorrow…oh Susan, I've met Ben." Izabella closed her eyes briefly and smiled from ear to ear.

Susan groaned.

Chapter Thirty-One
September 22, 2011
9:30 AM

The Texas Workforce, with state of the art technology, is organized, and today; not crowded.

Susan completed her paperwork and returned it to the clerk.

"Mrs. Penleigh, we will review your skills and call you when something is available."

Susan nodded, returned to her chair, and waited while Izabella interviewed. Flipping through a magazine, she came upon an interesting article and dove into it. Oblivious to her surroundings, she considered the authors pros and cons of living in San Antonio, Texas. *Love the River Walk and the scrumptious food there…*

"Mrs. Penleigh? Pardon me, Mrs. Penleigh, I hate to disturb you."

Susan casually raised her head and looked square into the face of Rex Monroe. She gasped.

"Mr. Monroe… of all people. How are you?" She stammered.

"Tolerable. Thank you for the suggestion to seek counseling at the Soda Lake Baptist Association center. I am comfortable there and realize how deplorable I treated others. One can get so caught up in pressure, it becomes a lifestyle you're not even aware of. You push forward, regardless of whose feelings you step on. Forgive me for stepping on yours."

"I forgave you long ago and include you in prayer."

261

"Much appreciated. *I am praying* and begin each day reading scripture. By the grace of God, before you today stands a changed and, thankfully, saved man."

"Congratulations, Mr. Monroe. You seem so happy."

"Yes, and now to find employment. It's difficult. Schools in neighboring towns issued contracts weeks ago. No positions are available."

"Why not consider private tutoring? Place an ad in the classified section of the newspaper."

"Certainly wouldn't hurt to try. Clients usually require references, though."

"List me as one. I'd be proud to help."

"Thanks, Mrs. Penleigh." He paused. "Nice to see you again."

"You too," Susan replied. He turned and left.

Overwhelmed, Susan reflected on their conversation, quickly said a silent prayer for him, and sighed deeply. *How ironic, Mr. Monroe tutoring. I was fired after the tutoring episode at school. Life is full of surprises. Lord, forgive us all…*

"Hey girl, you look lost in thought."

Susan flinched. "I was. How did it go?"

Izabella held an index card in the air and smiled. "Come on, I have an interview at a grocery store in fifteen minutes."

"A grocery store?" Susan rose to her feet as they rushed outside to the parking lot. "Tell me more."

Izabella flung the door open on her car, and they jumped in. She started the vehicle and quickly made her way to the main road. "Well, area school positions are all filled. I need to work and the grocery store job includes group insurance."

"Who would have guessed?"

"I know. Seems like a great work environment, too. Here we are."

Izabella parked at the entrance, and they hurried inside.

"Where is the manager's office?" Izabella called out to an employee wearing the companies trademark uniform.

"Right here." The worker pointed a few feet away.

"Thank you," Susan gushed, and whispered to Izabella. "I'll be checking out the book section." Susan watched Izabella knock on the door. A stocky man, with a bald spot on top of his head, whisked her in, and Susan strolled off.

Nearly an hour later, and countless books scanned through, Susan glanced around, saw Izabella, and did a double take. Carrying a folded uniform and brochures, Izabella rocked her body back and forth in jubilation, and sang out, "I got it, I got it."

"Good for you, girlfriend, way to go." Susan's face lit up.

"I have a lot to learn. You have to know a code for each produce item, and of course, recognize what it is to begin with, ha. I'll even be tested on it. Training is for six weeks. They'll teach me procedures for counting money, all sorts of things."

"You can do it."

"Thanks. I'm so relieved to get a job. Are we done here?"

"Yes, I have a date with Logan this evening, remember?"

"Too much going on, I totally forgot. Let's go home."

◆◆◆◆

Susan overheard Izabella talking to herself. She'd say a produce item and immediately yell out the code. Susan smiled, shut the bedroom door to drown out the produce lesson, and tried to concentrate on what she'd wear tonight. *I think I'll wear dress pants and a lacy top with a short-sleeved jacket.* She took the ensemble from the closet, laid it across the bed, and stared at it. *Maybe not.*

Interrupted by a shrill ring, Susan bolted to retrieve the cell phone from her purse.

"Hello? Logan, I can barely hear you. Wait, I'll put you on speaker phone."

"I'd like to get an early start tonight, if it's okay?" Logan sounded out of breath.

"Yes. What time?"

"Five –thirty? We'll arrive by six at the restaurant."

"Sure, see you then."

Susan glanced at the alarm clock and made a frantic decision on what to wear. In less than an hour, she withdrew from the bathroom; clean, dressed, and perfumed.

Izabella burst in the bedroom. "Logan is here. Oh, I love the pant suit. Nice."

"Thank you. Got to run." Susan tugged at her jacket, spritzed a light body spray over her hair, and calmly walked into the living room.

"Hi Logan."

"Hi yourself, you look great."

"Well, thanks, so do you."

He escorted her to his truck, and they drove in a direction unfamiliar to Susan.

"I hope you'll enjoy the restaurant I've chosen. Their specialty is Cajun cuisine."

"Sounds delicious. Are you feeling up to this? You haven't been out of the hospital long."

"I'm good. At first I felt drained, but I'm back to normal, now. Well, as close to normal as possible, under the circumstances. Strange to live in an apartment." He glanced at Susan as he drove. "I do miss my home, but thankfully I had fire insurance."

"Are you going to rebuild?"

"Depends. I'd like to have water front property, first."

"I did enjoy the river behind my house. It's a shame all the houses are gone."

"Local contractors are bulldozing the rubble and hauling it off in dump trucks. Should be cleared by next month. I wouldn't be surprised to see new houses popping up all along the river."

"New houses will be such a welcome site."

"Local people are already starting over. Well, here we are." He parked and helped Susan from the truck.

A waiter met them at the restaurant's entrance. "Reservations, sir?"

"Yes. Wakefield, party of two."

"Right this way, sir."

Seated in a secluded alcove, they scanned the menus as the waiter stood nearby.

"I know what I want. Susan, need more time?"

"No. I'll have the chicken and sausage gumbo with unsweetened tea, please." She smiled.

Logan handed their menus to the waiter. "Make mine the crawfish etouffe, and I prefer sweet tea."

The waiter took off, and Logan folded his arms. "So, how does it feel to finally have a regular date, after all we've been through?"

Susan put her elbow on the table and held her chin in her hand. "Hmm, it feels like old times, but who'd ever think wildfires, and hospital stays would happen? I remember our cook-out and lazy afternoon. Seems like so long ago. "

"You are right. It puts a whole new perspective on things. You appreciate what you have and don't take anything for granted."

"So many starting over realize the same thing," Susan added.

"Well, as a Christian, it's important for me to start over with like-minded people."

"Logan, I'm glad you brought this subject up. The same principle applies to many situations."

"Yes, it does; school peers, work buddies, even marriage." Logan raised an eyebrow.

"Especially marriage." Susan nodded.

"Excuse me, sir...your meal and drinks." A young man placed their food and tea before them. "Will there be anything else?"

"No, thank you." Logan turned from him and glanced at Susan. "Ever heard of someone being unequally yoked?"

"Heard about it? Are you kidding? This is something I am passionate about. I will never be unequally yoked in a marriage again. Either I am married to a Christian, or I won't remarry."

"Excellent. You understand completely. So many people do not realize the importance of being with like-minded people. No one needs to deal with people being against you in your daily life. That's called stress."

"I agree."

"Well, enough discussion. I'll pray so we can eat." Logan bowed his head and blessed the food. They ate heartily, and Logan soon motioned to the waiter who remained nearby. "Check, please."

He presented it to Logan, who immediately paid, and left a sizable tip on the table.

"There is another place I'd like to take you if you are finished here." Logan looked at Susan.

"This was delicious, and I am done. I can't possibly eat anymore." She laughed. He pulled her chair out, and they walked outside.

"It's too hot to stay out here. Care to go browsing?" He helped her into the truck.

"Browsing? Are we talking about shopping?" She strapped the seat belt on, and he started up the engine.

"Yes, I need your help with something, you know; a woman's point of view. A guy can only do so much at times." He tilted his head and gave a sly grin.

"Wait, can we write this down and frame it for general purposes?" She teased.

"No ma'am." He turned on the radio and hummed along while he drove.

Logan eventually pulled off the main road and into a shopping center. He parked and they got out. "Let's look around."

They strolled by several boutique shops, stopping to look in a few windows. Passing up a furniture store, a health food store, and a bakery; they continued walking down the sidewalk.

Logan suddenly pulled a door open.

"Here, let's go in."

They entered the store and a clerk nodded at them. "Be right with you."

"No hurry," Logan called.

Susan spotted a case full of matching necklaces, earrings, and bracelets and walked briskly toward it.

"Oh, Logan, it's turquoise. How beautiful."

"I think you already have stuff like that."

"Stuff?"

"Yes ma'am. Stuff. Come over to this other case."

He nudged her to another display case.

"Now, this is where I need help." He blocked her view by leaning over the case. Susan peeped past his shoulder to look and gasped at the diamond jewelry.

"I'd be honored to have you for my wife. I love you so much. Susan, will you marry me?"

"I can't believe this. Logan, we hardly know each other."

He flung his arms around her and lifted her in the air. "Lady," he drawled. "Pick out your wedding rings."

"I can't. Oh, Logan, marriage is too important to jump in so fast. I have to pray about it, and I want us to have counseling first by a preacher."

"Counseling?" Logan frowned and set her back on the floor. "I believe in God. We are both Christians. I can't understand you making an issue about counseling."

"I have one failed marriage behind me, I don't want another. When I remarry, I want both myself and my spouse to be prepared by building a solid foundation in Christ."

"When *you* remarry? I made the decision to marry *you*. Apparently, Susan, *you* are not used to the man of the household being in charge."

"Logan, I am sorry, but your views are sounding one sided. Counseling is helpful to any couple considering marriage."

"Considering marriage?"

"Yes, I told you I'd have to pray about it."

He stepped directly in front of her and sputtered. "I'll tell you right now, my personal life will *not* be discussed with any counselor."

She felt his breath on her face as he stood rigid. Chest rising in sudden intakes of air, he drew his mouth together in a tight line, narrowed his eyes, and glared angrily at her.

This is not the Logan I know. Susan turned and hurried to the exit door.

"Where do you think you're going?" Logan demanded.

"Izabella's."

"Wait, I'll take you." He walked with a cocky sway toward her.

"No, Logan. You aren't taking me anywhere." She darted out of the jewelry store, ran around the building and hid in a huge bush against the back brick wall. Susan could hear Logan calling her name. *Sounds like he's running down the sidewalk on the main street.* Shaking, items fell from her purse as she dug for the cell phone, and clicked speed dial for Izabella. Her heart pounded in her ears while the number connected and finally rang."Izabella, I can't explain now, but I'm across the street from the Post Office. Come and get me, and hurry."

"I'm leaving now."

Within minutes, Susan spotted Izabella's car entering the street and slowing at the Post Office. She ran to it, jerked the passenger door open, and collapsed inside.

"Logan is history. It's his way or no way. He sure fooled me." Susan vented.

"I thought he was a nice guy. Hang on, we're going home." Izabella swung the car in the opposite direction. "I don't think you'll hear from him again."

Chapter Thirty-Two

October 1, 2011
8:00 AM

"Thanks for driving us to Tyler. I can't wait to see Lisa." Susan shifted her weight in the seat and watched Izabella drive.

"The drug/alcohol rehab center boasts great statistics with few returning patients. I am proud she decided to try it. The alternative was grim." Izabella grimaced.

"One report I received last week stated she qualified for free dental work. Talk about a confidence boost, Lisa deserves it." Susan heard a muffled sound and reeled back. "There goes my phone." She ransacked her purse and retrieved it.

"Hello? Scott, how are you?" Susan paused.

"I'm fine. Yes, I would love it. I've got a weak signal; I understand every other word you're speaking. What? Okay, we'll talk later. Love you, bye." Susan plunked the phone back into her purse.

"My son called. He wants to plan a visit in the fall. I can't wait."

"Great. Did I overhear he's calling you back?"

A giggle escaped Susan's lips and her face beamed at Izabella. "Yes, and I'm savoring the moment. I treasure my family."

"Family is always well worth the wait. You'll have to update them on your recent experiences. Maybe introduce your son to a new friend. Susan, didn't you date Rick Yeager before Logan?"

"Yes. He moved to Tyler to be closer to his daughter, and I admire him for it. I thought I might hear from him sometime, but I never did. I called him once and helped two brothers get work with him. Rick took them in, offered free housing, as well. Guess Rick moved on with his life. It was his choice not to call me."

"I don't believe in chasing after a man. They lose respect for the women that do. If a man has to be chased after, he's not worth having."

"Sounds like a school lesson to memorize." Susan teased.

"Well, I don't work at a school anymore. One thing's for sure, we didn't chase after Logan and Ben. I almost have to hide from Ben." Izabella burst out laughing so hard her shoulders shook. "Ben is everywhere. I even ran into him standing in line getting fried chicken."

"I can imagine how surprised you were."

"Ben is the type to be in charge. I think it bothers him to see my independence. Hey, here we are." She swung into the parking lot and found an empty space not far from the main building. They grabbed several bags crammed with items they'd purchased for Lisa, and set off.

Lisa must have been waiting for their arrival. She bounced out the entrance door and ran all the way to them, receiving a big hug from both women.

An attendant trailed after Lisa and took all the bags.

"Purchases are examined by security. Sorry." She turned and walked back to the building.

"It's understandable… part of the rules." Susan shrugged it off, and glanced at Lisa. "Look at you, a smooth complexion, a pretty smile...girl…you must be doing something right." Susan hugged her again.

"Mrs. Penleigh, I'm better. At first, I was so sick, but it's like a breath of fresh air in the spring…after a dreary winter. This is a second chance at life. Making the most of it is my goal, and more important to me is learning God's Word. Mrs. Penleigh, I am saved."

"I'm so happy for you, and God is not finished with you. His work has only begun."

"Lisa, your bags have cleared. Visitation is over. Remember only thirty minutes this time. Next week, an hour," the attendant called out.

"I have to go." Lisa glowed with happiness. "Thank you both for coming and for your encouragement. I don't know what you brought me, but I appreciate your kindness."

A quick hug, and she returned to the building.

Izabella walked with Susan back to the car. "She has really blossomed and is seeing life through a new perspective. I know you Susan, and I know you helped influence her Christian viewpoint."

"I cannot take the credit, Izabella. Lisa was receptive and is still soaking up God's Word. I can only steer someone in the right direction, the Holy Spirit does the rest."

"You are a good example to her and to the other kids, also."

"Thanks, Izabella. I am mighty proud of how Lisa has progressed."

"Susan, if most people pictured Lisa a few months ago, they wouldn't think progress was possible."

"Remember Matthew 19: 26, "With God all things are possible. Another favorite of mine, Philippians 4:13, "I can do all things through Christ Who strengthens me." Susan paused, hearing footsteps behind her, and turned quickly.

"It's Rick Yeager…running to me…" Susan sputtered.

He caught up with her. "Susan. I'm so glad to see you." Rick immediately grabbed her in his arms and happiness clearly burst forth from his face. With exuberance he'd never displayed before, he looked straight into her eyes. Susan was strained and tried to pull away from him.

He loosened his grip and frowned. "Susan, what …what is wrong?"

"I'm surprised to see you. I didn't know if I'd ever hear from you again. It's been quite awhile." Susan tried to smile, but her bottom lip quivered. "I have to go." She pulled away from the grasp he had on her arm and both women hurried to Izabella's car.

"I've been helping my daughter and she is progressing. Susan, I've missed you. Can we talk later?"

"Maybe."

The women climbed in the car, Izabella turned the ignition, and backed out of the parking space. No one spoke. As Izabella drove onto the main road, Susan turned and looked out the window. Her heart raced at what she saw.

Rick stood in the empty parking lot, still staring straight at her.

Could it be possible? Does he really care about me?

To Be Continued ...